# Praise for *Behind*

Carrie Fancett Pagels creates a wonderful stor[y] *Behind Love's Wall*. Set on the amazing historical Mackinac Island, the auth[or] [does a] creative balancing act of time periods and characters, bringing it all together in one story that I found hard to put down. I believe readers will enjoy the twists and turns, and I highly recommend *Behind Love's Wall*.

 - Tracie Peterson, best-selling, awarding winning author of over 125 novels including Ladies of Lake and Heirs of Montana series

In *Behind Love's Wall*, beloved author Carrie Fancett Pagels skillfully weaves two generations' worth of romance and secrets to craft a captivating story set on breathtaking Mackinac Island. With unforgettable characters, a moving faith element, rich historical details, and two tantalizing mysteries to unravel, Pagels provides a highly satisfying tale that kept me reading far past my bedtime!

 - Susanne Dietze, RWA RITA® nominated, Selah Award-winning author of *The Blizzard Bride* and *A Small-Town Christmas Challenge*

*Behind Love's Wall* takes the reader on a double journey of intrigue and romance on Michigan's Mackinac Island. Author Carrie Fancett Pagels does a well-balanced job in this dual-timeline story. From 1895 to 2020, the setting of the famous Grand Hotel immerses the reader in the grandeur and elegance of a time gone by that is still accessible today. While Lily and Stephan do their best to hide their pasts in 1895, Willa and Michael are equally determined to unearth them in 2020. There are enough tangled webs in this story to keep the reader happily turning each page. This may be my favorite book by this author yet.

 - Pegg Thomas, award-winning author of *Sarah's Choice*

"Set on beautiful Mackinac Island, Michigan, Carrie Fancett Pagels has woven together intriguing historical and contemporary plots that will grip you heart and keep you up late at night, turning pages to discover the outcome for her heroines. Mystery, romance, and inspiration give this story what readers are looking for!"

 - Carrie Turansky - award-winning author of *No Ocean Too Wide* and *No Journey Too Far*

# BEHIND

## *Love's*

# WALL

*Doors to the Past*

## CARRIE FANCETT PAGELS

BARBOUR
PUBLISHING

*Behind Love's Wall* ©2021 by Carrie Fancett Pagels

Print ISBN 978-1-63609-069-6

eBook Editions:
Adobe Digital Edition (.epub) 978-1-63609-071-9

All scripture quotations, unless otherwise noted, are taken from the King James Version of the Bible.

This book is a work of fiction. Names, characters, places, and incidents are either products of the author's imagination or used fictitiously. Any similarity to actual people, organizations, and/or events is purely coincidental.

Cover image © Magdalena Russocka/Trevillion Images

Published by Barbour Publishing, Inc., 1810 Barbour Drive, Uhrichsville, Ohio 44683, www.barbourbooks.com

*Our mission is to inspire the world with the life-changing message of the Bible.*

 Member of the
Evangelical Christian
Publishers Association

Printed in the United States of America

To Susan Daniels Mullen
My dear friend
A blessing, always
Come to Mackinac Island with me!

# CHAPTER ONE

*Outside Detroit, Mid-June 1895*

*A* hatchet, a Bible, and a revolver were Lily's best friends—and Cousin Clem next door with his shotgun. She eyed the flimsy wood-paneled door of the dank room over the tavern. The "music hall" job was supposed to be her venue for the entire summer. Indeed, it was popular as the proprietor had advertised but in all the wrong ways and for rough clientele. This was no "Opera House," as was clear from some of the obscene lyrics being belted out by the buxom redhead downstairs. Off-tune soprano notes pierced the thin floorboards beneath Lily's feet, and she shivered.

She shimmied a rickety chair beneath the black metal doorknob. This was definitely not how she'd imagined her new singing job would turn out. But now that she'd traveled so far, she wouldn't let fear continue to run her life.

*God, I don't know why You allowed this. What are we gonna do?* Lily slipped to the floor and knelt on the worn rag rug that covered the wide pine floorboards. Downstairs, the hooting and hollering of patrons escalated. What elicited such a response?

She drew in a deep breath, rose, and stepped toward the water basin set in a wobbly oak stand. Lily poured the cool water into the bowl and dipped the dingy washcloth into the water. She'd pulled a new soap cake from her travel case earlier. She ran the wet cloth over the lye soap that she and Mama had made together. She shivered as she washed her face, inhaling the pungent scent. Mama was gone, and in the wake of her misdeeds, she'd driven Lily and Clem far from their Appalachian mountain homes.

As catcalls continued to ensue from downstairs, every nerve stood on edge. Fear had followed her all the way from the Kentucky mountains. Might not be any sleep until all the revelers at the inn had gone home.

Lily closed her eyes as she began to unbutton her blouse to get ready for bed. *Lord, keep me safe.* She dropped her hand and patted the sheathed knife in her pocket. *And guide me in Your plan.*

*Escape* was the word that came to mind. Or was it a word from Him?

Next door, Clem's snores marked him as sleeping. Heavy footfall rambled up the stairs outside her room.

A knock at the door startled her.

She rebuttoned her shirt. "Who's there?"

"Miss Jones?"

With her fatigue, Lily wasn't sure who Mr. Bly was asking for. Jones, yes. That was the name she was using right now. Lily Jones not Kerchinsky. "What do you need?"

"Thought we'd review the terms of your contract." An undeniable slur marked the manager's words as liquor tainted.

*Songbird of Kentucky* she'd been called. Sang at the governor's mansion even. With her mother's terrible action, Lily could rightly be called a tavern singer now that she and Clem had performed here—that was unacceptable.

The door rattled, and Lily stiffened.

In three steps, Lily grabbed her pistol in her right hand and positioned her hatchet on the bed. The knife in her pocket would be a last resort.

*Lord God, don't make me have to use these weapons.*

In Appalachia, pretty much any uninvited person arriving at the door would have met the same "welcoming committee" from her parents as she now had with her. She strained to listen for Clem. The doorknob rattled again, and she shook but took aim at the door.

"I will speak to you in the morning, Mr. Bly." Not a chance. She and Clem needed to leave this place.

"Well, Miss Jones, there are a few things I need to make clear about expectations." He hiccupped.

The door rattled violently, but the chair held firm.

"Clem!" she called out. Lily drew in a steadying breath, aiming at the center of the doorway. Surely if the man made it through and he saw the gun, he'd stop—at least that was what Pa had always counted on when he'd sent them on the road.

Where was her cousin? Through the thin walls, she heard Clem's bed creak. She held her breath as she heard his door open.

"What the—" Mr. Bly let loose a string of profanities. "Put that gun away, Mr. Jones."

Although they'd had run-ins in the past, Clem had never actually had to threaten someone with a weapon. "You get your sorry self right back downstairs so I don't get tempted to use my fists on you." At six foot one and 220 pounds of mountain muscle, Clem Christy hadn't lost a tussle yet.

She cringed, for she knew what this meant for them.

"If that's how things are going to be, then you two can pack up and leave right now." Mr. Bly sounded a little more alert.

"You get us our pay, and we'll head outta here in the morning."

"Have it your way, you backwoods imbecile."

How dare he insult Clem like that?

Bly's heavy footsteps headed away.

"You all right, Lil?" Clem called through the door.

She exhaled in relief, her heart pounding. "Yes."

She allowed him in, surprised to see Clem still dressed. "I thought you were asleep."

"I was, but from the way that vermin was eyin' you during our performance, I kept myself propped up in bed. But I fell asleep. Sorry, Lil."

"Thanks for being there for me."

"But now we've gotta move on again." He stretched his arms wide like he did after a performance, to ease his shoulders.

"I'll pack my things, and you do the same."

"We can't catch a train 'til morning, Lil."

"Right." And it wasn't safe to sleep out in the open in this city and certainly not in this neighborhood.

"Good thing we saw all those ads in the paper for singers at the resorts up North."

She huffed a laugh. "I wonder if those resorts will end up being shanty villages?"

"I already verified one of them—that place in Mackinaw City—as legitimate."

"Good. I appreciate you checking on it."

More laughter pealed from below as the singer launched into a popular beer-hall song.

"Let's pray they still have an opening when we get there."

If not, what would they do? "We'll have to hope so."

"I'll get my stuff together, Lil, and collect our pay. Then we best try for a bit of shut-eye. Maybe head out at daybreak?"

"All right."

Clem left her, and Lily hastily assembled her belongings.

Soon, she'd finished packing in the stuffy room. She raised her window, which was on the back of the building and right over a stoop. So much for allowing in a little fresh air. The scent of cigars drifted up toward her, and she coughed. She'd detested the scent of smoke ever since Mama had accidentally burned down their old cabin. Surely it had been an accident. And how strange that she'd blamed Lily for the incident.

Clem called through her door, "Lil, let me in."

She opened the door, and Clem quickly closed it behind him.

Her cousin pointed to her carpet bag. "You've got yer little friends in your case, don't ya?"

"Sure do. I need them and the good Lord helping me, seeing how things are going up here." She shook her head.

"We're gonna need Father God most of all in getting us a new spot to play. But even if it all goes bad, my Christy cousins can put us up at the lumber camp, and I can work there."

"You'd risk your hands working as a lumberjack?" She frowned.

"If that's what it takes." He shook his head just a tad—as he used to do when he was bluffing.

"But then you might never play piano again."

"The way I figger it, we've had some glorious years—me playing for the Kentucky Songbird all over the South."

Lily gritted her teeth. Once people realized who her infamous mother was, most of her contracts had disappeared. "We did have a good go of it, didn't we?"

"Dang right we have."

"I pray we've more years to continue our act."

A nearby door opened and then closed. Had others heard their argument with Bly?

Clem remained silent until footfalls passed their door and descended the stairs. "Let's get ourselves up to Mackinaw City on the morrow. My uncle says there's no place prettier on earth."

"Let's pray he's right."

"For now, though, let's doze while we can." He patted his chest pocket. "I went down and got our pay."

"Did he say anything?"

"Nah, just scowled and gave me the money."

She exhaled hard. "We'll need new names for our act."

"I reckon so, in case Bly sends out any bad word on us."

Why did things have to be so difficult?

Clem sat on the floor, his back against the foot of the bed frame. "I can sleep right here while you take a lie down."

As late as it now was, sunrise would arrive before they knew it. "All right."

She got a thin wool blanket from the bed and one of the feather pillows and handed them to her cousin and pianist.

Lily put the lamp out and lay down. How strange to be sleeping in her clothes while in bed. She and Clem had to do so on many of their train trips throughout the South—but they'd always been upright in their seats. She used to think she'd never be able to slumber while fully clothed. Now she knew better.

Lily drifted off into fitful sleep with visions full of men chasing her down long endless halls.

"Lil!"

Someone was shaking her and calling her name. It was a terrible dream. Smoke made her cough and gag.

"Lil! Get up!" Clem pulled on her arms.

"What?" She coughed as she inhaled the thick smoke.

"Come on! This place is on fire."

She could hear the cries of other guests and movement in the hallway.

Her cousin opened the hallway door, but when heat rushed in, he quickly closed the door. After checking below, Clem threw their bags from the second-floor window, then pulled the sheets from the bed and tied them quickly together. She knew what he was doing.

They had rehearsed this scenario before, but they'd never had to act it out. Her heart hammered erratically in her chest, like the way Mama played her dulcimer in one of her off moods.

"You first, Lil, I'll hang onto the sheets, make sure they hold to the bed frame."

Clem pushed her, none too lightly, to the window and handed her the end of a knotted bedsheet. "Now go!"

Clem lifted her, and with her feet dangling, he lowered her over the side. She held tightly, but when she coughed, her hands almost gave way. Below, people fled the building and ran toward the street. When her feet touched the ground, she released the sheet.

"Pull it up," she called to Clem.

With a rapid movement, he retrieved the sheet and then quickly descended from the building. Lily grabbed her carpet bag in one hand as Clem grabbed his.

"Run!" he shouted.

Her lungs protesting, she obeyed, and as they turned and ran away from the conflagration, the sounds of hell seemed to explode behind them, shooting debris wildly into the air.

They stopped in a copse a fair distance away. Even from where they stood, heat seared through her clothing.

Beyond the trees, the faintest glow of sunrise showed on the horizon.

"Gotta get to the train station, Lil. Can't stay here."

"Like this?" She pointed to their dirt-streaked clothes and her bare feet.

He bent and opened her bag. He handed her a pair of fancy shoes that she wore on stage. "These'll have to do. It's only about a mile walk."

"We'll have to find a water pump where we can clean up."

"But we're alive."

She inhaled the ashy air and coughed. "Yes, we're alive." Unlike her mother. Unlike the residents of the Kentucky asylum. She didn't need to be questioned by the police about her background. That wouldn't do at all. Would she ever escape from this nightmare that her life had become?

"Reckon we'll head up North to that place advertising for singers."

"I'll need a new name. Just in case. . ." In case someone thought she'd helped set this fire.

Her most valuable possession, a cedar box, held several items, including a small watercolor painting of a fort on a tall white hill. Someone else might not find the carved box, the additional birch bark painting of colorful homes on a clifftop over bright blue water, a whittled horse which she'd learned was a Percheron, and other odds and ends to be worth much—but they were hers. She'd toted them with her to every singing venue. The painter of the two pictures signed his name as—"*Swaine*, that's the name I'll use. Lily Swaine."

A memory rushed over her. "Lillian Swaine," a white-haired man with sad eyes called to her from a vast cotton field.

She shivered as they walked on to the pump.

"You all right?" Clem began pumping water for them.

What if she was never all right again?

*Mackinaw City*

If one considered garish deep red-and-blue velvet Victorian decor as pretty, then indeed this possible venue was so. Lily pulled on her elbow-length gloves, lifted her voluminous skirts slightly, and carefully mounted the four steps to the platform. In contrast to their Detroit venue, the Tavern at the Straits welcomed tables of families with adorable children. Customers also included broad-shouldered lumberjacks dressed in flannel shirts and sturdy workpants and various businessmen attired in the latest fashions straight from the advertisements in the *Detroit Free Press*.

No haze of smoke hung in the air, for a sign at the entry requested men to "abstain from cigar smoking until after eight o'clock in the evening." That fact alone helped calm Lily's nerves some.

Standing near one of the tall, mullioned windows, a dark-haired man with piercing, almost-black eyes stared at her. Lily felt her cheeks heat. Was he a detective? Did he think she and Clem had started the fire that they'd escaped? She shuddered.

Lily stepped toward the center of the raised stage. "Clem, can you start us off?"

"Sure thing." Her cousin began playing some introductory music.

The manager told them that it wasn't necessary to announce themselves, since a large chalkboard had been placed outside proclaiming Miss Lily Swaine and Mr. Clemuel Christy would be performing.

Clem transitioned to the beginning notes of her first song. Families who'd been chatting quieted. Businessmen in the midst of conversations paused and turned toward the stage. Lily continued to sense the gaze of the handsome dark-haired stranger. If indeed a detective, he was better dressed than she'd imagined one would be.

Clem paused for a moment, her cue that he'd begin the intro to her first song. Would these Northerners object to the popular but old-fashioned Stephen Foster song "Nelly Was a Lady"? It was a somewhat mournful tune that never failed to elicit emotion from a crowd. She began the sad song, her voice steady, Clem's piano playing perfectly matching her own pacing.

As she continued, each diner became quiet, even the children. At the end, she dipped a little curtsy, eyes downcast, and waited for applause. And waited. Sweat beaded on her brow.

Suddenly the entire room seemed to be clapping, and she looked up. Many in the room dabbed wet eyes with their handkerchiefs. Lumberjacks in the back whistled loudly. She smiled, relief coursing through her. She gestured toward Clem, and he launched into a livelier number.

An hour later, all the tables had been replaced by new diners—all save for the watchful man.

"Break time, Lil." Clem stood and addressed the crowd, "We'll be back soon, folks."

Polite applause broke out.

Clem joined her and took her elbow possessively, steering her off the stage and out the side door. As they entered the hallway, the three lumberjacks from the back table strode forward.

"If you're not a Christy cousin, then we don't know who is," the tallest man exclaimed. He extended his hand. "I'm Richard Christy and my pa sent me down from our camp up north to check on you. He got your message."

"Pleased to meet ya finally." Clem extended his hand.

When the big lumberjack pulled Clem into a bear hug and lifted him easily off the ground, Lily took a step back. She hoped he'd not try that with her.

Richard jerked his thumb toward the rear exit. "Come on. Let's go chat a spell before you'uns have to get back on that stage."

Clem turned toward her. "Lil? That okay with you?"

"Go ahead." She planned to drink the lemonade the proprietor left in the hallway for them. She'd sit for a spell in the burgundy wing chair nearby.

She'd no sooner settled down and sipped the sweet drink than someone strode up the gas-lit hallway.

The man who'd been watching her drew nearer, his steady gait expressing confidence.

Drat, she didn't have Clem, and she had only her pocketknife on her. She reached into the folds of her skirt and wrapped her hand around her friend.

"Miss Swaine?" The man drew closer, clutching a black bowler hat.

He could possibly be the most handsome man she'd ever laid eyes on.

"I'm Dr. Stephen DuBlanc, the new psychiatrist for the Grand Hotel on Mackinac Island."

Lily's vision blurred slightly, and her breath caught in her throat. Had someone from Mama's asylum caught up with her? Did he recognize her? With her free hand, she touched her throat. Wasn't the psychiatrist who ran the asylum also named DuBlanc? On their trip north, she and Clem had learned that French names were common in the area. The French had settled the region and held it for over a hundred years before the British and then Americans took possession. Indeed, on their trip to Mackinaw City, they'd already met a handful of people with French names: DuBois, Duvall, DuPeister, and a few more.

"I don't mean to alarm you, miss. Are you all right?" He knelt on one knee beside her. This close, she could see his eyes were a melting pool of chocolate and not black obelisks.

"We're not supposed to converse with guests, Dr. DuBlanc." Surely that would send him on his way.

He gave a short laugh. "If the owner knew what I was going to say, he'd definitely not wish me to speak with you."

"Why?" Her words emerged almost as a croak. What would this psychiatrist say? That he knew all about her and her mother? That she'd end up just like her? Cold fear, like taking a dip in an icy creek, coursed through her.

"The Grand Hotel has desperately been searching out a replacement for their contracted singer this summer."

Lily drew in a slow breath, the hint of lime and something musky emanating from the psychiatrist. Had she heard him correctly? "You wish to tell me about a missing singer?" That didn't come out right.

Dr. DuBlanc turned and looked down the hallway. "I'm saying that if you've not entered into a binding contract here, you may find your talents better suited to a very discerning crowd."

And just what would they be discerning? Would they be able to learn who she really was?

When she didn't reply, he stood and brushed off his knees. "I've heard it on good authority that the pay at the Grand is significant."

She blinked at him. "How much?" The question slipped from her lips before she could stop it.

He named the amount, and she swallowed hard.

"I apologize. A gentleman shouldn't be discussing financial issues with a lady, but since you are so talented, and since I would be fortunate indeed to have the chance to hear you sing each night, I couldn't help but ask. Forgive my impertinence."

"It's no trouble." She raised her hand to dismiss his apology. "Thank you for sharing that information with me. I'll discuss it with my pianist."

Clem and his cousins rambled up the hallway. Dr. DuBlanc extracted a flat silver box from his pocket. He unhinged the lid, pulled out a small ivory-colored card, and handed it to her. "If you're interested in the job, send a message to me at the hotel and I'll let the hotel manager know right away."

"I'm interested." She inclined her head toward Clem, who was regarding Dr. DuBlanc with suspicion. "I'll ask my cousin how he feels about it." But she knew what Clem's response would be.

Was that her imagination or did something like relief flicker over Dr. DuBlanc's face as he looked between her and Clem?

He offered his hand to her cousin. "Dr. Stephen DuBlanc currently of Mackinac Island."

Clem shook Dr. DuBlanc's hand. "Clem Christy, currently of wherever we're playing."

Dr. DuBlanc laughed. "I shared with Miss Swaine about an opportunity for the two of you to consider."

"What do you mean?"

Lily touched her cousin's arm. "I'll tell you later, Clem."

"Yeah, I reckon we best get back on stage."

Dr. DuBlanc pulled a brass watch from his vest pocket and examined the time. "I've a ferry to catch back to the island. Thank you both for the lovely performance. I enjoyed it very much." He grinned at Clem and then at Lily before he nodded at the lumberjacks and left them.

For the first time in a long while, a sense of aloneness washed over her, despite having her cousin right by her side. That didn't make a lick of sense. Then again, neither did her life. And those nightmares about the one-armed and one-legged man she'd begun to have—those definitely didn't make one bit of sense. Or did they?

# CHAPTER TWO

*Yellowstone National Park, Wyoming, June 2019*

"Are we in 2019 or 1895?" Willa removed her favorite oversized cheap sunglasses—so unlike the Chanel cat-eye pair she'd chosen for this year's television season—and stared up at the large cabin-like structure of the Old Faithful Inn.

Her assistant, Sue Pentland, parked their rental Subaru Outback, and the two of them unbuckled their seatbelts. Sue pushed her fringed blond bangs back. "It's not bad. Probably much nicer on the inside."

"Maybe there's a reason they don't show many pictures of the interior of the Old House rooms," Willa observed, referencing the central, original part of the structure. But experiencing the old lodge rustic vibe had been their aim.

"Check-in time doesn't start until five. Outrageous for what you're paying for that room." Sue touched the liftgate button to release the rear hatch, and the two of them exited the vehicle.

Sue grabbed her bag, an oversized black leather monstrosity she'd bought on their recent business trip to Dubai.

Willa pulled her own super-lightweight nylon rolling bag down from the back. "One of the benefits of traveling incognito is only having one teeny tiny bag this trip."

Shaking her head, Sue touched the button to close the hatch. "If I never see another lime-and-blush camo ensemble on you, I'll be happy."

Willa elbowed her. "Hey, you helped me pick that look."

"It's certainly memorable." Her assistant began pulling her bulky luggage toward the stairs, which led up from the parking lot.

"I should've dropped you out front." After the long flight from Virginia to Wyoming and the many hours driving into the park, her brain wasn't exactly functioning on fully charged capacity.

"Tell me again why we've come here." Sue sighed as she lifted her bag up one step and then another.

"Rustic chic inspiration for the new line." As one of the country's rising stars in hotel design and redesign, Willa had longed to get a look at one of the oldest rustic hotels in the country. "I've never been here."

"Um, yeah, me neither." Sue continued her slow sojourn upward.

"Let me help." Willa grabbed the handle too. She tried to lift, but the suitcase seemed full of bricks. "What have you got in here?"

Her friend's cheeks flushed pink. "I heard the weather can change fast out here. I brought boots, winter clothes, and everything in between."

"Seriously?" Willa cocked her head at her. "It's in the seventies today and I'm warm." Dressed in cargo shorts and a subdued off-white polo shirt, Willa desired to blend in with the other tourists.

"Can I help you ladies?" At the top of the stairs, a handsome, golden-haired man stood alongside an equally attractive woman, two blond girls standing between them.

*What a beautiful family.* Willa stared up at them. She didn't normally allow herself to think about what she was missing behind the walls she formed over her heart. Her stellar career was enough, or so she told herself.

The broad-shouldered man quick-stepped down the stairs and soon stood two steps above them. "Looks like you could use a hand."

Sue gaped at the man, and Willa bit back a chuckle. This guy really was a little too perfect in all the right ways.

When Sue didn't answer, Willa nodded. "Thanks, that would be great."

At the top of the stairs, the stranger's wife pulled out her phone and appeared to be checking something. The two little girls held each other's hands and swung them back and forth. They were adorable.

The stranger grinned at them, dimples forming in his suntanned face. "Let me take them both, eh?"

Willa stiffened. They were in Wyoming, not Michigan's Upper Peninsula. But the man's distinctive "Yooper" accent triggered the anxiety she associated with her birthplace. She swallowed hard but allowed him to take her bag.

The man bounded back up as though Sue's luggage held only down feathers.

"What's the matter, Willa?"

She shook her head. "Let's catch up with him."

As they neared the top, Sue slowed and grabbed Willa's arm. "Oh my goodness, do you know who that woman is?"

Willa narrowed her eyes, taking in the woman's lovely profile. "As you know, I don't watch television unless it's about hotels or resorts, and I don't go to movies. So just tell me."

"That's Bianca Rossi, one of those *Housewives of Beverly Hills.*"

Drop-dead gorgeous with an equally attractive family, Bianca likely enjoyed showing off her fantastic life for all the nation to see. Her husband sure looked like a happy man, with that huge smile on his face as he rejoined his family.

When they reached the top, Sue reached for her suitcase. "Thanks so much, but I can roll it on in from here."

Bianca's silvery blue eyes locked on Willa. "I know you, don't I?"

"No." The numbers were improving for her HGTV segment, but without her makeup, Willa's crazy hair thanks to wigs, and her outré clothing, how could this woman know her?"

"Yes, yes I do."

Her handsome honey glanced between the two of them. Mr. Yooperman with Hollywood Glamour Gal? How had that happened? Still, they looked awesome together.

"You're Willa Christy."

She dipped her chin in acknowledgment. Willa had taken her grandfather and birth mother's surname as her professional name. Willa Forbes was her adoptive and legal name.

"You redesigned my father's resort in Jamaica last summer. He raved about you. And I love your new segment on HGTV!"

*Ohmygoodnessgracious, Bianca Rossi is having a fangirl moment.* Too bad that Willa couldn't return the favor.

Sue leaned in. "And I love watching you on TV too, Bianca."

Bianca raised a perfectly manicured hand and feigned locking her lips. "Mums the word for all of us while we're here, right?"

Hunky Yooperman grinned. She didn't care how good-looking he was, if she had to listen to that UP accent every night, she'd be a nervous wreck, even though she'd never been able to say why. Natives of the UP of Michigan, or the Yoop as some phonetically sounded it, had finally gotten their designation as *Yoopers* in the dictionary only in the last couple of decades. The designation had been commonly used by residents for a century though. Her sweet grandpa was a Yooperman, albeit an elderly one, but his strong regional accent didn't bother her.

"We're keeping our trip on the down low too," Sue confided.

Bianca glanced around as if making sure no one could overhear. A bus of tourists, most of whom were speaking an Asian language, arrived at the front of the lodge. "So are you researching something at the Old Faithful Inn?"

"Nothing your father could have used in Jamaica, believe me." Willa winked at the other woman.

Bianca laughed. "I know. This look would never have worked for Pops."

The older of the two little girls tugged at her mother's navy patterned tunic. "Let's go, Mom."

Willa briefly locked eyes with Yooperman. "Thanks again for your help."

"No problem." Was it her imagination or did he suddenly look sad? Did it bother him when Bianca talked shop?

"Nice to meet you two." Bianca beamed at them.

"Us too," Sue gushed.

Soon they'd made their way inside, registered, and headed to their room.

Willa unlocked the door and opened it. Sue had specifically chosen one of the inn's original rooms to obtain a more genuine rustic feel. This was certainly that.

Sue stepped in behind her. "Oh my."

"Yikes. Where's the bathroom?" Willa looked around the spartanly furnished room, as though a bathroom might show up if she looked hard enough.

"Um, it's down the hall."

"Down the hall?" A fact Sue had forgotten to share.

Her friend chewed her lower lip. "You wanted the rustic experience."

It wouldn't help to complain. Willa would put on her big girl pants and deal with the situation. "At least the windows are pretty."

"And old, very old." Sue crossed to the window.

Willa joined her. "Look at that, a geyser is going!" Willa pointed out. "Wow, that's pretty cool."

The two of them watched as the geyser continued to erupt.

"Don't see that every day, do you?" As the geyser stopped its flow, Sue reached to turn the window's locking mechanism to open it. "Oh, this was already unlocked."

"Maybe that's why it's so cool in here."

Sue struggled to lock the window again. "Hmm, this might be original equipment here."

"Let me try." On work sites, strong-handed Willa was the one who could often get things unstuck. She tried repeatedly but failed to connect the brass pieces. "I think we needed Mr. Yooperman for this."

"Huh?"

"That guy's accent is pure Upper Peninsula of Michigan."

"Yeah?"

A distant memory of a man in uniform with the same accent and cadence to his voice whispered to her from the past. Goosebumps prickled her arms. This was silly. Although Willa began her life as a Yooper, she'd grown up in Virginia with her adoptive parents. But born a Yooper, always one. "Let's try together to get this goofy window to close."

The two of them leaned into it and finally succeeded.

When they woke the next morning, Sue went to the window and drew the drapes back. "Good thing we got that window shut tight."

"Why?" Willa stretched beneath the covers.

"Come look."

She rose and took a look outside, where a winter wonderland had replaced the sunny summer's day. "This is the first day of summer."

"Mother Nature doesn't care."

More snow swirled around, and in the distance, rows of pine trees sparkled in white shimmery elegance. So pretty. *So dangerous.*

"It looks like a Hallmark Christmas movie." Sue threw her arms wide overhead.

Willa never ever traveled where there might be snow. She trembled, shaking where she stood. *It looks like death.*

A memory assaulted her. Twenty-eight years earlier, she'd stood looking out her grandparents' window and stared at the swirling snow, waiting for Mommy. Unbidden tears, like she had with every rare snowfall in Virginia, pricked at her eyes. The whisper from earlier became louder. A tall man in a policeman's uniform knocking on the door. The deep voice asking if Angela Christy's husband was there. Grandpa calling Grandma to come. Then the pronouncement that had hissed for years in her nightmares: "We have some bad news."

# CHAPTER THREE

*Mackinac Island, June 1895*

After explaining the terms of their offer, Mr. Costello, the manager of the Grand Hotel, held Lily's gaze for a long moment. "Since the former songstress left her entire wardrobe of gowns, you're welcome to use them. She left without a by-your-leave. Which is why you'll notice that, in your contract, you must remain the entire season to receive your full payment."

Lily calculated in her head. The hotel was housing both her and Clem; all meals were covered, as was transportation around the island; and they'd receive half-pay with the remainder coming at the end of August. Clem could send home money to his mother and sisters, and Lily could continue to put aside money for when she might no longer be able to earn her living as a performer—which could be any time if people learned about her true history.

"Seems purty generous to me." Clem leaned forward and gazed hard at the contract. Despite his ability to play music, his reading skills were almost nonexistent. He'd been raised in the "hollers" away from the more settled areas in eastern Kentucky. Lily had been fortunate to both have a school nearby and visiting librarians. And it didn't hurt that her mother had been an educated and well-bred young woman from Virginia.

The manager rubbed his lower lip. "I should tell you that Miss Swaine's suite of rooms is undergoing some minor construction."

Clem arched an eyebrow. "How minor?"

"It involves changing a storage area that is shared with an office adjacent the suite. Our main craftsman, Garrett Christy—"

"That's my cousin." Clem grinned, but Willa cringed at him for inter-rupting the hotel manager.

"Yes, well, your cousin can explain what all is involved."

"Sure enough. We'll speak with him."

"Thank you, sir." Since Lily's name wasn't legally Swaine, would this contract even be binding? She ran her tongue over her dry lips. "This seems fine, but I'd like to review it with Clem before we sign."

"Certainly." The manager pushed his chair away from his rosewood desk and rose to offer her a copy. "Let me give you a moment alone."

"Thank you."

Mr. Costello closed the door behind him as he left.

"What do you think of them offering us that suite that's gettin' tore up?" Clem rubbed his chin. "Mightn't that put people in and out of our quarters?"

"Yes, I wondered about that too." Lily scanned the document.

"Mighty inconvenient, Lil, if you're trying to get in and out to change clothing."

"We've changed our wardrobes in rooms too small for church mice."

"Reckon that's true."

"I'll just have to ask the workmen to be careful not to end up with dust on my, or rather that former singer's, clothes and accessories."

"Maybe ask for some old sheets to cover them up in between wearings?"

"Good idea." She finished looking over the contract. "This all looks fine, Clem."

"Good."

The door reopened, and the manager stepped back inside, a dark-skinned man in business attire at his side. "Let me introduce Mr. Willi-ford to you. You'll see him around the hotel quite a bit."

Clem stood and extended his hand. "Good to meet ya, Mr. Williford."

Why were they being passed off to an assistant manager?

Mr. Williford met Lily's gaze with soft brown eyes and smiled. He looked like the kind of man you wanted to trust. "We hope you'll be very happy at the hotel, Miss Swaine."

He was already assuming they were going to sign. She exchanged a quick look with Clem.

Mr. Costello clapped his hands. "Also, you'll be assigned your own maid. Miss Alice Smith is her name."

"A maid?"

"Because of the inconvenience of the construction—at no cost to you." Mr. Costello slipped his hand into his jacket pocket. "And no doubt you'll have many wardrobe changes."

Clem cleared his throat. "Might solve some of our concerns."

"Shall we sign, then?"

"Reckon so."

"Wonderful." The manager went behind his desk and arranged the document copies on top of it, as well as his writing implements.

Mr. Williford cocked his head. "By any chance is Robert Swaine a relation of yours? He's a stockholder for this hotel and owns a Great Lakes shipping line."

"Not that I know of." She didn't know the artist of her little paintings any more than she did this new Mr. Swaine.

The manager's assistant stepped to the side of the desk. "Captain Swaine is known to be a fine fellow. I'm sure you'll run into him here at the hotel."

Perspiration broke out on her brow. Maybe borrowing the name Swaine hadn't been a good idea.

They all signed the forms.

Mr. Costello waved his hand over the signed documents. "Thank you, Mr. Williford, for serving as witness."

"A pleasure." He gave a curt bow and left the office.

"Let me show you to your rooms." His features twitching, the hotel manager gestured for Lily and Clem to follow. His loose-fitting, gray-and-cream herringbone pants flapped a bit against his legs as he continued down the hallway.

"Since we're passing, let me show you Garrett Christy's workroom." He turned at an alcove and stepped in then rapped on the oak-paneled door.

A broad-shouldered man with dark wavy hair opened the door. "Hello."

"I thought we'd stop by on our way to Miss Swaine and Mr. Christy's rooms. The hotel manager stepped aside as Clem moved forward.

"I'm Clem Christy."

"Oh my goodness. Haven't seen you since you were knee-high to a grasshopper." Garrett shook hands heartily with Clem.

*Please, dear God, don't let Clem share we're all from Kentucky.* She didn't need anyone questioning her origins, lest it led to her mother and her misdeeds. But with Clem's twangy Appalachian accent that he couldn't seem to cover, it may only be a matter of time.

"Lil, this is my cousin on my ma's side. She's singin' here this summer while I play the piano."

"You don't say." Garrett's white teeth shone against his black beard.

Lily took a step closer to the two men, inhaling the woodsy scent. Wood shavings littered a small area beneath a wide pine worktable. "It smells so good in your workroom."

Garrett laughed. "Reminds me of being out in the lumber camps sometimes."

Mr. Costello gestured to Lily. "She's taking over Ivy's suite of rooms."

"Ah yes, my crew won't be in there every day."

She'd never had to deal with a work crew before. The repairs to their log cabin had always been accomplished by Pa until he'd died. "Clem and I have regular practice times."

"And performances," her cousin added. "Do your men also work at night?"

Garrett's lips twitched. "Up here, men work all manner of hours, especially when it's light outside until ten in the evening."

"Could they get in there while we entertain?"

The craftsman exhaled slowly. "We could stretch the repair out until the end of season if you'd like. Have them come in for a few hours a couple of times a week while you're in the entertainment room downstairs."

"That should work well." Except that they had a maid to consider too. "We do have a helper, Alice, who will be in my room."

"The maids here are used to adjusting their schedules to accommodate others," Mr. Costello said and pointed to the hall behind them. "Like that new girl, Maude, who has been moved from one site to another since she's started."

Lily turned as a maid awkwardly maneuvered her cart, the linens stacked atop it precariously balanced.

"That's going to—"

"Fall," Clem finished for her.

Another maid, blond curls peeking out from beneath her cap, hurried to help poor Maude.

"Word is she won't last long." Garrett scratched at his beard.

"My housekeeping manager, Mrs. Fox, has little tolerance for errors." Mr. Costello tapped the toe of his brogan impatiently. "Ada Fox is very helpful, but this place has to run like clockwork."

Clem pulled his brass timepiece from his vest. "Speaking of clocks, we'd best get upstairs to our rooms."

"Nice to meet you, Mr. Christy." Lily offered a smile.

"Call me Garrett."

Clem puffed out his chest. "Now we'll have two Mr. Christys in this place."

"You only ever go by Clem." She couldn't remember the last time he'd used his surname.

"True."

And there were also two Swaines, even though only one was the genuine article.

Stephen's breath hitched as Lily, a vision of loveliness in her blue dress, strolled down the Grand Hotel hallway with her cousin and the hotel manager. By the smiling faces, hope grew that they'd signed a contract to perform on the island.

"Ah, just the man I wanted to thank," the manager called out. "You've brought us fresh new talent."

"Happy to oblige."

A blush colored Lily's high cheekbones. "Good day."

Perhaps she felt the same attraction that drew him to her.

"Good day all around. I'm very happy for all of you." He locked gazes with Lily. "I've an appointment to get to now." He hoped she heard the regret in his voice.

"Oh yes, do be on your way." The manager made motions as if to shoo him on, which didn't sit well with Stephen.

Technically, though, he was this man's employee, at least until his position opened at the Newberry Asylum in September.

Strange to think that only days earlier, before he'd encountered Miss Swaine, Stephen had believed September couldn't come soon enough. Now, the time may pass all too quickly.

Stephen dipped his chin and went on his way to his appointment with Mrs. Butler, a matron struggling with melancholia. Given her lengthy concerns about her husband, it was no wonder the woman was depressed.

After finishing his sessions for the day, Stephen freshened up for dinner. As usual, he had no definite plans. Certainly none of his patients wished to sit with him. He often sat alone by a window overlooking the Straits of Mackinac. On occasion, Captain Swaine would join him. Was there a connection between Lily and Robert? He'd ask.

After donning his dinner jacket and brushing his unruly hair into place, he left for the dining room. In the long queue, ladies and gentlemen chatted amiably, their dulcet tones carrying through to the end, where he stood.

Someone touched his shoulder, and he swiveled around.

"Hey Doc, how about sittin' with us tonight?" Clem Christy grinned at him.

Beside him, Lily fidgeted with the strings of a pink satin reticule. "Clem, the doctor likely has other plans." Her tone suggested that he *should* have other plans.

"No, indeed I don't." That had come out a little too quickly, and heat surged up his neck.

"Then join us." Clem tugged at the straining lapels of his brown jacket.

"I'd be honored."

When they finally entered the dining room, Stephen was aware of the stares they attracted. With a beautiful woman on his arm and her bodyguard of a pianist, they must have made an interesting sight.

Clem leaned in. "Am I dressed all wrong?"

"No, you're fine." The pianist could use a little sprucing up, but there were plenty of old guard bluebloods in the room who were attired similarly. Not only that, but with the hotel attracting new money, in particular industrialists, those men wouldn't look down their noses at someone not attired in the height of fashion.

Soon they were seated at a table for four, with the fourth seat left empty and covered with an opened linen napkin.

The waiter, attired in a close-fitting jacket and slim black pants, poured water for them. "Would you like coffee or tea or a choice from the wine menu?"

"Tea for me and my cousin, please." Lily indicated herself and Clem.

"Coffee, Dr. DuBlanc?"

"Yes, thank you."

When the waiter departed, Lily took a sip of her water and set the goblet down. "Dr. DuBlanc, why don't you tell us about yourself? Where did you grow up? Where have you lived?" Her gaze seemed hard, her questioning tone accusing.

Accustomed to being the one asking questions, he was taken aback. He certainly wasn't going to share the full truth of his life. "I grew up in lower Michigan, where I lived all of my life, and my father was a physician." He omitted that his father, Étienne DuBlanc Sr., a brilliant psychiatrist, had died in the tragic fire at Kentucky's newest asylum, a massive wooden structure that collapsed quickly, killing everyone inside, including his father. "Sadly, both my father and mother have passed away recently." He averted his gaze. Perhaps if he made his countenance appear to be filled with more grief than he felt, Lily Swaine might cease further inquiry.

"Sorry, Doc. Lil's an orphan too. A grown-up orphan, I guess." Clem lifted his glass to his lips and proceeded to toss back half the contents.

"Let's find happier conversation." Lily waved her hand as if to dispel such talk. "Tell us of the recreational opportunities here on Mackinac Island—we've heard many suggestions this afternoon about things to explore in our free time."

A much better topic to pursue—especially if Miss Swaine and her cousin allowed him to accompany them. After the disastrous early part of the summer, with a ship sunk in the harbor, a fire on the main street, and a journalist's exposé quashed, Stephen could use a respite. The remainder of this summer could be pleasant indeed.

Lily perched on the narrow chair at the ebony desk in her room—a fancy piece of furniture with gold engraving on tiny drawers that had matching golden knobs to pull them open. She dipped her pen into the inkwell and tapped off the excess ink. She began recording in her journal—a habit she'd had for over a decade. Lily wrote about landing the job at the Grand Hotel.

She recorded her first few days' impressions of the building, which reminded her very much of an oversized hunting lodge, despite the fancy decor in this suite.

She wrote of the most astonishing moment so far—when Stephen had taken them on a carriage drive through town and past the fort. She recorded her reaction:

> *When I saw the fort, atop the white limestone walls, I begged Stephen to stop. It was the exact image from my painting. What I'd taken for a white hill were actually those gleaming white walls, set into the high cliffside. I almost stopped breathing, so taken was I with seeing my little watercolor come to life. I began to cry. I sensed a connection to this place. For an instant, I could hear a man saying, "Lillian, I made this for you," as he passed the image to me with his one good hand. When Stephen urged me to share my feelings with him, I simply shook my head. Clem said, "Golly, it's purty, but it ain't that special to make a body cry." I laughed at that. Thank God for my cousin.*

A knock sounded at the door.

"Who is it?"

"'Tis Alice, miss." The maid's heavy Irish accent held a musical lilt. "And Mr. Mace, the bellman, is helpin' me too."

Lily rose and hurried toward the door. Why would the bellman be helping Alice with anything? She opened the door.

"It's all cleaned now, miss." Alice bobbed a curtsy.

The bellman's ruddy cheeks looked even redder than usual—and no wonder with the load he pushed. The quantity of garments, shoes, hats, scarves, and even costume jewelry that occupied every square inch of a huge, brass rolling wardrobe rack was astonishing.

Lily didn't move out of the way. "Those aren't mine. I already have what's left for me in the closet." She waved toward the cherrywood armoire, which held a handful of fancy frocks similar to these.

Alice exchanged a quick glance with Mr. Mace. "Oh yes, miss. These were Miss Ivy Sterling's items that she left behind."

Lily frowned.

"These were sent out for cleaning before you arrived." Alice wrung her hands. "Mr. Mace let me know just now that they're all ready."

"So here we are, miss." The barrel-chested man had a deep voice to go with his appearance. "Allow me to transfer them to your wardrobe."

Lily stepped aside.

The bellman transferred gown after gown into the closet. Alice set the hat boxes aside. They'd need the stepladder to get those into the top of the closet. She folded each scarf neatly and transferred it into the tall mahogany chest of drawers nearby.

Mr. Mace quirked a bushy eyebrow. "Your predecessor didn't lack for anything, did she?"

Alice whirled around, a gleam in her green eyes. "Well, sir, Miss Sterling must've lacked for a beau, because she married Mr. Lasley just as quick as you please."

Lily stifled a grin.

Mr. Mace cast Alice a cautioning look.

Alice dipped a curtsy again. "Pardon me, miss, I liked Ivy ever so much, but I have never seen a lady so quick to be wed."

The bellman cleared his throat. He finished hanging the gowns and wraps.

"Whatever is a body to do with all that?" Lily's Kentucky accent evidenced itself a little too loudly. Her lips twitched as she worked to articulate more like a Northerner. "That is, I was quite happy with the garments I had."

The bellman shrugged. "You'll have plenty to choose from now. And if they don't fit, we'll put the extra in storage to get them out of your way."

"Thank you so much."

"My pleasure, miss."

Alice continued to move items to their proper places. "Did you see those ivory kidskin pumps with the buckle, miss?"

"No." Some of Ivy's shoes were just a smidge too small and tight for

Lily, and Alice had tried to stretch them by filling them with crushed paper when a wooden shoe-stretcher failed to yield results. Even Zeb, the shoeshine man, could only work so much magic on them. "If you like them, why don't you try them on and see if they fit you?"

Alice's already pale face grew creamier yet. "Truly, miss?"

"What am I going to do with twenty pairs of shoes?"

"The young ladies here often change several times a day. My last assignment before Miss Sterling was the daughter of a steel baron, and she brought thirty pairs of shoes to the island. Her footwear filled one complete trunk."

"I'm truly grateful for all the options these outfits give me, but I can't see us trying to stretch out another twenty pairs of shoes." And she couldn't afford to keep paying Zeb to try his hand on them.

"Try on your very favorites, miss, and I'll set to getting those as good as I can."

"Thank you, Alice. You're a dear." Lily smiled at the young Irish woman.

Alice's cheeks pinked, and she averted her gaze. "Thank you kindly, miss."

The maid didn't seem to handle compliments or gratitude very well. Lily would be careful not to upset her by overdoing either. "Let's go through the shoes and see. Some of them may fit."

But she best not let herself get too comfortable here at the Grand Hotel. *Only here till the season ends.* Then she'd have to move on. For the first time in all of her years performing, Lily longed to stay put. Those items in her treasure box had a link to this place, and it was time to discover how—and why.

# CHAPTER FOUR

*Mackinac Island, July 2020*

*W*illa sat on the edge of her ferry seat, white-knuckled, as she and Sue crossed the Straits of Mackinac to Mackinac Island. *This is ridiculous, feeling so anxious about this trip.* To distract herself, she focused on the St. Ignace newspaper on her lap. "Lily Jones or Lily Kerchinsky?" read the headline. She scanned the article. A Pinkerton agent had tracked a suspected arsonist from Detroit up to the straits in 1895. The agent's notebook had recently been discovered and offered a treasure trove of insights into how the investigative agents, who often had earned rough reputations, operated. She sighed. This was not a cheerful distraction. She drew in a deep breath. "Remind me again why I agreed to do this."

Sue adjusted her multicolored boho-cloth face mask with one hand, holding the seat with the other. "We're here because the Grand Hotel has been sold, and the new owners would like to hear your ideas."

Her stomach churned. "Why?"

"Since you're one of the premier hotel redesign consultants in possibly the world." Her friend's laughter failed to calm Willa's nervousness.

"Does the choppy water bother you?" Sue glanced out the window.

"It does."

Light whitecaps dotted the water between Mackinaw City and Mackinac Island. Each vibration of the seat, accompanied by rumbling noises, threatened to launch Willa into the aisle. Other than a private water vessel, there was no other way to get across the Straits of Mackinac to the island.

She had a vague recollection of being on a far rougher ride as a small child. Maybe her heart beat wildly because of COVID's impact on her ability to make a living. Since their HGTV show, *Real Resorts Reimagined*, had gone on hiatus because of the pandemic and most vacation properties were struggling, she and Sue had scoured the United States for work.

Finally the ride smoothed out. Willa released her grasp on the seat-back. "This ferry seems to be slicing right through the waves."

"Smooth sailing now." Sue pushed back in the bench seat.

Too bad her career wasn't on smooth sailing. All that trouble establishing herself as a bona fide top professional in hotel and resort redesign, and here she'd come crawling back to a place she could barely stand to be. Still, Grandpa was happy about this turn of events. "Silver lining," he'd said.

It had been a while since she had been home. *Home?* Why had she even thought that word? She'd lived in the nearby village of Hessel until she was three. She shook her head, not wishing her thoughts to go down that path.

Sue's eyes twinkled. "Do you think we'll see any celebrities?"

Willa couldn't care less about that. What did concern her was who her biological father had been. She'd get Grandpa to spill the beans if it took a trip to the mainland every week to find out. And she'd speak with some of the locals. She didn't buy the notion that her birth mother's boyfriend had been her father. That would have been too simple. Grandpa said they'd broken up well before her sixteen-year-old mother had become pregnant. The guy had even come up to Willa after church during her last visit and said that, although he'd happily be her father, if he were, then it was some kind of immaculate conception. At the time, she'd been shocked that her birth mom's old boyfriend would express that out loud. Now she stifled a chuckle at the memory. He'd also shared that her birth mother, Angela, had implied that Willa's father had died.

"Willa?"

"Um, sorry, what was that?"

"Do you think Jane Seymour might show up?"

"Not with this virus." The actress had starred with Christopher Reeves in the 1980 movie *Somewhere in Time*, set on Mackinac Island. Seymour returned annually for the Grand Hotel's special event in honor of the movie. With the new owners, might all that change even after the coronavirus resolved?

"I wonder if that hunky guy we met at Yellowstone is back on Mackinac Island? You know this is where Bianca Rossi met him. It's where he's from."

The way Sue said the reality TV star's name, one would think she and Bianca were best friends. "No, I didn't know that, even though I think this is the third time you've told me their meet-up story."

According to Sue, Mrs. Rossi had met the gorgeous man on the island when he was landscaping her summer rental. After her separation from her husband, Bianca lured him off to Hollywood.

"They said on *Celebrity Tell All* that she used him to get revenge on her husband."

Willa huffed a sigh. "Yeah, and now your BFF Bianca is back with her hubs again, right?"

Sue gave her a hurt look, and guilt immediately assaulted Willa. "Sorry."

"It's all right. Do you remember him coming out of his room and trying to chase away the paparazzi swarming around Bianca and her kids' room?"

"Yeah." She'd wondered why the dad was sleeping in another room— but she'd later learned he wasn't either Bianca's husband or the father to those cute kids.

Would they run into him, again? He might not have any common sense when it came to love, but Yooperman was the best-looking guy Willa had ever laid eyes on. He put the wonder of Yellowstone to shame. Not only that, but he was kind and a gentleman. Could he be a believer? God only knew how she'd struggled with her own faith ever since John's betrayal.

Chimes sounded, and Sue pulled her iPhone from her overstuffed purse. She glanced down at the screen. "Ugh, my cheating ex-boyfriend sent me a crying emoticon and for the hundredth time says he's sorry."

Willa hadn't dated anyone steady after the disastrous relationship she'd had in college. With her busy career, she'd been far too busy and traveling too much to get to know any guy well. Her habit of dressing in rather wild outfits to establish her brand had partially been formed to put off men whom she met in her work life. "At least you have had some kind of love life."

"Yeah, a *bad* love life." Sue rolled her eyes. "You could be dating if you wanted."

"Sure." She waved her hand dismissively. "On another topic—maybe this is good for you to be solo. You've got your own crack at a show once this pandemic clears out. You can stay focused on your own branding. You need to start moving more front and center." She bit back the thought that maybe it was time for Sue to take over their current show if Willa didn't get her chutzpah back. That deep ennui had nothing to do with the pandemic and everything to do with having been in the design world for almost half of her life. She'd gotten jobs starting at sixteen—the age her poor mom had gotten pregnant—and Willa hadn't stopped working since.

"I need us to get this job in order to pay my mortgage." Sue had just bought her first home.

Willa's home, overlooking the York River, served as both living and work space. "You could always bunk in with me again." But Sue liked her privacy and had been thrilled to get her own place.

Sue ignored her comment and leaned closer to the window. "Holy cow, this water is so blue."

In front of them, most of the passengers sat still, almost like they were in church. An unbidden memory rushed at Willa. People laughing, children pointing toward the island. The scent of vanilla and apple. A blond teenager smiling at her with love in her eyes. Slim arms wrapping around Willa and lifting her to look out the window. Cold anxious feelings as her mother talked about something sad. Chills coursed through Willa. A kiss pressed against the top of her head and a long warm squeeze jolted love through her in her memory.

"You all right?" Sue's golden eyebrows joined in concern.

Willa shook her head. "I think I'm remembering my mother."

"Oh, wow." Sue placed her warm hand over Willa's.

Unbidden tears dampened Willa's eyes. "I felt my mom's love so strongly, Sue." She wiped away the tears, and Sue reached into her purse and handed her a tissue.

"Maybe this gig will be good for you, chickadee."

Willa sniffed and gently blew her nose. "Maybe so. I have to say that the memory of the pure love shining in her eyes just nailed me. It was beautiful." More tears threatened, but she pushed her back into the stiff seat. She needed to distract her concerned friend. Willa pointed toward the huge white structure dominating the cliffside. "There's the Grand Hotel."

"Pretty impressive. And that's the longest porch in the world."

"Sure is."

"Oh my goodness, this water really looks like the Caribbean, doesn't it? I can't get over that."

"Yes." Funny, but when they'd been on their last job in Jamaica, Willa had thought the water looked like the Straits of Mackinac. "It's the limestone underneath reflecting the sunlight up."

"It's gorgeous."

Same colors as her current signature style. All items packed up in the two huge trunks being shipped to the island. For now, she was just an ordinary tourist, dressed like half the rest of the women on the boat in a multicolor but subdued tunic top, leggings, and a pair of walking shoes. At thirty-one, she no longer felt the pressure of wearing fashionable but foot-torturing high-heeled sandals like the twenty-something girl seated two rows ahead of her.

"That's near where we'll be staying." Willa gestured to the left of the Grand.

Sue's jaw dropped. "You said a cottage. Those aren't my idea of cottages."

"Yeah, I know, but the islanders do call them cottages." Victorian mansions would be a better description. "We can't see ours from here. Aimee said it's set a little farther in."

"I'm surprised they didn't put us up at the Grand since reservations are down this summer. Someone said by almost fifty percent." Sue raised her fair eyebrows.

"That could change." If the hotel's new owners didn't care for Willa's ideas, they had an option in their contract specifying accommodations could change and other little annoying details that previously she'd never have accepted. But with Sue paying a mortgage on her own and her ex bailing on her, and with their options for income dwindling, Willa had to do something.

"What a hardship if we have to move to the Grand." Sue laughed.

It was wonderful seeing her friend happy after all the heartbreak her no-load boyfriend had put her through.

"I've never slept over on the island, much less stayed up there." Her parents had been there once for a physicians' conference, but Willa had stayed behind to care for her younger sister, Clare.

Only fifteen, Willa had been left in charge of a willful toddler all by herself for a week. That was one reason she'd asked to spend the next summer with her grandfather in Hessel, in Michigan's Upper Peninsula.

"Oh, this is so quaint. It's even better than all those pictures in the Addicted to Mackinac Facebook group."

Behind them, two men chatted about a heritage softball game being cancelled at Fort Mackinac. They had to be locals, with those accents.

When the ferry docked, Willa rose and attempted to head out into the aisle, but the people from the front were pushing through instead of waiting for those at the back to exit first.

"So much for that 'Up North' hospitality you told me about." Sue shook her head.

Finally, they were able to step out into the queue and disembark. On the dock, bikes were parked in the way of the travelers, who streamed around them. A worker driving an electric luggage cart headed toward them, and the mass of people parted.

"Like Moses parting the Red Sea." Willa pulled Sue's arm hard, veering her away from the determined man.

"Good thing I'm not wearing heels or you'd have broken my ankle."

Sometimes she felt like she was Sue's big sister rather than a friend and colleague. "There are heaps of travelers here, and we need to get off this wharf."

Sunny and in the seventies, the weather couldn't have been any more perfect even with the strong breeze. As they moved away from the crowd, Willa removed her mask, and the scents of sugar, chocolate, and fresh air mingled in a welcoming embrace.

"Look—a candy shop where they're making fudge right now!" Sue pointed across the street, where workers could be seen through the window working with long slabs of fudge.

A memory of running across the street to a fudge shop danced through Willa's memory. Her mother's tinkling laughter. Her singsong voice. Sweet nostalgic memories mixed with anxiety assaulted her. Would the entire trip be like this?

"Michael, I know you've got the reputation for being arrogant, but that fit you threw with the Grand's new management was uncalled for." Kareen Parker pushed back a strand of silver-white hair from her face.

"I'm sorry." He stared down at his filthy work boots, glad that Kareen had come to him on his worksite instead of requiring that he go to her hotel for this talk. He'd known the woman all his life but only recently as his boss. She and her husband owned a gorgeous boutique resort on the East Bluff. She used to be pretty chill, at least in a reserved sort of way, until her daughter-in-law had died from an overdose. Then she'd morphed into a hypervigilant in-your-face grandma type of person. As for her comment—he wasn't as cocky as she thought. He was struggling with his mood today, and the storm the previous day hadn't helped any.

"I know you've been a highflier, and we appreciate that—and your name recognition—but we're trying to hang onto that contract with the Grand's new owners." Kareen pointed to her grandson, Carter, who was tending a garden of colorful mixed annuals below where they stood. "And our clients do love your work. You're hugely popular on the island."

He lifted his head, meeting her direct gaze. "Thank you." Michael didn't have addiction demons to struggle with, as had Kareen's daughter-in-law, but keeping his mood in check was like always having a big animal with him that he had to manage while also doing his work. Sometimes it was like having a big bear who had to be kept behind the walls of a cage. Other times, his mood problems were like an antsy puppy, distracting and needy.

She exhaled a big breath. "Look, go apologize to Aimee, and let her know that you'll be happy to work with Willa. My gosh, Michael, you've worked with other high-falutin' designers all over the world. You can manage this. Just do your job and keep your mouth shut." She pushed her expensive-looking sunglasses up onto the bridge of her tiny nose.

He dipped his chin in agreement. Since his breakup with Bianca ten months earlier, his life had changed. He'd loved her two kids, especially since he'd decided no kids for him because of his mood issues. That had ended a couple of previous relationships. But Bianca had dumped him because she'd never intended to be with him permanently. Her relationship with him had been a publicity stunt. The betrayal had stung him worse than he'd imagined. The good thing was that it had helped him accept that this mood problem was never going away, and he'd have to deal with it.

Kareen cast him a sideways glance. "We're so glad you decided to make Mackinac your permanent residence, but you have to remember that we're a small community."

"True." With only about four hundred year-round residents, you had to either get along or isolate, which he often did.

"I'll do everything I can to make Willa feel comfortable as a consultant." And then she could go and leave him in peace. With that thought, he headed toward the one place that recently calmed his nerves.

"You just missed the carriage to the Grand." The dock porter pointed to a fully loaded carriage pulling away from the curb. "For the regular taxis, you have to call ahead."

Why hadn't Willa known that? "How far a walk is it?"

The dark-haired man scratched his chin. "You could probably get there before a carriage would be here for you."

"Thanks."

The downtown area was far more congested than Willa had imagined it would be, with tourists bustling up and down the main street.

"Should be under a mile." Sue pulled out a travel itinerary. "We could manage that."

"All right." She estimated the walk could take up to a half hour or less.

Soon they'd crossed the main street and walked up a side street where the Village Inn's sign boasted, "Home of the Planked Whitefish."

A loud siren pierced the air, and Sue grabbed Willa's arm.

"What's that?"

Around them, no one else seemed to react. Willa glanced down at her phone, noting the time. She recalled the sound blasting years ago here on Mackinac Island. She'd squeezed her mother's slim hand hard. "It's noon.

It sounds then." The same words her mother had spoken. She blinked back the mist in her eyes.

"Oh good. So it's not the local nuke plant melting down?"

"Oh my gosh, Sue! They don't have a nuke plant on the island." Willa laughed, and the two of them continued on past quaint Victorian-era homes.

"There are tons of people on bikes."

"Watch out for them. People who haven't been on one in decades think they can ride through town—and often end up having accidents."

"Yikes. Those streets are crowded even though there are no cars."

"Yeah."

A dray hauling huge stacks of hay rolled by.

By Hoban and Market Streets, young workers were seated outside a large plain building that was likely their housing dormitory. Across the road, a lovely B&B proclaimed itself as Cloghaun's. Flowers bloomed everywhere along the street this July day. She was no landscaper or gardener, but she admired the many types of daylilies, white and pink groundcover, hydrangeas, and geraniums. Baskets of flowers hung from posts all along the roadway.

They passed shops with all manner of lilac items in the windows along with Michigan-made items and other touristy tchotchkes.

Ferns, evergreens, and topiaries outlined a number of structures. Landscaping appeared to be almost a religion on this island. And who-ever was responsible for all the beauty was to be commended. A flowered carriage rolled by, a bride in her white dress and groom in his dark suit waving at the pedestrians.

"There are many weddings here on the island, and a lot of the people stay at the Grand," Sue supplied.

Mackinac Island had been one of the places Willa's mom had pushed for the wedding to John. *A fairy-tale wedding.* The fairy tale was that he had loved her. Her nose crinkled in disgust.

Through an opening between two homes, she spied the brilliant azure blue of Lake Huron. From this angle, it was even more breathtaking than when they'd crossed on the ferry.

The many tall trees ahead on their left, as they continued walking, reminded Willa of Europe—Switzerland near Lucerne—as did the tall evergreen hedges that completely hid some homes from view. Birds sang sweetly in the trees. The *clip-clop* from horses' hooves as they passed in the street was oddly comforting.

"You sure it's under a mile?" Sue swiped her hand across her forehead.

"I think we're over halfway there once we get around this corner."

They continued walking as a trail of horseback riders, mostly young girls, rode by in the street.

Her friend clipped her long blond hair up. "Oh, I can see the hotel now. But it's all uphill."

Ahead of them, Willa spied the Little Stone Chapel. She knew she'd been there before but couldn't remember her grandfather taking her there. "Let's stop at the church and rest a minute."

"And get out of this sun."

"We'll feel the breezes better now that we're away from downtown." Granted, downtown was about as small as Yorktown's Riverwalk area. At least here they didn't have the stifling heat and humidity they experienced during a Virginia summer.

"I should have listened to you about the walking shoes." Sue, who was younger by a few years, had scoffed at Willa's suggestion to wear a pair of tennis shoes.

"Let's cross here. And watch for the manure in the road."

Sue crinkled her nose. "Will do."

Rose hedges encircled the next building, and all manner of lilies blossomed in groups centered in low gardens filled with pansies. "Pretty much everyone has their property landscaped."

"That might be why Aimee said the owners of our cottage"—Sue formed air quotes as she said the word—"have called in a landscaper."

"Especially with the place having sat empty for over a decade."

Sue stopped walking. "Um, did you forget to tell me something? I mean, is this place going to be full of cobwebs and spiders?"

Willa laughed. "I sure hope not. If so, we'll move up to the Grand."

"Who would leave a place up on that cliffside empty for years, maybe decades?"

Willa affected a mock British accent. "We'll have to sleuth it out."

Her secret addiction was watching British mysteries.

"You love your whodunits, don't you?"

*Maybe not such a secret.* "How do you know what I watch?"

Sue blushed. "I sometimes sneak into the living room to watch a little of *Real Housewives of DC*, and I see your Netflix list."

Willa cocked her head at her. "Seriously? Is that why you sometimes claim you're more comfortable with your laptop out there?"

"I can't believe you've never caught me." Sue turned to look at the family driving a small carriage past.

"You always use the remotes to put it back to Netflix each time you're done?"

"Yup."

Willa shook her head.

"I'm just checking out the decor of all those housewives. It's all job-related viewing."

Willa raised her eyebrows.

Sue plucked a bent peony that grazed the sidewalk. Bicyclists passed by in the street. Sue sniffed the creamy flower. "It smells so great."

She handed Willa the flower.

She inhaled. "Beautiful." A rush of memories flew through her mind—Grandpa singing "Happy Birthday" to someone—the blond teenager who must have been her mother—her grandmother holding a Polaroid camera and snapping a picture of them, a vase of pink-and-white peonies set on a linen tablecloth embroidered with bluebirds. "I've always loved peonies."

But the flowers evoked a bittersweet longing—something that Willa didn't love.

# CHAPTER FIVE

## 1895

$\mathcal{S}$tephen DuBlanc, born Étienne DuBlanc Jr., scrawled his signature, not his actual legal name, across a patient's case notes. The Chicago matron was becoming increasingly more anxious and depressed, despite her husband's telegrams indicating he was well and would be at the Straits soon.

The psychiatrists arriving to attend the conference at the hotel would probably be envious of his plush position. But he'd not trained to treat women trapped in their gilded cages. He needed to ensure that there was still a permanent position available for him at the asylum in the growing Upper Peninsula town.

His dinners with Lily and Clem would be disturbed for the rest of the week. He rubbed his hand across his jawline, feeling the stubble that shadowed his face late in the day. He'd shave again before dinner and change from his work clothing to dinner attire. But at least he'd have another night to relish Lily's company without distraction.

An hour later, Stephen descended the stairs to the parlor area and waited until he spied Clem's shaggy head above the crowd. Stephen grinned, happy that he no longer found himself seated alone. Instead, he dined with a beautiful and talented woman and her equally gifted cousin.

Stephen made his way down the queue of dinner-goers, some guests nodding slightly as he passed. When he reached Lily, his breath fled—she was attired in a gold and olive-green satin gown that wrapped around her bodice in a crisscross manner with a skirt made from a matching silky material. A filmy gold scarf hugged her neck and was secured to the bodice with a gold lion's head broach. She was loveliness itself.

"You all right, Doc?" Clem tipped his head to one side.

His cheeks heated. "I'm simply stunned by your cousin's perfection."

Lily laughed lightly as he took her hand in his and raised it to his lips. He pressed a soft kiss atop her hand, which smelled faintly of lilac water.

"It was Miss Sterling, or rather Mrs. Lasley now, who has made such finery available to me."

Clem dipped his chin. "We're mighty glad that she and Lil are close to the same size."

"Providential," Stephen agreed.

The line began to move forward, and they too inched along toward the massive dining room. The scents of rich beef broth, coffee, yeast rolls, and roast potatoes mingled with the aroma of whitefish and pork—the two main entrées for the evening.

"Smells mighty good." Clem waggled his eyebrows.

Stephen chuckled. "It does." But the patrons likely wouldn't express their appreciation so eloquently as Clem just had with his simple gesture.

"Dr. DuBlanc?" Someone tugged on his elbow.

Stephen turned to face a silver-haired man with round spectacles. His sharp features were familiar, but something about the navy-striped dinner suit didn't fit with his memory.

"Dr. Rightler from the Newberry Asylum."

"Oh." He straightened. "I almost didn't recognize you without your physician's coat on, sir."

The older man extended his hand, and Stephen shook it firmly.

Dr. Rightler gestured to a slim younger man with a well-trimmed moustache and dark hair that pressed against his high collar. "And this is a new colleague, Dr. Thomas Bottenfield."

Stephen shook the other man's hand too. He tried to not show the regret he felt at having his dinner plan for tonight ruined. He swallowed hard. "I was expecting you tomorrow." His words sounded rude even to his ears.

Lily turned toward the men. "You're welcome to join us for dinner, gentlemen."

Stephen shot her what he hoped was a cautionary look.

"Or Dr. DuBlanc may wish to dine with you at another table." Her cheeks were pink, but he wasn't sure if she was upset with him or embarrassed.

Stephen had to salvage the evening. "Oh no, I'm sure Dr. Rightler and Dr. Bottenfield would be delighted to join our new singer and pianist here at the Grand."

The older man beamed at Lily. "Is that so? You'll be entertaining us?"

"Yes."

Dr. Rightler beamed. "I do so enjoy musical entertainments, and we're still building up Newberry in that department."

"There's a delightful new music hall there." The tall Dr. Bottenfield, whom Stephen had to admit would be described by others as dashing, pressed a hand to his chest. "I'd be honored to join you."

And the man possessed charm, something Stephen found himself lacking. He felt a little sheepish at having wanted to keep Lily to himself, seeing how appreciative the other men were. It was indeed a privilege to enjoy her company.

Clem rocked a bit sideways. "Let me go and let that maître d' know that we'll need a bigger table tonight." He lumbered off toward the desk at the dining hall's entrance.

"That's a distinctive accent," Dr. Rightler commented.

Lily straightened. If these men were psychiatrists like Stephen, she didn't need them knowing they were from Kentucky. Mama's disaster was too recent in the making. She affected a tinkling laugh and then linked her arm through the older gentleman's. "Why we're from the South, sir, but we try not to make it too evident around here."

"No?"

She pretended to glance around at the other well-dressed dinner-goers in the queue. "There are many Yankees who'd chase us off." This man may have served in the war himself.

His bushy white eyebrows drew together. "I think you have a point, miss. There are quite a few of us who served in that terrible war."

So she'd guessed right. She wished she could confess that she'd grown up in Kentucky, a proclaimed neutral state. "My father served with the Virginians." Where in God's green earth did that come from? Lily pressed her fingers to her lips as her heartbeat ratcheted up. This silver-haired man reminded her of an older man, someone in Virginia, someone—her grandfather. Chills shot through her.

"Are you all right, miss?"

The handsome younger doctor bent to look at her. "You look awfully flushed. It's not your fault your ancestors were Virginians. Why Dr. Rightler knows my grandfather served with Lee's army from the Shenandoah Valley."

Images of dirty, dusty, gray-suited soldiers struggling toward Grandpa's farmhouse flooded her memory: *Papa's chestnut gelding carried a one-armed man toward her and Mama. Mama was crying. She ran toward the poor injured man, who Lily could see also missed one leg. "Papa!" Lily had cried out. That was Papa? What had happened to him?*

Lily wiped tears from her eyes, aware that both of the doctors were holding her by the elbow.

"Is it a fit of apoplexy?" Dr. Bottenfield asked the elder psychiatrist.

"I don't think so."

"Lily?" Dr. DuBlanc leaned in toward her.

She tried hard to focus on his dark eyes.

"Yes?" she managed.

"Are you all right?"

Clem rushed toward them, fear coloring his broad features. "What's goin' on?"

"We were talking about your family in Virginia, and she suddenly became very pale." Dr. Bottenfield explained.

Dr. Rightler frowned. "And then very flushed."

"Did you lose your father in the war?" Stephen asked.

"Yes," Lily blurted out even as Clem's lips formed the word *No.*

"I'm so very sorry." Dr. Bottenfield moved toward her and took her hand in his. "Please forgive our impertinence in asking such personal questions, but as psychiatrists we're accustomed to making inquiries all day long about sensitive matters."

Lily's cheeks heated. The man released her hand.

Clem frowned at her, a question burning in his eyes. But he turned toward the two psychiatrists. "Where we come from, we don't discuss our family business in front of strangers."

She clutched a handful of her gown and was about to cut Clem off from explaining just how things were done in the mountains of eastern Kentucky, when Stephen splayed his hands broadly in a gesture of surrender.

"I'm not sure most Virginians would know what to do with us uncouth Yankee psychiatrists nosing around." Stephen shrugged.

This seemed to placate Clem, whose shoulders relaxed. The other two men exchanged an amused glance.

The line moved forward, and their little group followed. Before long, the maître d' indicated for the waiter to seat them by the window at a table for five. Stephen pulled Lily's chair out for her, a nicety she appreciated, having never experienced it before, not even from Clem, and was beginning to become accustomed to—perhaps a little too readily. She smiled at him. He took a seat beside her and Clem sat on her other side. Across the table, the two psychiatrists gazed out the adjacent windows, taking in the gorgeous view of the Straits of Mackinac. Lake Huron's cerulean blue–, turquoise–, and sapphire–colored waters changed hourly, swirling and mixing and turning gray when storms approached.

Dr. Rightler gestured toward the view. "What a delightful way to start your career, Dr. DuBlanc."

"You couldn't ask for a more beautiful location in all of Michigan," Dr. Bottenfield added.

"I agree." Stephen beamed at the men.

The younger doctor redirected his attention toward Lily. "And with such a lovely companion beside you."

"Why, thank you." Lily dipped her chin.

Beside her, Stephen's elbow brushed hers. "Considering that I am a psychiatrist and no one in this establishment wishes to sit by me, lest I psychoanalyze them, I am doubly blessed."

Lily stiffened, reminded once again why she should be avoiding Stephen. The waiter poured her glass of water and then moved counterclockwise around the table, filling the remaining crystal water goblets.

"The first course tonight will be a creamed asparagus soup."

Dr. Rightler glanced up at the server. "They grow asparagus in

Newberry, where we both work at the. . .hospital there."

The slim waiter finished pouring Clem's water and stood back a bit. "The main course choices are apricot-glazed pork and baked whitefish. Both are served with whipped chive potatoes and orange-glazed carrots."

They all gave their entrée choices, and the server departed.

The handsome young psychiatrist across from her offered the equally handsome man beside her a tight smile. "So, Dr. DuBlanc, will you be speaking at the upcoming psychiatrists' conference here?"

Lily lifted her water glass to her lips. A whole conference of psychiatrists here? She swallowed her water hard.

"No, I'll be busy with my patient load. I fear I can't attend much of it."

"We should discuss that with your employer and let him know how important such training is." Dr. Rightler sounded like one of those men who was quite confident in his own opinions.

"Since our comrade is a recent graduate, I doubt his boss will think he needs extra educational opportunities right now." The younger doctor had a point.

"True. But you should be glad, Bottenfield, that our hospital superintendent didn't feel that way about your attendance here."

Clem shifted uneasily beside her. "Say, are any of you fellas interested in going down to the dog races after dinner?"

The two older men exchanged a quick glance. The younger of the two patted his breast pocket. "I've got odds on the terrier."

Dr. Rightler shook his silver head. "I think the greyhound will win."

Clem laughed. "Well, all right then. We'll all go down after a stroll on the porch after dinner."

"Who'd you bet on, son?" Dr. Rightler asked in a conspiratorial tone.

"She's a street dog that one of the island kids put up for this. She's a long shot, but I'm a fan of the underdog."

The other two men nodded slowly in acknowledgment.

"How about you, DuBlanc?" Bottenfield asked.

Stephen shook his head slowly. "I have other plans."

The server approached the table with a cart covered with bowls of asparagus bisque. Soon they all were dipping their silver-plated soup spoons into the narrow china bowls to taste the savory soup. Beside her,

Clem slowly and methodically dipped his spoon and carefully lifted the bisque to his lips. At home, he'd been accustomed to lifting the entire bowl and drinking the contents if it suited him.

"I can't stay long at the races, though." Clem lightly elbowed Lily. "We've got a performance at eight, and I'll have to change first."

"We should come and watch you tonight," Dr. Bottenfield suggested.

"Indeed," his older colleague agreed.

Before long, the meal was served, and thankfully conversation topics ran from politics, to the economy, and finally horse-racing results instead of the guests' profession. After a decadent dessert of chocolate mousse, Lily pushed back from the table, and Stephen rose to assist her.

"If you'll excuse me, gentlemen, I'll be on my way."

"Thank you for your companionship, my dear." Dr. Rightler rose, as did Dr. Bottenfield.

"Reckon we can take our leave and go stroll the porch." Clem finally stood.

"It's the largest one in the world." Dr. Rightler smiled benevolently at Lily.

He reminded her of a kindly grandfather. She'd never known such in Kentucky. But the man who'd called her "Lily Swaine" in her memory— he had to be her grandfather. She knew it in her heart.

Dr. Bottenfield adjusted his tie. "After that, we should depart for the dog races before the crowd gets too big."

Lily resisted the urge to shake her head at the notion of the men squandering their money on a dog race. "I'll see you later."

Amid a general murmur of assent, Lily headed out of the dining room. When she reached the parlor, an elegant, slender woman in a gray gown descended the stairs. "Miss Swaine?"

"Yes?" She recognized the hotel guest as one of those in attendance at the previous night's performance. Although Lily and Clem had performed across Kentucky in some of the finest ballrooms, she still wasn't sure how these wealthy Northerners would accept them.

When the lady reached Lily, her faded blue eyes sparked with good humor. "I so enjoyed last night's event."

"Thank you," she exhaled. These hotel guests were accustomed to the highest level and quality of performers. Although she'd been told repeatedly how talented she was, Lily had her doubts.

"Would you do me a great favor and sing *My Old Kentucky Home* tonight?"

*No!* No, she wouldn't sing that song. Lily longed to shout the words and run. Instead, she clasped her hands tightly at her waist and twisted Mama's garnet ring around her finger. "I will see what I can do, ma'am, but"—Lily searched frantically for an excuse —"but often my pianist has our entire selection all laid out." Somewhat true, but they had on occasion taken requests, especially when it was a well-known song like this one.

"Perhaps another night then?" the woman asked hopefully.

"Maybe so." Another night when she'd worked up enough nerve to sing of her home state.

"Thank you, my dear." The matron stepped away with a confidence and smoothness in her step that Lily might never acquire.

Hours later, Lily stepped onto the stage, the smooth oak platform slick beneath the new hard-soled and tight-fitting pumps. She'd have to be careful when she gestured during her songs. Should have stuck with her own shoes, which were older than Ivy's and had enough wear on them to prevent her from sliding on a highly polished floor.

Heart pounding, mouth dry, sweat broke out on Lily's brow. Why now? Why this new reaction that she'd never experienced in all of her years of singing? Was she becoming like her mother? Would she have an attack of the nerves and have to take to her bed?

Clem stepped alongside her. "You all right, Lil?"

"I don't know," she whispered.

"Come on over by the piano for a minute." Clem took her elbow and led her carefully across the stage to the piano.

When they got there, he turned her away from the guests who were beginning to fill the seats. But not before Lily saw Stephen there.

"I'll be all right." But there was a quaver in her voice. No, no, no this couldn't be happening.

She could hear her own heart beating in her ears over the sounds of the audience members talking as they awaited the start of their program.

"You and I have every right in the world to be up here on this stage,

Lil, so don't be thinkin' that we don't." Clem's firm voice jolted her.

His emphatic words recalled another man's, long ago, when she was a child. Warm but firm words that had brought tears to her eyes. "Don't forget you're a Swaine, and you've a right to claim your heritage—no matter what happens to me."

Her breath fled and her knees weakened. Clem swiftly pulled her to sit on the piano bench beside him. "Whoa, Nelly, what's goin' on here, Lil?"

She forced herself to breathe slowly in and out, as Mama's doctors had instructed her to do with her when she had an attack. God wasn't supposed to let this happen to her. *Why now, Lord?*

Clem reached for her water goblet on the nearby stand, where the hotel staff always left them. "Sip this real slow."

She did as he asked.

"Now listen to me. We're gonna sing for these people, and it's gonna be the best stuff they've ever heard." Where had her soft-spoken kindly cousin gone? This new Clem was a lot more commanding.

She sipped the sweet water, her heartbeat returning to a more normal rhythm. Footfall softly sounded behind them as someone ascended the back steps to the platform. A warm hand settled on Lily's shoulder, and she inhaled Stephen's masculine scent before she looked up into his sympathetic eyes. The panic that had been rising in her fled.

God help her, she was falling in love with the one man who could never accept her if he knew her truth.

# CHAPTER SIX

## *2020*

*W*illa hurt simply watching her friend limp along. She pointed to the nearby church. "Let's go in there and sit."

"My feet really are killing me." Sue pointed to the building's sign. "The Little Stone Church would be a great place to pray for a taxi to show up."

"I'll call one." Willa dialed for a taxi but got no answer.

Beyond the beautiful stone building lay the Grand's golf course. How incongruous to hear laughter and conversations carrying from the field. They slipped on their masks as they stepped inside the sanctuary, where the atmosphere grew hushed.

They sat in a pew, and Sue slipped off her shoes and wiggled her toes. "Look how swollen my tootsies are."

Willa's eyes adjusted to the dim light. "I see an ice-water bath for those toes in the near future."

"Maybe cold water, but no thanks to the ice water—that's even more painful."

"Let's sit for a minute, and I'll try calling again."

Sue leaned back and closed her eyes.

Willa pulled her newspaper out from her bag, and as sun shone through the nearby Tiffany windows, she continued reading the article about the 1895 suspected arsonist. Although Pinkertons had earned a bad rep after busting up labor strikes, some agents were a little more sympathetic to the people they were pursuing. A lumber baron, whose tavern in Detroit had burned, had hired this particular agent to pursue a singer who'd fled the scene, along with her supposed cousin, believed to be her husband or lover. The Pinkerton had already been at the Straits investigating a possible maritime fraud case when he'd been assigned Lily's investigation. His initial contact with Lily had led him to believe she was innocent of any wrongdoing in the fire. The reporter ended the article by writing that perhaps Lily wasn't as ingenuous as she seemed and for readers to watch for more information to come.

Willa set the paper back down. It sounded like this Lily Jones or Kerchinsky might be guilty of something that happened later. For her to possibly be traveling with a lover was certainly not something done by virtuous women back in the day.

At the front of the church, a cluster of tourists retreated, revealing a broad-shouldered man bent over a floral arrangement. He added greenery to a huge crystal vase on a side table that was loaded with pink roses, vibrant red gladiolas, and white lilies. When he turned, his face mask had PARKER LANDSCAPING printed on the front in block letters. His blond hair was shaved close on the sides but was slightly longer on top. He wore a tight-fitting white T-shirt that hugged his muscular torso and cargo pants with short leather work boots.

When he began walking toward them, Willa elbowed Sue. As he neared, she looked into clear blue eyes that seemed familiar. He nodded at them and headed out the door.

Sue turned to her. "Bianca Rossi's former boy toy?"

"I think so." Her accelerating heartbeat agreed. This was the guy they'd met in Yellowstone last year whom she'd nicknamed Yooperman. "Parker Landscaping is the Grand Hotel's contractor."

"Do you think we'll be working with him?"

Willa was glad that Sue couldn't see her gaped mouth behind her mask. She pressed her lips together and swallowed hard. "I hope so." Really? Had Willa just voiced that thought aloud?

Sue shoved her feet back into her shoes. "I *hope* you can reach the carriage taxi service now."

Someone tapped Willa on the shoulder from behind, and she jumped. She turned to look up into sky-blue eyes.

The man took two quick steps back. "Sorry. But could you use a lift?"

Sue brought her hands together as if in prayer. "Horseback, bicycle, or carriage?"

"A dray with plants on it and equipment. But there's room at the back."

"Our knight in shining armor," Sue proclaimed as she rose.

Yooperman laughed, a nice manly sound. "Just a landscaper with fairly dirty work duds."

Willa liked how he said duds, like Gramps would have. "Regardless, you're really saving my friend. We're on our way to the Grand."

"I figgered as much. Going there myself. Come on with me."

Should she tell him who they were? That they'd met him before? Not just yet. Because if he didn't know, then when he officially met her, Willa would be attired in her latest costume, because that's what her work attire really was.

They followed the tall man outside and removed their masks. The flatbed dray was mostly covered in geraniums, greenery, and trays of annuals.

As Sue drew close, she hesitated and turned to give Willa a wideeyed stare. "Really? In that?"

In the blink of an eye, Yooperman turned, lifted Sue like she weighed no more than a down comforter, and set her on the back.

When he faced Willa, she felt those beautiful eyes taking her in, and he hesitated for a moment. My, oh my, was she glad that he wasn't Mr. Rossi.

Not only were these two women the cohosts of *Real Resort Redesign*, but Michael had met the duo a year earlier at Yellowstone. Bianca was one of their fangirls and had been disappointed that they hadn't met up again. He'd even watched several of the duo's shows in preparation for this project at the Grand.

Now, he stared into Willa Christy's truly unusual eyes. They were a green-and-gold swirl surrounded by a thick ring of navy blue and fringed with dark lashes. He sucked in a breath as he surveyed the woman before him. She was dressed in what Mom would call "typical touristy clothes" that were intended for comfort. In Wyoming, the year previously, she'd been dressed similarly.

The television version of Willa Christy was so heavily made up and dressed in such weird getups that her age could have been anywhere from early twenties to maybe pushing forty. Not this gal, though. With no makeup coloring her eyes or forehead, she might be closer to his age, which was soon to be thirty-one.

When he slowly lifted her onto the wagon, something passed between them. And his carefully constructed walls around his emotions threatened to crumble. He'd have to fight any attraction he might feel for this woman. He'd be working with her for the next month. And he was not in any shape to even consider getting involved with a woman again. He had nothing to offer and a whole bag of liabilities.

"There ya go." He released her and hurried to the front of the dray, where he stepped up into the driver's seat. He surely would not make that mistake again—falling for a celebrity who was only interested in her own agenda.

He checked the road, and when a string of bicyclists passed, he directed his horse to move out into the street. He had a job to do, and he wasn't about to disappoint Kareen or Aimee.

The notion that Yooperman had lifted Willa off the dray bed as though he was about to carry her off to his castle fizzled quickly when he deposited them at the Grand and rode off from the hotel without a backward glance. That frisson of attraction between the two of them must have been solely in her imagination.

She and Sue passed the beautiful landscaping that marked the side entrance to the hotel. No doubt their dray driver had contributed to its design and execution. Years earlier, Mom had sent Willa many images of these beds being filled with an array of colorful tulips and daffodils, as they'd have been for Willa's scheduled wedding in the spring of 2010. That had been before...before everything had imploded with her and John.

Sue pointed to Sadie's Ice Cream parlor, attached to the side of the entrance. Outfitted with bright red awnings and featuring a lovely, bricked patio leading up to it, the place should draw guests right in. "You and me later, Willa."

"Depends on how far our place is from here." The hotel manager had informed them that they'd be housed in an exclusive hideaway cottage to ensure their privacy. The hotel had an arrangement with the house's owners. "It could be a trek."

Sue's forehead wrinkled. "Yeah, you're probably right. But let's hope for the best." She raised her hand, fingers crossed.

"Let's get inside and find Aimee."

They both donned their masks.

A red-jacketed young Asian woman stood at the side entrance. "Are you guests?"

"We're here to meet with Miss LaFerier."

The girl gave Sue and her the side-eye. "And your names?"

Willa passed the girl a business card she'd prepared in case of such an event, which Aimee had warned her about. On the back of the pink card, Willa had written, "Please do not announce our names out loud. Simply tell Miss LaFerier her appointment is here. Look at the front of the card, but don't share our information with anyone."

The worker read the back of the card, eyes widening, and she briefly flipped it over.

Willa reached for the card. "Please call Miss LaFerier."

The pretty young woman turned away from Willa and Sue and spoke into her hotel walkie-talkie. She waited for a moment then turned to them. "She will be right here. Follow me please, ladies, to the alcove by the art gallery."

Inside, a queue of guests stood at a stand where two other workers were accepting payments.

"Ten dollars just to come inside?" a middle-aged woman complained to her companion, a man wearing a Pittsburgh Steelers T-shirt.

"That entitles you to tour the grounds as well," the man replied. "And don't forget, we're going up to the cupola at the end to have a few drinks before we walk back down to town."

Ahead on the left was a florist's booth. As they passed, the sweet scent of roses, lavender, and lilies permeated Willa's mask.

The color scheme was jarring, as she knew it would be from the photos, but somehow it all seemed to work. She didn't plan to tour the building and grounds until the next day. "I'm glad I told Aimee we would need fresh eyes for this project."

"Yeah, waiting to tour until tomorrow was a good plan. It's been a long day already."

"And more hours to come."

They followed the worker to an alcove on the right, where contemporary artwork was displayed. She turned toward them and gestured to a nearby hot pink divan. "Miss LaFerier will be here soon." Then she left them.

Sue leaned in closer to look at a painting of a woman holding a golden-haired child's hand. "This is really nice, isn't it?"

"They all are." Willa crossed the room to an abstract painting that appeared to be of two men standing beside two brown boats. She leaned in. The striation in the painting suggested these were wooden boats. A plaque to the right of the painting proclaimed, "The Dueling Moores," by Kareen Parker. *Strange name for a marine painting.* She checked the date on the painting. The year before she was born. Wooden speedboats, which these appeared to be, weren't really being built then—unless her grandpa was the one who'd built them. Something about them was familiar in a disturbing way.

*"Bienvenue!"*

Willa turned. From social media images, she recognized Aimee LaFerier, the French lead director for the hotel transition team.

"Welcome to you both."

With that impossibly pulled-together look that only French women seemed to manage, Aimee wore a slim black houndstooth pencil skirt, a three-quarter-length matching black top, and scarlet kitten heels. Her blond hair was pulled up in a chic chignon, with several tendrils falling down alongside her long neck. Understated black pearls with matching drop earrings completed her look.

"Thank you, we're glad to be here." Sue did a half-turn toward Willa, and she stepped forward.

"We hope we can offer some valuable input."

Aimee clasped her hands together. "I would shake your hand, like Americans do, or kiss your cheeks as we French do, but as things are. . ."

"Hopefully things will get back to normal before long."

*"Oui!"* Aimee pulled two small keyrings from her pocket. "In the meanwhile, let's get you two ladies over to your temporary home while you are with us. Get some rest tonight, because tomorrow you'll be entering our mystery room." She fluttered her hands theatrically.

Sue exchanged a glance with Willa.

Aimee handed them their keys. "You'll be redesigning a room that has been out of service for many years."

"How many?" Willa couldn't imagine the hotel not using every room available.

"Over a century."

She blinked at the French woman. "Why? Was it converted to a storage area or something?"

Aimee shook her head slowly. "No. The story I heard is that the maids from the turn-of-the-century refused to go into the room because of a death associated with it."

Sue shrugged. "But wouldn't that have been forgotten long ago?"

"Each era of servants has one excuse or another. 'It's got bad juju' is the expression the current staff use."

"I take it the new ownership isn't going to let superstition stop the usage of lucrative real estate space."

"*Exactement.*"

"You don't think we'll find a skeleton in the room we're redesigning, do you?" Willa stepped up into the open carriage that Aimee had procured for them.

"I hope not." Sue raised her eyebrows high as she took her seat.

Their driver, Judy, drove them past the grand Victorian cottages on the West Bluff. Soon she directed the horses into a turn, and they headed upward. Bells on the harnesses jangled as the carriage drove deeper into the woods. Judy wore the calm demeanor of someone long-accustomed to driving these old-fashioned conveyances.

The woods cleared, and a two-story blue-and-white cottage sat atop the cliff.

A wide, covered porch ringed the building. On the approach, a semicircular garden edged in old orange-red brick had gone to weeds. But on the right side of the property, a matching semicircular garden had been transformed into a vibrant mass of roses, peonies, gladiolas, and geraniums intermixed with various greenery.

Willa inhaled the floral and earthy scent of the new garden.

"Someone's done a great job on rehabbing that flower patch," Sue called out to Judy.

Judy directed the horses over to the turnabout on the far right. "Probably Michael DuBlanc or his assistant, Colton Byrnes. One of those guys from Parkers' Landscaping."

"The same landscapers the Grand Hotel has working with us on our consultation," Willa shared.

Judy laughed. "Mike DuBlanc has his hand in tons of landscaping projects on this island. But my money is on his assistant for this smaller job."

A tall blond man with the build of a linebacker rounded the side of the building. He waved at them.

"And I was right." Judy directed the horses to stop and then secured the carriage so Willa and Sue could step out. "Ladies, this is Colton Byrnes, one of the best landscapers on the island—or the *best* if you ask him."

Colton pointed both hands at himself. "What, me? Would I say that?" Then he laughed low and deep in his broad chest.

Sue stood staring at the landscaper, and Willa had to sidestep her as she descended from the carriage.

Judy brought the carriage back around in a tight circle. "Colton, I've heard you say it, so don't deny your claims."

"Aw, I probably had a couple of brews in me at that point."

"We were at the Ice House, so yes, I'd say you probably did." Judy grinned at him, then shook the reins and departed.

Colton rubbed his large hands together. "Glad to meet you, Willa," he said as he stared at Sue.

"I'm Sue, and this is Willa." Sue blushed and pointed to Willa.

So obviously Colton wasn't a fanboy and hadn't seen their show.

"Nice to meet you, Colton." Willa waved.

"I was just wrapping up for today, so I'll be heading out."

"Do you have to go so quickly?" Sue was definitely assuming a flirty posture, leaning in toward the tall man.

"Tell you what. When you get bored up here tonight, come on down to the Ice House BBQ, it's behind the Island House Hotel, and I'll buy you a beer." He was definitely looking more at Sue, even though his brief glance included Willa.

Sue winked at him. "You're on."

Willa resisted the urge to roll her eyes. Sue was on to her next heartbreak. This was a summer temporary consulting gig.

"Catch you later then." Colton went to the side of the house and grabbed a dinged-up blue Trek bike. "If I hurry, maybe I can catch up with Judy and she'll give me a ride back to the Grand."

He was off in a flash.

A dreamy expression washed over Sue's face as she stared after the departing gardener.

"Come on. They were supposed to have delivered our stuff." Willa pulled the house key—an old-fashioned brass one—from her purse. She headed for the back door, which was painted a bright turquoise. Inside, black-and-white porcelain tiles covered the square entryway, whose walls were a garish mustard yellow.

"Yikes," Sue muttered as she stepped inside. She covered her eyes. "I think I'm blinded."

"Ha, maybe you're blinded by Colton's beauty!"

"Very funny," Sue returned dryly.

Willa entered the narrow hall that led from the back to the kitchen. A huge farmhouse-style sink was set in a wide butcher-block countertop that by its patina looked to be over a hundred years old. "At least that sink has faucets instead of a pump."

Sue pointed to the stove. "Whoa, look at this."

By first appearances, Willa thought it was an antique. She stepped closer. "Oh my goodness, that thing cost a fortune." The Elmira Stove Works reproduction oven, which was outfitted with gas, was immaculate.

"I've never actually seen one in person."

"I know. Do you remember the hotelier in Vermont who wanted them last year for their cabins?"

Sue slapped at her forehead. "I wish I could forget."

"Do you remember when we redid the budget three times, and they still couldn't see that the budget wouldn't cover it? It's a good thing the husband finally convinced his wife to settle for something we could get installed quickly."

"Yup. But this really is gorgeous." Sue ran her hand over the surface of the stove, which appeared as though it had never met a spatter.

Willa stepped to the kitchen cupboard, 1920s or 1930s in design with an art deco flare. "Gramps said that once furniture was brought to the island, it never left again. That's why we'll likely see a mishmash of all kinds of different antiques in this house."

Soon they'd toured the house, which held an 1860s one-piece black-and-gold hall mirror and bench combo that Willa would have killed for. Maybe not killed for, but boy did she ever want it. "We'd only ever see one of these in a museum."

"Yeah, I'm drooling over these too." Sue pointed to several pieces of art hanging on the wall by the curving oak staircase.

Stifling her inner cautionary critic, Willa stepped forward. *No way.* Her mouth gaped open when she recognized the artwork as original—and überexpensive. "I can't believe these paintings look this good after being left in a building with no climate control." Or had they been?

"Ohmygoodness!" Sue's words flew together as she pointed out two impressionistic sailboat paintings. "Those are by Thad Moore."

Willa leaned in, reading the signature. "Wow. I wonder how they got those? As my grandma would have said, 'They're rare as hen's teeth,' right?"

"Right. He died before he'd even turned twenty, and his pieces are highly prized."

Willa cocked her head, examining the brushstrokes on the canvas. "Who would leave such valuable artwork here?"

"Maybe someone so rich it doesn't matter to them? Or what if this was his cottage or his parents' cottage and they can't bear to do anything with them?"

Chills brushed down Willa's arms. "That would be sad."

"But it would make sense, wouldn't it?"

"Yeah, but there are other expensive paintings here too."

"Right."

"Regardless, we'd better be careful of all those valuable paintings."

They headed upstairs, Sue in the lead. "I get first pick this time, right?"

"You sure do." This past year, Willa had consciously made sure Sue got equal crack at picking her room on assignment. Sue was coming into her own and would soon be offered her own show, if Willa guessed correctly. What would it be like for Willa to be on her own again?

The oak floors creaked as they stepped down the long hallway.

Willa peeked inside the first bedroom. A sage-colored wool, circular rug softened the hardwood floor, while a chest of drawers, circa the 1940s, hugged the right wall. A four-poster cherrywood bed would have looked more appropriate in some Southern plantation home. The sole picture on the walls was a framed newspaper clipping. She moved in closer to read it.

July 1, 1895, was the date across the top of the newspaper. A photo of a pretty woman with upswept hair and what looked like a white Victorian lacy dress dominated the framed page. "Songbird Lily Enchants at the Grand Hotel" was written beneath her picture. Could this be the Lily being pursued by the Pinkertons, as written in the article she'd read earlier? But Lily was a very popular name back then. And this woman had gainful employment. She scanned the article. *Nope.* This was Lily Swaine, not Lily Jones/Kerchinsky.

Sue frowned as she moved alongside Willa. "Doesn't it seem strange that there are no other pictures in here?"

"Yeah, but let's look at the other rooms."

She and Sue continued on. Willa peeked into the next room, painted a deep navy. An oar hung on one wall. The drawers had rope pulls, and overhead a ship's brass bell had been outfitted with an electrical light. Color photos, likely from the 1990s, showed two teenage boys aboard various sailing vessels. Two twin beds were placed opposite each other on the left side against the wall. The lamps atop the nightstands resembled anchors, secured to dark wood platform bases with a light at the top covered by gold pleated lampshades.

Sue shook her head. "This room really stands out, doesn't it?"

"Yeah, and not in a good way—although Gramps would think so."

Pointing to framed photos on the wall, Sue took two steps forward. "Do you think one of them is Thaddeus Moore?"

"I have no idea." Willa shrugged. Sue was getting carried away by her imagination again.

"I'll google it when we have Wi-Fi. Speaking of which, when will we get that?"

"Better be soon, or we'll move up to the Grand." Willa couldn't function without Wi-Fi and her MacBook.

"Let's look at the rest."

Willa followed her friend to the end of the hall. Inside the room, she could have been transported directly back to the Victorian era. The ornate bed, the bulky black armoire, the Eastlake chair and its hideous matching desk belonged in a haunted mansion movie. "Is this what we'll find in the 'bad juju' suite that we're going to remodel?"

"Maybe, but I'll take this one." Sue grinned.

"Seriously?"

"Yeah. It's cool—kinda Gothic."

Willa resisted the urge to roll her eyes. All the light fixtures appeared to be converted from gas to electric. She lifted one of the electric cords, its old-fashioned gold-and-brown cloth cover fraying. "I wouldn't feel safe using this thing."

"Me neither. I'll just unplug it."

Willa followed Sue up the hallway. They ducked inside a bathroom with ivory Italian marble tile. "How did that happen?" Willa stepped forward and touched the subtle but elegant new wallpaper.

"Appears to have been recently remodeled, which is fine by me."

"Right. Those new gold-plated fixtures are from Königs' Emporium in Chicago, and they were only available in their catalog this past winter." Willa ordered many of their products. "So, somebody's coming here or paying someone to fix things."

Sue raised an eyebrow. "Or they have a really weird squatter who enjoys remodeling things."

They both laughed.

"I'll take the first bedroom, then." With the picture of the pretty young singer. She'd read the rest of the article later. It seemed strange to realize that this cottage must have existed here over 125 years earlier. Who had lived here then? Who owned this place now?

Willa's cell phone buzzed. "Yay, we've got a signal up here." She glanced down at the message from Gramps: WHEN ARE YOU COMING TO SEE ME?

She texted back—HAVE TO LOOK AT ROOMS TOMORROW AT GRAND. WILL COME NEXT DAY. Hopefully, the mystery suite at the Grand Hotel would be an easy redesign to solve. Then she could sketch out her ideas tomorrow night.

OK, Gramps texted back.

She was ready to push harder to get answers about who her biological father might be. And for her nightmares to finally stop.

# CHAPTER SEVEN

## 1895

*H*ow strange for Lily to have a maid sleeping in the adjacent room instead of her cousin Clem—and no need for firearms either. What a blessed relief. Lily unfolded Mama's thin quilt and spread it atop the fancy bedcoverings. She couldn't remember much about her early years in Kentucky, but the recollection of Mama stitching the quilt outside their cabin always made her smile. Those were happy times. Mama would hum and sometimes sing—she had a pretty voice and everyone in the hollow said, "That's where Lily got her purty sangin' voice from."

Back in the day, Pa would come home from his work as a laborer, toting an armful of food, and Mama would always be hopeful that he'd also have brought some coins with him. Anton Kerchinsky was a handsome man, quiet, and dedicated to his family. His kin populated their eastern Kentucky hillside. Every Sunday without fail, Pa would ride them to church on the buckboard. That's where Lily's crystal-clear voice first was noticed. She wasn't vain about her ability—this was something God had given her to cherish and use.

She smoothed out the quilt and went to her desk and sat. Lily pulled her journal out from the side drawer and prepared her new fountain pen.

Soon Lily began to write:

> *Tonight, I had my first attack like one of Mama's. I'm so scared. I have prayed that nothing like what happened to her would befall me. Yet here I am behaving in a similarly strange manner. And I fear the terrible headaches that plagued her are now attacking me. I had scarcely begun*

*my evening ablutions when my temple began to throb. I*
*pray this is brought on only by the distress of meeting those*
*psychiatrists tonight. I must make a plan to avoid Dr.*
*DuBlanc. It's not safe to be around him. I don't trust him.*

She stopped writing. That wasn't exactly true. She did trust him but not with her secret.

Alice tapped at the door as she entered. "Sorry I'm late, miss." She dipped a curtsy.

Maybe Lily should have inquired what had kept the servant away, but it hadn't really mattered. She'd been able to undress herself and get ready for bed without any assistance. Truth be told, Lily preferred her privacy, but the hotel was insistent that she have help. Alice had been especially useful in getting Lily dressed properly for dinner and then changed for her performances.

When Lily said nothing, the girl visibly relaxed. "I went for a long walk on the cliffside. It's ever so lovely this time of the day."

Lily quirked one eyebrow. "Or night."

Alice laughed. "Aye, it is after ten o'clock now, but it seems much earlier with the sun just now setting."

"I hope to explore the surroundings further myself, once I have my free evening."

"Have Dr. DuBlanc take you to all the romantic places." The maid clutched her hands to her chest. "He's so very handsome."

Lily raised her eyebrows in warning. "Dr. DuBlanc is a kind gentleman who has helped Clem and me to get settled in with our work. He is not a beau."

"But you take dinner with him every night, miss."

Lily exhaled a breath. "The poor man has no one to sit with since he's a psychiatrist." That was exactly what he'd told Clem and her.

"Oh, I see. Sorry, miss, for getting above my station."

"It's all right, but please don't bring up these silly romantic notions with me again. I am here for my job, and I'm not like my predecessor, Miss Ivy Sterling, seeking a wealthy husband."

"Aye, miss." She bobbed a curtsy again. "I'll ready myself for bed."

"Good night."

Lily should never have accepted Stephen's offer to accompany her and Clem on a tour of the island on Sunday. It was too late to bow out now. Clem would be too disappointed, and it would be rude for Lily to cancel. She simply wouldn't accept any more invitations from Stephen. And she'd speak with Clem about changing their dinnertime. That should take care of things. But would it? She'd only be here for a season. She'd kept suitors at bay before, and she could do it again. Why then did the thought make her so sad?

Sunday arrived with a brisk breeze and full sun overhead. Lily couldn't help but feel exhilarated, as though something were waiting just around the bend for her. After service at Mission Church, with an excellent sermon by Rev. Brian McWithey, Clem, Lily, and Stephen set out on their adventure.

"Let's stop and eat our sandwiches by the fort's garden," Lily suggested. She wanted to look up at the view of the fort that had inspired someone, maybe a relative of hers, to paint it.

"Pretty soon this national park will be transitioned over to a Michigan state park." Stephen pointed to Fort Mackinac.

"Seems a shame." Clem pulled an apple from his pocket and took a bite. "This here place, and much of this island, is part of the second national park in America, but now it won't be."

Stephen shrugged. "I think the government can't keep up with things, and the state is willing to step in, so I'm happy about it."

They walked through what had been the fort's garden area, which was now lying fallow, with the soldiers gone.

Stephen removed his jacket and set it on the ground for Lily to sit.

"Thank you." He really was a considerate man. She arranged her skirts around her.

Butterflies flitted between lilac trees now bare of their blossoms. Seagulls soared and dipped, squawking when people threw bits of bread to the ground. How unlike her home in Kentucky.

When they finished eating, the men rose. Stephen assisted Lily to her feet, holding her hands just a little bit longer than was necessary. Her cheeks warmed.

"Time to continue our walk back to the Grand Hotel."

"That was a lovely little picnic." Something that she would treasure when it was time to move on again.

"The first of many, I hope."

*If only that could be.*

They set out again along the boardwalk, passing through town, where the stores were closed for the Sabbath.

Quite a while later, when they approached the base of the hill to the Grand Hotel, Clem pointed ahead to where tents were arranged in a large cluster. A mix of longing and concern played across his features. "This is the Chippewa encampment."

"Have you visited it?" Stephen cocked his head to the side.

Clem's Adam's apple bobbed. "Yes. I've found the folks here to be right friendly."

A boy zipped past them in the street on a bicycle, holding his hands high in the air. Lily gaped at the child. "He's a daredevil."

"Jack Welling—he's a good kid, but he lost his mother last year."

"Oh my. I'm sorry to hear that." Lily knew how it felt to experience loss, and her heart ached for the boy.

"Jack should be safer than usual with all the physicians arriving."

"Don't you mean psychiatrists?" Lily raised an eyebrow at him.

"Well, we are also physicians."

Clem scratched his cheek. "Don't rightly think of them that way."

Neither did Lily. Psychiatrists were the people who had to lock her mother away in an asylum because she'd become a danger to herself and others.

"Indeed, we're trained as medical doctors as well as in maladies of the mind."

Lily stiffened. Yet another reminder why she shouldn't be out with this charming man after today. She and Clem had already agreed they'd begin varying their dinnertimes.

Nearby, a man in a brown bowler hat and a plaid brown-and-mustard suit pointed out the encampment to the woman at his side. "See how they live, Sarah? They're like animals. That's why we have a responsibility to make sure their children are taken from them and educated properly."

The woman nodded.

Anger surged through Lily. How dare they speak like that?

Clem's face reddened. "Why that. . ."

Stephen's lips tightened. "What the man says is a topic to be discussed at the conference—education and environmental changes versus genetics and heredity. The main focus of the conference is this eugenics movement."

"What's that?" Lily squeaked out her question.

"The conference chairman believes strongly that genetics are the primary influence for the development of mental illness."

Lily's hands began to sweat beneath her crocheted gloves. Maybe she and Clem should attempt to get their job back in Mackinaw City. How could she bear it if she had to listen to such conversations all week at the hotel? But then they'd lose the money that they'd been promised if they lasted the entire season. Still, if she had to listen to such terrible sentiments, how would she refrain from losing her temper and telling them off?

Clem squinted one eye closed. "So some folks think it's best to take these Native kids away from their folks, yet others would say they are, uh, genetically worse off so leave 'em alone. Is that right?"

They continued toward the encampment, where women were weaving baskets and creating intricate beaded designs on small looms.

"It's more complicated than that." By his tone of voice, Stephen sounded frustrated, but hopefully not with them.

"Always is when there's politics involved." Clem shook his head.

"Yes, I see it that way too." Stephen blew out a breath. "Why don't we go for a ride after this and stick with some happier topics?"

"Yes," Lily agreed.

"I think I'm gonna stay down here, if'n you two don't mind." Clem stuck his thumbs in his vest pocket.

"But. . ." Lily would have no chaperone, and she'd be alone with Stephen. Tongues would wag. But then again, at her age and with her profession, people already were gossiping about her, as her maid had confirmed on more than one occasion.

Nearby sat a pretty young Chippewa woman with a long dark braid, attired in a light-colored buckskin dress. She looked up from her beadwork. "Clemuel Christy! You have returned."

Clem blushed. "Yes'm." He removed his hat and clutched it in his hands. "This here is my cousin Lily, and Lil this is Marie."

"Nice to meet you, Marie."

Clem gestured to Stephen. "This is Dr. DuBlanc."

"Come. Sit. I'll bring you some tea."

Stephen gestured toward Lily. "I believe Miss Lily and I shall be taking a drive around the island this afternoon."

"Otherwise, we'd be happy to join you." Lily could see the relief in Clem's eyes.

"I'd love some tea with honey, Marie, if'n you don't mind."

How long had Clem been coming down to the village, and when?

Stephen took her by the elbow and steered her back toward the street. They headed to the line of taxis parked along the walkway. "We'll have to take one of those from town. Ah, I see Stan Danner is driving one of his own carriages today. Let's go with him."

Before long, Stephen had assisted her up into the shiny carriage, and Mr. Danner directed his matching Percheron horses out into the street.

As the carriage passed the encampment, Lily spied Clem laughing. Marie's pretty face shone in delight. Was her cousin falling for her? What might that mean? Lily and Clem had been together for so long now.

On the boardwalk to the left, ladies and gentlemen in their Sunday finery strolled arm in arm, some with well-dressed children trailing behind them. When a gust almost lifted Lily's beribboned hat, she grabbed it. A few of the ladies' menfolk had to chase their blown-off bonnets to retrieve them. Some of the women had the good sense to attach their pretty hats with scarves tied under their chins. It would take more than hatpins and hairpins to secure a bonnet from a stiff Mackinac wind. Would it take more than a convention of psychiatrists to drive Lily off?

"What do you think of the island?" Stephen shifted a little beside Lily so that he could look more clearly at her. His opinion of the place had grown even more favorable ever since her arrival. But he didn't have much time before he'd have to find a position elsewhere.

"It's so beautiful." Lily gazed out at the curved beach area, strewn with rocks.

"There's a nice little spot over there." A large, smooth-topped boulder would be the perfect place to sit. "Let me get out and help you down."

Mr. Danner called over his shoulder, "It's a popular place, especially for Sunday outings."

Stephen glanced around at the wide expanse of green lawn. "But there's no one here right now."

He exited the carriage and assisted Lily out, her hand soft and warm in his. When she was on terra firma, she released his hand and smoothed her skirts. He offered his arm and steered her toward the huge rock.

A carriage full of silver-haired men and women rode by, many attired in somber colors. The islanders, he'd noted, had mostly dressed in drab clothing, but perhaps that was because most were workers or owned businesses and weren't here on holiday. The open carriage rolled past, pulled by a pair of matching bay horses.

"I'll miss this place when I'm gone." Lily gazed out at Lake Huron and the Straits of Mackinac.

"Strange to think that's Lake Michigan over there." Stephen pointed to the west.

"But it all runs together."

"Yes. Lake Michigan and Lake Huron join together up here."

"Why not simply give it one name?" Lily frowned.

"Who knows? But it's all breathtaking, isn't it?"

She nodded. "Have you traveled much?"

Stephen blinked. He'd traveled to Europe after finishing his college studies and would have returned after finishing medical school were it not for his father's death. "Some. How about you?" He didn't feel right talking about his travels unless he knew the person with whom he was speaking had similar experiences. He didn't want to seem to be putting on airs.

"Only for my work. And I didn't usually have much time for enjoying the sights." Lily's lower lip trembled. "My mother was ill for a long time before she died."

"I'm so sorry. My father died rather suddenly. I'm not sure which is worse." He gently released her arm from his, removed his coat, and set it atop the boulder. He gestured for her to sit.

"Thank you." She chewed her lower lip.

"Do you have brothers or sisters?"

"No. What about you?"

"I have a much older brother and a sister—both married and living in other states." He slipped onto the stone beside her. "I was the baby, and my mother favored me, which didn't serve me well with my siblings."

Lily laughed softly. "Do you look like her side of the family?"

He shook his head. "No. I'm the spitting image of my father, and she loved him almost worshipfully—which I don't believe is a good thing."

"Better than neglecting him."

"Certainly. But I'd not want my wife to fail to see me as the very real human that I am."

She quirked an eyebrow at him. "You have a wife somewhere?"

He chuckled. "No. Not yet." But lately, his imaginings of such a wife were of this beautiful woman.

"I don't think I'll ever marry. I'm quite an old maid at this point." Lily watched a sailboat speeding through the waves. "And I believe that some people should never marry and have children."

Her cheeks turned rosy.

"You sound like some of my ridiculous colleagues who are pushing for this heinous eugenics movement."

"You don't agree with them?"

"No. Such men wish to make themselves gods and determine outcomes that they should have no control over."

She drew in a long breath and exhaled slowly before turning to him. "But what if you had a patient who you could see would be a terrible parent? Wouldn't you lock them away?"

He sighed. "I wish we had better treatments, and we do what we can to restore people to their families. But this eugenics movement goes far beyond the pale. For instance, what if someone as talented and lovely as you had never come into this world because her mother had gone insane?"

Lily gaped at him.

Heat seared his neck in embarrassment. "I apologize. I was so insufferably rude. I forget myself."

Lily struggled to recover her composure. Surely, he didn't know. Stephen couldn't possibly realize her background. She breathed in slowly, imagining herself by the peaceful field she always took herself to in her mind when she was upset. She still didn't know where that place was, but it always made her feel calm.

Stephen stood and ran his hand through his hair. "This is the problem with being a psychiatrist. I say the most socially inept things."

Lily waved her hand dismissively. "Don't worry about it. Let's not speak of such things again." *Never again, preferably.* He was speaking of marriage, yet he'd never expressed that he loved her.

The *clip-clop* of horses' hooves sounded behind them, along with the jingling of harness bells. Lily turned to see that the driver was the handsome man who had been staring at her during last night's performance. Oh no. She'd dealt with many men who believed that songstresses were easy pickin's, as Mama used to say. Thankfully, she had Stephen beside her today. Clem kept most male fans away from her at their venues.

Beside the dark-haired driver sat a young woman with chestnut-colored hair. She looked quite familiar, although Lily couldn't quite place her. She was certain she'd seen her at the Grand. In the carriage's second row, a young boy about twelve or so years old jostled in his seat and pointed toward the beach. Clearly he wished to stop, and his father obliged. What was it with married men who thought they could ogle singers and actresses and then went back home to their families acting as though they were perfect saints?

"You seem deep in thought." Stephen frowned at her.

"I saw that driver, the father, at my show last night."

"Him?" He inclined his head to where the stranger expertly eased his carriage into place behind theirs. His wife and son both greeted Mr. Danner warmly.

"Yes. I'm guessing they are islanders." The boy patted Mr. Danner's horses and opened his palm to offer one what looked like a bit of carrot.

"That's the most eligible bachelor on the island."

"Who's with him?"

"That's Jack—we saw him earlier racing down the street on his bicycle.

Jack Welling is his nephew."

"Yes, I recognize him now. The little daredevil with no hands on the bars."

"He's twelve years old and quite full of mischief." Stephen inclined his head toward a young woman with beautiful dark auburn hair. "He's with his older sister, Maude. Their family owns the Winds of Mackinac Inn."

Maude. That was the name of the clumsy maid. Surely this couldn't be the same young woman.

The trio headed down toward the water. Attired in a flowing, cream-colored muslin day dress, Maude held a matching parasol over her head. The boy removed his boots and socks and ran barefoot into the water despite all the rocks on the beach.

To Lily's distress, the handsome man strode deliberately toward them. Rich and a bachelor or not, Lily wasn't interested in dealing with him today on her one free day in the week.

The man slowed his steps as he neared them, his facial features tugging as if in disbelief. He ran his hand slowly over his chin—like a man accustomed to sporting a beard would do.

Stephen extended his hand. "Good to see you, Captain."

The man nodded, continuing to stare at Lily with that strange expression on his face. It wasn't like that of an admirer, though.

She smiled in what she hoped was a genteel manner. "I'm Lily, the new singer. But I believe you attended my last show—so you would know that."

"Yes, I enjoyed it very much."

"I'm glad we could entertain you."

He looked much too young to be Maude's uncle, but up close some silver glinted in his hair. His face was unlined, though, and she judged him to be near her own age. He examined her face closely as though searching for something. "I'm Robert Swaine."

Her heart did a little lurch.

When she didn't respond, Robert continued. "I understand your surname is Swaine?"

"It's. . .it's a stage name," she stammered. Should she confess where she'd taken the name?

"I see." His face relaxed. "It's remarkable, but you greatly resemble a portrait of my mother when she was young."

Stephen leaned in. "What is your real last name, Lily, if you don't mind me asking?"

She did mind—very much.

Robert took another step closer, and she could see amber flecks in his hazel eyes, like she had. Like someone else had. *The man with no arm and no leg.* She shivered.

Mr. Swaine turned toward the water. "Maude! Come here for a moment."

Stephen cast her a quizzical look. "Is something wrong?"

When the captain turned, perspiration dotted his brow despite the cool day. "Where did you grow up, Lily?"

"Virginia," Stephen supplied before she could even open her mouth.

Robert straightened to his full height. "My grandparents lived in Virginia."

"Mine as well—near Fredericksburg." How on earth had this lie slipped past her lips so blithely? Yet in her spirit, she felt the conviction of its truth.

Maude joined them, a smile wobbling on her face as she glanced between her uncle and Lily. "What is it?"

"Do you see a resemblance to grandmother's portrait?"

"Yes."

"This is Miss Lily Swaine, who I wonder if may be kin to us."

Stephen placed his hand over Lily's. "I think you're out of line here, Captain Swaine. Lily said the name she uses is only for her performances."

"I apologize." Robert had the good grace to look a bit sheepish. "But if you're willing, Miss Lily, would you meet with us this evening and share your real name and story? I'd be happy to escort you after your performance at the Grand."

Jack ran up to them, soaking wet and panting. "Hey, that's the lady you said looks like Granny did! Is she the one you told us about?"

His sister gave him a cautionary glance, but the boy continued, "You sure do look like her painting, lady—except you're not dressed in some ugly, old-style clothing."

Lily couldn't help but laugh. This child was full of the energy she wished she'd had at his age.

Captain Swaine locked his hazel gaze on her. "Do you know the bright yellow cottage near the Grand Hotel?"

"On the cliff?" She'd seen it from the ship upon her arrival and thought it resembled the painting in her treasure box.

"Yes, that belongs to our family."

Lily swallowed hard. On the back of the birch bark painting had been written "Home Sweet Home" in a masculine scrawl. "I'd be happy to meet with all of you."

"Should I come fetch you in our carriage?"

"No, I believe I'd prefer to walk and get some fresh evening air."

Jack angled in front of his sister and uncle. "You can see the sunset real good from the front porch."

She laughed. "I'd have to stay mighty late to see that, wouldn't I?"

"We can play horseshoes and croquet if you want. And I have checkers and cards too." He leaned in conspiratorially. "We don't have to spend all our time talkin' about boring family stuff—we can have some fun."

"You're definitely on then." Impulsively, she pulled the boy into her arms. No children of her own and no extended family. Maybe God was granting one of her most secret desires—for more family. And maybe one day she really could find a future for herself, one not tainted by her mother's terrible deeds.

# CHAPTER EIGHT

## *2020*

*W*illa woke with the buzz of excitement that always accompanied the first day on a new job. Today Aimee would show them their design project, which was to represent a sample of their style. They had to complete this challenge as well as present an acceptable overall redesign.

Willa donned her leopard-print skinny jeans, an asymmetrically cut turquoise tunic, a signature piece necklace of dangling sea glass pieces, and matching bespoke earrings. It had taken a while to get her over-the-top makeup in place, but her hair extensions had gone in pretty easily. Looking in the mirror, she wasn't sure anyone would recognize her as the woman who'd arrived at this cottage yesterday. Sue had already warned the landscaper Colton to keep quiet about both who they were and what they looked like when functioning as "normal" people.

Sue knocked on the door.

"Come in."

Attired in a boho maxi dress of fire engine red, yellow, and green swirls and an inch layer of makeup, Sue had been transformed. "Do you realize that if we got some average twenty-something women—"

"Thirty-something for me."

"Okay, twenty to thirty or so, and put our hair pieces, clothing, and makeup on them and sunglasses and then top it off with the mask. . ."

Sue seemed to have run out of breath. Willa laughed. "So you think there are people who want to be Willa and Sue impersonators?"

"Yeah, like the Elvis impersonators."

"All that stuff doesn't make the person. It's just an image they are projecting."

"Maybe they'd do our job for us, and we could just be tourists." Sue stepped toward the bureau mirror and swiveled left and then right, watching her image. "Have to say I'm looking beastin' good today."

"Beasting good?" Willa hadn't heard that one before.

"Colton said our gardens were starting to look beastin' good today, so I'm giving those flower beds a run for their money."

Willa shook her head slowly. Would her friend ever learn about the pitfalls of quick romances?

"Come on, we better get out there for the taxi."

Sue grimaced. "We're gonna be on foot."

"No taxi?"

"Nope. I called too late. They're all taken. Sorry." Sue's lips formed a pout.

"No wonder you've got flats on." Tomorrow, Willa would order the taxi early.

Soon the two of them had trod through the woods, across a footpath, down a hill, and onto the sidewalk that led to the Grand Hotel.

Sue patted her pocket, which held her cell phone. "We'll definitely have over ten thousand steps on our health apps each day if we walk."

Willa had already snuck a look at her app and seen that they'd walked a mile, even though the staff at the Grand had assured them that the cottage was under a half mile away. By the time they reached the steps to the hotel, they'd no doubt have logged another quarter of a mile.

Inside, they approached the concierge, Pedro, their contact person. He left his desk to join them. "Good morning. Are you ready for our first stop?"

"Sure thing." Willa adjusted her turquoise and silver face mask.

They took the elevator up to the third floor. Pedro led Willa and Sue down the long, carpeted hallway.

Sue frowned. "I can feel the unevenness in this floor, even beneath the heavy carpet."

"Our historian, Bob Tagatz, could tell you stories about that. But trust me, it's all solid."

Sue cast a glance at Willa that suggested she didn't think so.

The young Latino man's braid dangled down his back, swaying back and forth as they followed him. He stopped almost at the end of the hallway. "This is the room Miss LaFerier wants you lovely ladies to redesign."

Sue clapped her hands. "We're psyched to get started."

"This room has been, um—how do you say—untouched?" Pedro turned and looked at them.

"Aimee mentioned something like that." Because the mystery room hadn't been utilized in over a hundred years, Willa knew it would definitely not be decorated in the fashion that Carlton Varney had done with the other rooms.

Pedro pulled an old-fashioned brass key from his pocket and unlocked the door.

"Ladies?" He waved them into the dimly lit interior.

Sue entered first, and she paused midroom. Willa remained at the entrance, wanting to soak in whatever it was this bedchamber was supposed to tell her. Was that her imagination or did roses and lilies scent the air?

Faded pink roses dotted the cream-colored wallpaper, crisscrossed with equally faded green vines.

"Wow. The 1890s since this room has last been decorated?"

"Yes. No one in here since then." He clasped his hands together.

The woodwork wasn't painted white, as she'd expected, but was stained or varnished in a golden oak hue that would be consistent with the earlier time frame. The room was deep and spacious, with a huge window dominating the far wall. A desk and matching chair sat midroom. A tall rosewood framed screen shielded one corner. Willa pointed to it. "So that was the dressing area?"

"Has to be." Sue pointed to a massive armoire adjacent the wooden screen. "And that chifforobe is ready for a ton of clothes. I'm guessing this was a wealthy young woman's room."

Pedro's lips twitched. "We are told a singer used this room."

Willa strode forward, past a brass bed covered in a bedspread so dusty that she couldn't discern the color of it. "There should also be a servant's room if this has been untouched. She reached for the walnut paneled door on the right wall and turned the brass doorknob, engraved with leaves.

When the door didn't budge, Pedro pulled another key from the same round brass keyring and opened the lock beneath the knob. "Here you go, ladies."

"Thanks." Willa stepped past him into the small side chamber. As she expected, in contrast to the outer room, this one possessed an austerity that was almost chilling. A rumpled white sheet covered the narrow pine bed. Atop that lay a moth-eaten wool blanket.

"Oh my goodness, my grandma had a pitcher exactly like this." Sue went to the washstand atop which set a blue-and-white porcelain bowl and a small, cracked pitcher.

Several shabby dust-covered dresses hung on hooks on the wall. "It almost looks like someone left and planned to return soon."

The dark-eyed man shrugged. "Maybe."

"What do you know about these rooms?" Willa slowly scanned the main area, which was generously sized.

"I know you are supposed to showcase your style here." A tic jumped in Pedro's jaw as he made that clipped statement.

"Was there a murder here?" Sue got right to the point.

"We don't believe so. But the rumors—they keep circulating that there was a death that happened. The previous owners said these always were called 'the Songbird's Rooms'—Lily was the singer's name."

"Lily?" The woman in the picture in the article back at the cottage.

"No one talks about this woman." The concierge made the sign of the cross on his chest as he backed out of the room.

"Ah." Sue arched an eyebrow.

Pedro looked like he was going to do a runner on them, as he eased closer to the door.

"What's our budget?" she called after him. She knew the set fee for doing the job but hadn't gotten the specifics on what the redesign budget was. She'd been so happy to get immediate work for them that she'd not pushed for that info.

He named the amount.

Willa crossed her arms. This thing was a big job for a short consultation. "Who do we have access to for the work crew and supplies?"

Pedro pulled an envelope from his pocket and set it on a tiny wooden table by the door. "Here are the specifics."

Sue walked over, grabbed the envelope, and opened it.

The smirk on Pedro's face told Willa that the young man knew the details. Willa moved in and peered over her business partner's shoulder.

She scanned the document. This project would have been almost impossible to have managed even if they weren't on an island during a pandemic. Anger shot through her. Was this some kind of setup for failure?

"We can do this," Sue assured Pedro.

*Seriously, she just said that?* Willa clamped her lips together.

"*Saludos.* Best wishes then." He handed them each a key.

"Thanks," Willa mumbled. *For nothing.*

The concierge departed, almost like a puff of smoke. She sank onto a nearby chair. "This is impossible."

They both removed their face masks.

Sue clapped her hands. "I'm really excited about this. I tell you what—I'll make this my main project while you do the rest of the legwork for our consultation."

"Do you think they knew this was a two-designer job and that's why they hired us? A twofer?"

"I don't know, but I am jazzed that we could turn this into something truly stunning."

"Yeah, we could if we had twice as much budget and four times as much crew." Willa made a sarcastic face.

"It is a pandemic. Maybe they don't have enough manpower right now."

"True. Still—"

Sue raised her hand. "No worries, my friend. I've got this. And hopefully this Williford guy is a construction genius."

What had happened to Willa's enthusiasm? Had all that playfulness and fun she'd had on their HGTV projects been an act? No, she loved her profession, all the travel, the challenges, meeting new people, and climbing up the ladder in prominence among national designers. But now it wasn't enough. There was a hole in her heart that had been left when she was a child and widened by John's betrayal. She knew she had to repair that void if she was ever to live a full life.

She'd start by pushing for some answers in Hessel.

Willa settled in for her second night's sleep at the cottage. She had an early morning departure to get to her grandfather's dock by his lunchtime break. She adjusted her white Vellux blanket around her, glad she'd packed it. Much easier to sleep having her own blanket and pillow. She really needed her rest before she headed to Hessel and pushed for more answers about her father.

"So 11,055 steps today," she whispered. Too tired for bad dreams tonight. *If only.*

Willa drifted off to sleep.

*"You've got a fever, Willa." Pretty mommy held the thermometer up for Willa to see the numbers, but she didn't know what they meant.*

*"I wanna go."*

*Gramps smacked his newspaper down on the wooden kitchen table. "You can't go, and that's that."*

*"Dad, let me handle this." Mommy lifted Willa from her chair and carried her to the front window. She pulled back the blue curtain and white sheers and pointed outside. "I'll be back before the sun sets."*

*"But my friends. . ." She began to cry. Her head ached and she was hot, but Willa wanted to spend time at the playtime building while Mommy took her classes.*

*"You can go when you're better. You don't want to get your buddies sick, do you?"*

*"You're a nurse. You can fix them."*

*Mommy laughed. "Not quite yet, but soon I'll be a nurse." She brushed Willa's nose with her finger. "But even so, I'd still want you to stay home and not infect anyone else."*

*She didn't know what infect was, but it didn't sound good. "Bring me a big cookie?"*

*Mommy tilted her head. "I bet you want oatmeal raisin," she teased.*

*"Nooo, oatmeal raisin is yucky. I want a chocolate chipper."*

*"All right." She bent and kissed Willa's head.*

*"Don't go!" Willa wailed.*

*Someone shook her. "Hey, Willa, try to remember this dream, but you need to wake up, my friend." That voice belonged to someone beside Mommy, and Willa didn't want to leave her yet.*

*Mommy squeezed her hands. "I promise you a chocolate chipper cookie, and I'll be back before you know it and we'll be together again!"*

*"Don't go, don't go." Willa didn't want this time with her mother to end.*

"Willa, listen, it's Sue. You have to wake up; you're having that night-mare again." Her friend shook her shoulder hard.

Willa sat straight up in the bed, sweat drenching her sleep shirt.

"Tell me right now what you remember."

"My mom, Gramps, snow, I was sick." Willa hiccupped back a sob. Sue had woken her from her night terrors many times over the years, but Willa always retained only a fragment of this dream. Not really a dream but a memory. "It really happened. My mom, I. . .um, I was supposed to go to a play group at her university in the Soo. And I was sick." Tears poured down her cheeks.

Sue turned and grabbed a tissue from the box on the nearby dresser. "Here. But keep going, try to remember it."

"I had to stay home. My mom kissed me, and then she left."

"And never came back?"

Willa tried to stifle a sob. Her therapist had told her she had to access and release these memories if she was ever going to get past this emo-tional roadblock she had with men. Her psychologist, Dr. Svendsen, didn't believe that Willa's overachieving behavior was simply success driven, nor did she believe that John's academic betrayal had caused it.

"I, oh, wow, she was so young, Sue. I know she was only twenty when she died, but to see her again in my memories like that. A decade younger than I am and with a three-year-old."

Sue brushed her tousled bangs back from her oval-shaped face. "Maybe you should write this down while you remember it best."

Her friend went to the midcentury oak desk by the wall and grabbed the peach-colored notepad Willa had placed there earlier. "Here ya go," Sue said, handing Willa the pad. "And congrats on finally remembering some more stuff."

"Thanks for helping me." If Sue hadn't spoken into that dream, would Willa have remembered it now? Probably not. Willa had suffered from night terrors for years, and the only thing she could remember was a feeling of deep loss. Her adoptive parents tried to help, but they seemed as frightened of her dreams as she was.

It wasn't until she was sixteen and they'd finally revealed her adoption that the nightmares made sense. They'd disclosed that her mother had died in a car wreck in a blizzard, driving home from her nursing classes at a college in the Soo, what the locals called Sault Ste. Marie. Willa had stayed with her grandparents, with whom she and her mother had always lived, until she'd been adopted by her childless aunt and uncle.

"I wonder if your being up here and seeing your grandfather tomorrow has triggered this one?"

Willa nodded slowly. Then she began writing down every detail she recalled.

"Good night, my friend." Sue patted Willa's arm gently.

"Good night."

Willa sat there, writing other things that came to her. Standing on the porch as snow blew down. Sticking her tongue out to catch some flakes. Gramps pulling her back inside the house. Gramps frantically calling people asking about her mom. A policeman coming to their door. Grandma collapsing onto the couch and sobbing. The word *dead* had been one she'd only just learned before her mother's death, when her dog had died.

"Buster," she spoke aloud into the night. She'd forgotten her dog—her and her mother's golden retriever. Now images of flashing tan fur, her mother laughing, the two of them tumbling with the dog in the grass flooded her mind so fresh they could have occurred yesterday.

Willa wrote down more memories and finally turned off the light and tried to go back to sleep. She wanted to remain in the recollections of her mother, afraid that if she went back to sleep she'd lose them again.

Healing had to start soon. She couldn't continue like this. Sometimes it felt like she was losing her mind.

# CHAPTER NINE

## 1895

"*D*r. DuBlanc, come sit with us." Dr. Perry, the superintendent of the Newberry State Asylum, gestured for Stephen to join the suited gentlemen seated around the polished oak bar in the men's parlor.

Stephen lingered in the entryway for a moment. The pipe and cigar smoke in the room repelled him. If only his father had set aside his smoking habit. If only he'd not been so absentminded. Maybe he was becoming like his father, because that morning he'd put on two different shoes, a Loake loafer and an Oxford style, and had to correct his error. Stephen's thoughts of a certain singer were likely the cause of his distraction, though.

Dr. Bottenfield waved Stephen over. Reluctantly, Stephen moved forward across the plush wool carpeting. But he should extend all courtesy to his future employer.

He slid onto one of the padded leather seats beside Dr. Perry and extended his hand. "I attended medical school with your son." This man possessed the same dark eyes and rosy cheeks as his classmate, but his wavy dark hair was well-laced with silver.

"Then you may know that he's working at the hospital with our brain-injured patients."

"No, I didn't know that, but it was an interest of his throughout our training."

"Indeed." Perry's ruddy cheeks grew even redder as he beamed with pride. "He's gaining a reputation for helping in even the most desperate cases."

Dr. Rightler and Dr. Bottenfield nodded.

Dr. Perry sipped the amber liquid in his crystal goblet. "With the growth of our Malingering Neuroses Unit, we could use a man like you at our facility."

"I'll toast to that." Rightler lifted his glass.

The superintendent seemed to school his features. "Yes, we are looking for candidates with a sterling reputation and credentials." He raised his cigar to his lips and inhaled, then blew out smoke across the bar in the servers' direction.

If these colleagues knew about his father and his likely actions, they'd not consider Stephen for one second. He exhaled a breath he'd not realized had stuck in his chest. When he inhaled, he resisted the urge to cough. "Good to set the bar high." And may no one ever know what ill his father had begotten.

"We enjoyed your sweetheart's performance last night." Dr. Rightler leaned in and winked at him.

"She's not my sweetheart." Stephen pulled at his collar.

Superintendent Perry pointed at Stephen's face. "There's a tell that would get you in trouble in a game of poker."

Rightler laughed. "I think games of poker are out for you, Dr. Perry, but I'm sure a little harmless betting on the horse race this afternoon would be fine."

"Horse race?" Stephen had been on the island for over a month and not heard of such races—only that dog race yesterday.

Bottenfield and Rightler exchanged a sly look. Obviously, they had means of discovering things that Stephen didn't possess.

"Yes, a couple of island men are racing in a field over beyond the Grand's stables." Bottenfield drummed his fingers on the wood counter.

"Is that part of the conference then?" Stephen quipped.

Perry guffawed. "It is for me and Rightler. We've got five-to-one odds on a beautiful bay mare."

Rightler shrugged. "It's during that idiot Dr. Fraufein's presentation."

"He's certainly jumped on the eugenics movement." Dr. Bottenfield's scowl suggested he shared Stephen's concerns.

"As a Christian as well as a psychiatrist, I think Fraufein should take his notions back to Germany." Rightler scowled.

"Maybe not even there." Perry lifted a brandy snifter to his lips and tossed the contents back.

Rightler inclined his head toward the door, and Stephen turned. Lily stood there as if in search of someone or something. "Now there is someone so beautiful that she's bound to have something wrong with her." The older man laughed.

What a rude thing to say. Who knew what other ungentlemanly things these fellows said and did in private? But by the way the others were chuckling, Stephen realized this was the way they joked about their profession, to ease the tension in coping with mentally disturbed individuals on a daily basis.

Lily waved to him, and Stephen rose. "Let me see if I can help her."

"Assuredly, do so." Perry turned all the way around, and his face brightened. "Lovely lady."

"Yes, she is." Stephen dipped his chin. "I'll see you later, gentlemen."

He went to the entryway to join Lily, who was frowning. "Are you all right?"

"I am, but my maid wasn't in the room when I returned from breakfast. One of the other workers said she might be on this floor. But I can see this room is full of the psychiatrists here for the conference."

"Right you are."

Attired in a blue-and-green plaid day dress, Lily's hair was swept up in a fashion that emphasized her hazel eyes and high cheekbones.

"I'll check on this floor, but then I'm off to see if I can find her. I'll need help today with the extra performance for the doctors this afternoon."

"Have you asked Mrs. Fox to help you manage Alice?"

Lily shook her head emphatically. "No, I don't want to cause unnecessary trouble."

Lily didn't want to cause extra worries for herself or for Alice. But something had to be done if Lily was to effectively do her job. She strode down the hall toward Mrs. Fox's office. She didn't want the girl to get in trouble, though. Hadn't one maid, Maude, just been fired? She chewed her lip—surely that hadn't been the Maude who may be her cousin. The name was fairly common, so Lily dismissed the silly notion.

Ahead of her, a maid with an enviable figure and golden hair tucked up beneath a white head-covering looked up from her cart. She gawked at Lily. "You're Miss Lily Swaine, aren't you?"

"Yes. And what's your name?"

She bobbed an awkward curtsy, as if remembering herself. "I'm Sadie. Sadie Duvall."

"Nice to meet you, Sadie. I'm looking for my maid, Alice."

She frowned. "I saw her sneaking a smoke out back a few minutes ago."

What if Alice decided to smoke in their quarters? Employees were forbidden to smoke inside the wood structure, although male guests were allowed to partake in the smoking room and men's parlor, which she'd just left. She exhaled a sigh. The younger woman was still staring at her.

Sadie looked around the hall, which was empty. "I'm a friend of Robert Swaine and of his niece, Maude Welling."

Lily felt her eyes widen. "I met them yesterday, myself."

"They were right, you do look almost exactly like the portrait of Mrs. Jacqueline Swaine—even down to the way your hair does that little thing right there." She pointed to where a section of hair at Lily's brow frizzed into an unruly curl. "You can see it in her painting at Robert's home. I remember Mrs. Swaine having that when she was an older lady."

"Mr. Swaine and I. . .we're exploring our possible connection."

A matronly looking woman exited a nearby room followed by a young woman who clearly was her daughter. The twosome cast Lily and Sadie a sideways glance.

"Thank you for your help, miss," Lily feigned a forced cheerfulness. "When you see Alice, please send her directly up."

"Yes, ma'am." Sadie averted her gaze and dipped into a curtsy as the two women passed by.

"Nice to meet you, Miss Duvall." Even if what she'd said had disturbed Lily further. This was no chance connection. She knew Anton Kerchinsky was not her biological father, but her mother had refused to ever discuss who he was, only that she'd lost the one true love of her life.

Hours later, Lily and Clem completed their afternoon performance for the psychiatrists. Robert Swaine had arranged to meet Lily at the back door to the stage. Why was he close friends with one of the maids? Was he one of those kinds of men who took advantage of women? She'd give him the benefit of the doubt since Sadie claimed that she and Maude were friends.

Clem packed up his music as their audience departed the room. "I'm headin' down to the encampment for a bit."

"To see Marie?"

Her cousin's cheeks turned pink. "I reckon I might. I've got a right to a life of my own, Lil."

What did that mean? "I don't think I said otherwise."

Clem made some kind of grumbling noise of disagreement as he turned his back to her, and she followed him down the few steps out the back door.

Flummoxed by his unusual display of petulance, Lily watched her dear cousin walk away. She drew in a few deep breaths before she too left the stage.

Robert awaited, hands shoved in his expertly tailored jacket pockets. "Are you ready, Lily?"

Clem gave him a stern look. "You're responsible for her care this afternoon."

Captain Swaine mock-saluted her cousin. "Assignment accepted."

"I'm serious. You wouldn't believe the number of Lil's crazed admirers I've had to deal with over the years."

"I think I might. I have a dear friend, Laura Williams, who has suffered the same difficulties as an actress."

Clem's jaw dropped. "You know her? I saw her in the hallway. Supposed to be a great actress."

Robert chuckled. "That she is. But to me, she's a longtime dear friend."

Lily hadn't worked up the nerve to introduce herself to the stunning actress—and probably wouldn't.

Soon they'd left the back hall. The scent of fresh coffee mingling with sweet yeasty cinnamon rolls greeted them as they entered the parlor. Multiple coffee and tea carts were set up for the psychiatrists, as well as platters of baked goods.

"They had to contract with the Christy Tea Shop to supply afternoon tea for the conference," Robert confided. "I don't think the management anticipated the rate at which those psychiatrist vultures consume pastries."

Lily laughed. "Only in the daytime, though, I believe."

"Ah yes, nighttime seems devoted to imbibing various brandies and whiskeys."

"I've noticed."

He gave her a questioning glance. "Back to the Christys. Are they related to your cousin?"

"Yes, they're his kin."

"So, he's a relation of the hotel craftsman too?"

"Yes. Mr. and Mrs. Christy are so kind. They've offered to host a get-together for us at their tea shop this summer."

Robert pointed to where a cherrywood console, carved with grape-vines and grapes, hugged the wall. "Garrett built that piece, and he's commissioned to make a few things for my mother's home in the off-season."

"So your mother still lives on the island?" She'd thought the woman had passed on. Lily's heartbeat ratcheted up. Might the woman be her grandmother? Would she know the story of the one-armed, one-legged man named Swaine?

"I misspoke. The Cadotte cottage, or the Canary as some call it due to its bright yellow color, is now mine, since my mother passed."

"I'm sorry." Her heart sank. So she'd never have the pleasure of meeting her. "Why Cadotte?"

"That was my grandmother's lineage, and she was proud of her connection to this prominent métis family. She was a feisty lady. But she loved her children and grandchildren." A shadow seemed to pass over his face.

Robert palmed two of the coconut macaroons from atop the silver tray on the console. A matron attired in an old-fashioned black linen-and-lace day dress cast him a disapproving look.

As they exited the hotel, Robert handed Lily a cookie, and she accepted it. They both ate their cookies as they descended the wide steps to the sidewalk.

Robert offered his arm, and she took it. "It's a short walk. I could have taken you out the side door, but then we'd be wading through that group of pompous. . ." He made a throaty noise.

"I take it you're not too fond of psychiatrists."

"Dr. DuBlanc is fine, in fact he helped my brother-in-law out. But some of that mob, especially that Dr. Fraufein, just plain scare me."

"Me too." But in a different way than the eugenics men bothered Robert, no doubt.

"The world is a different place now. The journalists who were recently here sought only to procure a salacious story, no matter the cost to the person or persons they were maligning."

"Oh." Her hand tightened into a fist around her small reticule. Were there even now journalists seeking a headline story? Would they want to know about the daughter of the woman responsible for the Kentucky asylum tragedy?

"Our local newspaper staff is seeking out another culprit for the fire at my shop, the Island General Store."

"That was yours?"

A seagull squawked overhead as it was joined by two other gulls. "Yes. And my employee admitted that he may have left his pipe burning in the shop when he closed up."

"I heard that the shopkeeper was injured, and the fire brigade responded swiftly."

"That's true. Still, there are those who wish to place the blame on some other nefarious person—especially if they can point the finger away from the island."

"Oh?"

"Yes, we islanders have long memories, and my store manager's reputation is now in tatters."

At least he wasn't dead like her mother. But hearing Robert speak this way had her wondering. How had her mother gotten ahold of something to start a fire?

"I was fortunate to rescue Sadie Duvall from going back into the upstairs apartment to save her sisters, who were already gone."

"How frightening." Lily drew in as deep a breath as her corset would allow. "I met Miss Duvall today."

"She's a very special young woman but hard-headed." He pressed his lips together, and Lily didn't push him any further on that topic.

A carriage rolled past, a dark-skinned man in uniform driving while a well-dressed couple sat in the back.

"That's my home." Robert waved toward a beautiful Queen Anne yellow home.

Lily stopped and Robert did too. The yellow house was the one in her birch-bark painting. Her breath stuck in her throat.

He opened the gate that led to the walkway to the house. "My Sadie thinks this is the prettiest cottage on the bluff."

His Sadie? What was Robert's relationship with the woman? There'd been rumors at the Grand Hotel that he was sweet on Miss Laura Williams.

"Lily, what do you think of it?"

This was the same structure in the painting by Terrance Swaine. Several people had asserted that Lily resembled Jacqueline Swaine. Too much coincidence. "Tell me about your family."

"I am what you call a replacement son." He shrugged in a self-deprecating manner. "My mother lost two sons during the War between the States."

"Two sons? How horrible." She touched the cameo at her neck.

"It's worse than that. My eldest brother fought for the Confederacy, and the next born fought for the Union."

Lily frowned. "How did that happen?"

Robert huffed a sigh. "My paternal grandparents lived in Virginia, and my eldest brother stayed with them many summers. When the war broke out, his allegiance to his Swaine grandparents proved stronger than to my parents."

"What heartbreak for your parents."

"That's what my older sister always said."

"When did your older brother die?"

"The brother with the Union was killed at Appomattox."

Chancellorsville was a name that had echoed in her nightmares over the years, not Appomattox. "Oh. How terrible."

"My other brother was said to have died in battle in Fredericksburg in 1863."

*The year of the Battle at Chancellorsville.* She shivered as she recalled the men in the filthy grayish uniforms who'd marched onto her grandfather's property all those years ago. It hadn't been a nightmare; it had all been real. But Papa had been brought home.

A stray tear escaped her eye, and she brushed it away.

Robert patted his breast pocket. "We always thought Terrance had never married, but we have a letter from a long-lost cousin in Virginia who claims he had married before he'd enlisted."

"His wife's name?" She held her breath as they continued up the walkway.

"He didn't know. He suggested I get in touch with my grandfather's estate manager."

Lily exhaled. "Surely someone would have told your family if he'd had any children." But if they kept secrets as closely guarded as both Mama and Pa and all their Kentucky neighbors, then maybe not.

"I really don't know. My mother was convinced that Terrance had died. I've tried to find the letter from my grandfather informing her of his passing, to no avail. Of course I never knew either of my brothers. But my parents were able to retrieve my eldest brother's body and bury him on the island. They assumed Terrance was buried in Virginia."

"Maybe so." But not until years after the war had ended.

"My sister told me that Mother wouldn't accept his death for a long time, and then she had me. Hopefully, I brightened her life." His hazel eyes, so much like her own, flashed with humor.

As much as Lily wished to know more about her past, the idea of anyone discovering her mother's infamy terrified her. Yet here she was, preparing to enter the very house portrayed in the little painting from her box.

The yellow house featured matching cupolas and a front porch upon which two benches sat. The front door opened, and a thin elderly man stared out from within. Yet another person gawked at her today, much in the way Sadie had earlier.

Suddenly, the servant took two steps back into the dark hall.

"Hastings, are you all right?" Robert released Lily's arm and bounded up the steps.

Trembling, Lily slowly moved toward the house. A sensation of returning to something from her past yet completely unknown enveloped her.

Robert had the older man sit at a black bench just inside the house. "Are you sure you're well?"

"Yes, just a startle to my old heart. She looks so much like Miss Jacqueline."

Robert motioned her forward. "Lily, this is Hastings, our butler."

"Pleased to meet you, miss."

"Likewise."

Family portraits hung in a row in the huge entryway hall. In the center, the woman painted could have been Lily, save for the ebony hair. She pressed her hand to her throat. Even the woman's piercing gaze was one Lily had viewed in the mirror when she'd been perturbed.

"Oh, my stars." Her comment emerged with a distinct Kentucky accent.

"So, you see it too?" Robert cast her a sideways glance. "Isn't that something, considering Swaine is only your stage name?"

"Yes." Her one-word sentence emerged on a breath. How could she speak of her suspicions without revealing her mother's secret?

"I believe my brother fathered a child but didn't know about it before he died."

*He knew.* That remnant of a man who'd returned to the Swaine farm knew of his child—the one who ran and threw herself at him even when he'd sat in his chair, staring out the window, his limbs half missing.

"I wonder if that child might be you? My mother was so infuriated that Terrance joined the Confederate cause, that she may have cut off all ties with him—I don't know."

"And maybe that caused his wife to not contact the family about the child? But what about your Swaine grandparents?"

"Yoo-hoo!" Maude Welling, attired in a pale pink ensemble with a matching hat and parasol sailed into the house. "Goodness, what's going on?"

Robert pointed to the painting. "We all agree that Lily and Grandmother could be twins."

"Born what, forty-odd years apart?"

"Something like that."

Maude removed her hat and set it on the stand. "And she doesn't have Grandmother's black hair, although neither do I. It's a Cadotte woman's legacy that I was denied. No Ojibway princess's tresses for me."

Hastings rose, took Maude's parasol, and set it in a brass umbrella stand. "I'm fine now. Please come into the dining room where we have afternoon tea laid out for you."

"I have so many questions for you," Maude gushed.

Soon Lily was nibbling on tiny cucumber sandwiches, drinking fragrant black tea, and answering numerous inquiries. She had a small assortment of pastries assembled on the delicate china plate set before her by the Swaine's cook. She needed to keep fortifying herself for the continuing march of Maude's questions.

"So your mother likely remarried, you have some remembrance of possibly living on a large farm in Virginia, and you remember a Confederate soldier who may have been your father." Robert's pretty niece set her delicate china teacup down in its saucer. "Is there anything else?"

"Two things. One is that I have a small box full of things that do seem tied to this place, and I will share that with you. Perhaps that will also help solve the mystery." She sipped her tea and repositioned her cup in its saucer.

"And the second thing?" Robert quirked a dark eyebrow at her.

"The soldier came back from war without an arm and one leg."

"Oh!" Maude gasped. "How terrible."

"And, and"—tears piled up in Lily's eyes—"and later he died." She sniffed and reached for her reticule, set on the chair adjacent her. She pulled out her handkerchief. A vivid memory of her mother, attired in black from head to toe, sobbing over the fresh grave; a simple pine box lowered into the ground; and a silver-haired man, his faded blue eyes almost vacant-looking, and the salt-and-pepper-haired woman beside him shaking with unshed tears and stifled sobs. And then the wailing, the keening sound. That was when her mother's mind was broken. Lily had stood by the grave, hands clasped around the horse her father had whittled for her—a large Percheron horse like the ones on the island.

"Are you all right?" Maude left her seat and joined Lily. "Were you remembering something?"

Lily nodded.

Robert rose and went to the other room, a parlor area. He returned in a moment and handed her an ambrotype of a man and woman standing in front of a large white plantation-style house. It was them—the man and woman from the graveside but younger, and with life still in their eyes.

He handed her another ambrotype encased in black leather. "My brother."

The young man pictured stood tall, attired in a well-fitting suit. An easy grin highlighted his handsome features. He had his whole life ahead of him. But that same man, surely her father, had been destroyed by the war. He'd not died in that battle. He'd returned to the plantation in Virginia, where she and Mama had awaited him.

Lily touched the picture. "Papa. When he was whole." She didn't remember him like that. The fleeting recollections she'd had were of the sorrowful man waiting to die, who didn't want to be a burden to anyone.

"I think I need to go." Lily pushed away from the table, the demons from her past chasing her.

"Let me accompany you." Robert rose.

"No." She raised her hand, palm outward.

"Give her some time alone." Maude's words recollected the last thing she'd heard Grandmama say before Mama had packed up their belongings and taken off with one of the horses. There had been many days on horseback, times of her stomach rumbling, many tears. Then there had been the arrival at a burned-out farm in western Virginia. More tears from Mama. And a nice man with kind eyes. He had all his limbs. And the man who would become her new pa took Mama and her to Kentucky.

Lily didn't remember how she'd managed to exit the Swaine house and return to the hotel, but somehow she'd done so and ended up sitting down at the desk in her room. She pulled out her journal and prepared to write.

# CHAPTER TEN

## *2020*

*I*n just shy of three hours, Willa had taken a carriage ride, a ferry ride, a walk to retrieve her car, and a drive over the Mackinac Bridge. *Whew!* She drove north on I-75 until the exit to Hessel. Willa took the turn, hands trembling on the wheel. She needed to remain focused on this wooded drive on a two-lane road. Her flashbacks to her childhood were helping her to recapture her past, but she didn't need to have one while driving home. *Not home.* Prickles coursed up her arms as thick woods crowded in on either side of the road. But these were welcoming tingles, and she smiled at the familiar embrace of the north woods.

Willa tried calling her mom and then her sister, but there was no cell reception. She'd finally given up, when her phone rang. She tapped at her car's screen to accept the incoming call.

"Willa! Everybody wants to see you while you're here," her ebullient younger cousin Jaycie chirped.

Jaycie and her family had lived near Willa's family in Virginia. But then Jaycie's parents, Tamara and Brad, had split up. Two years ago, she and her mom relocated near the Straits of Mackinac.

"Are you off for the summer, Jaycie?"

"I am from my regular job, but I'm going to do some work on the island starting next week."

"Awesome! I'll be here for about a month." Unless the new owners hated her ideas, in which case maybe only another week.

"My mom will want to see you too."

Jaycie's mom, Tamara, was a sweetheart and had helped Willa out a lot back home in Virginia before she'd moved. "I'm thinking Pink Pony midweek." The Pink Pony was reported to have the best smoked fish dip on the island.

"Awesome. How about seven on Wednesday?"

"Perfect."

"Love you, Willie."

"Love you, Jay-Jay."

Willa grinned as they ended the call. No one had called her Willie in years. And no doubt beautiful Jaycie no longer answered to Jay-Jay or Jaybird anymore. Tonight Willa would call, text, or otherwise reach out to her younger sister until finally they connected.

As close as they were now, it seemed strange to think of all those years ago, when Willa had fled to Gramps's place so she wouldn't have to babysit Clare for the summer. The problem wasn't that she didn't want to care for Clare—it was the revelation that Willa had been adopted. That discovery launched her escape from Virginia. When she returned home, she had landed in therapy for a year.

At least her counselor understood. She perceived that Willa's adoptive mom, her biological aunt, was a rescuer. She always had a project going to save someone or something, and she'd kept so busy with her various causes that Willa had navigated her childhood mostly on her own. Even after Clare was born, which her parents had pronounced "a huge, unexpected blessing," Mom and Dad had both returned to their workaholic ways. In Mom's case, it should be called volunteeraholism if there was such a word—probably not.

Willa drove on and passed the guarded entrance to the dolomite mine on the right. Within minutes, she spied the sign for Hessel.

She drove slowly past the marina and parked on the street by Gramps's house. Same low white picket fence out front but with landscaping and floral design that rivaled that of Mackinac Island's Jack Barnwell Designs. Whoever had accomplished Gramps's landscaping redesign clearly knew their stuff.

Gramps rose from the swing on the wide porch, his smile broad. Tears tickling the corners of her eyes, Willa joined him on the porch. Gramps wasn't going to do a socially distanced reunion. He rushed toward her and gave her a bear hug, then kissed her cheek.

"Oh, Willa-girl, look at you."

She'd worn her regular thirty-something clothing today with low-key hair and makeup to match. "Not all glammed-up like on TV."

"Thank goodness." He ran his hand along his jawline. "I look at that gal on your show on TV, the one who is supposed to be you, and I shake my head till it rattles."

"It's just for show, Gramps." She'd not reveal that she dressed in an outrageous manner to keep men at a distance.

She'd fled to Gramps's place when she'd broken her engagement with John. Gramps knew all about the betrayal and her heartbreak.

"Maybe I don't understand show people." He scratched his cheek. "We've got a few of those famous types around here in the summertime, ya know, eh?"

She stifled a grin at his strong Yooper accent. "I guess I do know, eh?"

He laughed. "Now you're getting your accent right."

He gestured her inside. "Come on in. Sherry made pasties for us."

The last time she'd been there, her step-grandma had been traveling all the time with her job as a state accountant, and her grandpa was always at the dock. Willa had learned the lunch specials at the marina by heart on that visit because she didn't cook much and neither did Gramps.

Willa stepped inside. The last visit, Sherry and Gramps had been married only a short while. Now in retirement, Sherry's touch had transformed the home. This new version of the living room harkened back to the one she first remembered as a young child, with its bright yellow and peach colors.

"Come on through."

Willa followed Gramps to the dining room. She gestured to the dining set. "You set up the table and chairs I ordered for you." Pleasure coursed through her.

"Of course we did, Willa-girl."

She'd spotted the classic midcentury oak table and chairs in a Chicago warehouse the previous year and had them shipped up north. Gramps had given away an almost identical set, his wedding gift to her grandma, when she'd died, but had immediately regretted it.

"I'm glad Sherry was okay with me sending it."

"Aw, she was fine."

"Good."

"This set could near be the same one we had." Gramps patted the tabletop. "Lots of memories at that table."

Seeing it there, another memory rushed through Willa's mind.

*Her pretty blond mother sat facing her, the table covered in books, paper, and pens. "Just a little while longer and we can go out together and play."*

*"I wanna go now," Willa pleaded.*

*Grandma came into the dining room, a pot dripping water in one hand and a kitchen towel in the other. "Come help your old grandma dry the dishes."*

*But Grandma wasn't old. She didn't even have any gray in her hair and no wrinkles. Grown-ups sure were funny.*

*"All right, Grandma." Willa followed her grandmother into the kitchen, pausing just long enough to see her young mother's head bent over her work, her tongue sticking out from the corner of her mouth like Willa's did when she was thinking really hard.*

Gramps cleared his throat, bringing Willa back to the present.

"I'm glad you sent it, Willa. I kind of needed to put some ghosts to rest. Maybe you do too."

"I think you're right, Gramps."

Sherry stepped into the room from the kitchen. "Welcome, Willa." She pulled Willa into an embrace.

Gramps moved forward and put his arms around Sherry and Willa. "Group hug."

"I haven't had one of these since before the pandemic started," Willa said.

When they all stepped back, a sense of renewal coursed through her.

The scent of savory beef wafted from the kitchen. She sniffed appreciatively. "Smells great."

"Home-made." Sherry beamed.

"You're rockin' the grandma thing, Sherry." *No offense to you, my grandma in heaven.*

Gramps pointed to a nearby chair, at the position Willa had sat in since a child.

She gestured to the pretty coral-and-turquoise paisley seat pad covering the chair. "I recognize this." She sat.

"You ought to," Sherry called over her shoulder as she headed to the kitchen.

"That's from my 2018 Target line, isn't it?"

"Yup." Gramps sat across from her in the middle instead of at his usual place at the end.

Mom, or her "birth mother" as her adoptive mother liked to call Angela, used to sit in that place. Before Willa had discovered that Angela was her biological mother, she'd been referred to as "Auntie Angie," the poor unfortunate sister who'd died too young.

Willa forced her memories aside to focus on Sherry's comment. "You know what, they change stuff up so fast every season that I have a hard time remembering what I did a year ago, much less two."

Target might not extend her contract. With her HGTV show on hiatus during COVID, it wasn't clear when she'd be back to work. And no TV show meant eventually no more design contracts with big companies and retailers. But after working under so much time pressure for almost half of her life, Willa found herself questioning what had driven that strong need to prove herself.

"We're real proud of you. But you know, I'd still be proud of you if you were down at my marina dippin' out ice cream."

She laughed. "That was some kind of summer, wasn't it?"

"One of the best in my life."

Sherry carried in a tray of steaming pasties, a regional specialty. The crust surrounding the meat, potatoes, carrots, and rutabagas had been baked to golden perfection.

"I'll say the prayer." Gramps bowed his head. "Lord, we thank You for our sweet Willa being here with us, and bless this meal and our time together. In Jesus' name, amen."

"Amen," Sherry and Willa chorused.

"Dig in." Gramps forked into his meat pie.

"There's gravy on the stove if you want some, but we usually stick with ketchup." Sherry flipped open the cap on her Heinz and squeezed the ketchup out.

"Ketchup for me too."

"I'm next after you." Gramps drummed his fingers on the tabletop.

Willa accepted the bottle and squeezed out a circle of ketchup. Then she extended the upper middle section to look more heart shaped. Her mother had done that. *"Don't forget I love you,"* she'd say, kissing Willa and leaving her to eat lunch with Gramps and Grandma while she went off to school.

"You remember her doing that, don't ya?" Gramps accepted the ketchup.

Willa dipped her chin in agreement.

She cut her pasty into only one forkful at a time, as her mother had taught her to do.

"You even eat pasties like her." Gramps sectioned his off into equal portions.

A lump formed in Willa's throat.

Sherry frowned at him. "Now don't upset her."

"Sorry." Gramps squirted ketchup atop his four sections.

"It's all right. I actually think that now, more than any other time in my life, I'm ready to talk about and learn more about my early years." Thanks to Dr. Svendsen's therapy.

Over lunch, Willa caught up Gramps and Sherry on her sister's and her parents' activities.

Gramps thrummed his fingers on the table. "Did you know that your mom got your dad to agree to foster greyhound dogs? Says it's because Clare would be going off to college soon."

Willa snorted. "As if she needs an excuse."

"Arlene has always got to be in the thick of things."

Except Willa's life. "Right." Mom always had to have someone to save. "Do you think that's why she adopted me?"

Sherry patted her lips with her napkin. "People like your mom don't usually understand *why* they always have to have something or someone to rescue."

Gramps exhaled loudly. "That might be a bit harsh, but there's a lot of truth in it. Still, I'm so glad she unselfishly let you spend that entire summer with us, Willa."

With her sister, Clare, then three years old, clamoring for attention and Willa struggling with memories of herself at that age, she'd begged to go. "Dropping that bombshell on me could have been avoided if she'd been honest with me from the beginning."

"About being adopted?" Sherry cocked her head to the side.

"I was really hoping to talk with you some more about my mom. And who might have been my biological father." She needed to know.

"That's water under the bridge as they say." Gramps harrumphed.

The spell had been broken. If she knew her grandfather, he'd be busy from the time they got there until they left. Like her mom and her dad, he was a workaholic and would be interrupted by people all day long.

*A workaholic like me.* And anything with an *-ic* on the end was a problem, as Dr. Svendsen had warned her. Certainly all of Willa's efforts hadn't brought her the peace and joy she craved. But she wasn't about to give up on learning about her past.

"I'm going to give you two some alone time." Sherry gathered up the plates.

"I'm gonna take Willa-girl over to the marina and put her to work."

"See you later." Sherry headed to the kitchen.

"Let's go to where it all started—Willa Christy Designs."

Gramps's business in Hessel was where she'd had her first redecorating assignment—making over the frumpy marina building into a welcoming spot for wealthy boaters.

Willa's redesign had caught the eye of a Detroit decorator who'd helped her meet the "right" kind of people and had been influential in her decision to opt for Savannah College of Art and Design instead of a traditional college. Too bad that John's bad choices had made it impossible for her to finish her degree.

"What were you thinking, Gramps?"

"People loved what you did all those years ago, and we've done a bit of freshening since then, but I'd really welcome your ideas about keeping everything welcoming and contemporary."

"I don't think they really want current fashion, Gramps. Your customers are looking for a subdued elegance with a bit of rustic thrown in."

"Come take a hard look and tell me your thoughts."

Willa and Gramps headed to the marina, and she whistled when she counted the boats that had moored since she'd first arrived, including several high-end yachts. "High-dollar clients."

He swiveled toward her. "And we wanta keep 'em happy, eh?"

They turned and headed up the walkway to the marina's all-purpose office, store, ice-cream shop and deli, and wharf bathrooms. They both donned their masks and entered the building, where Gramps introduced her to the two workers inside.

The large building looked much as it had after her initial redesign. Aged planks on the walls and floors gave the place a decidedly rustic feel. The brown leather sofas in the seating area had been replaced by a pair of squarish black leather ones that didn't quite fit the vibe. Two picnic tables, covered with newspapers, offered a place to sit. Those had been her idea, but now they simply looked like forced retro rustic. *They need to go.*

The new ice-cream cases gleamed. "Those are really nice, Gramps."

"Posh." He affected a fake British accent. "That's what Sherry said."

"She's right."

"Hey, Garrett, can you help?" The young blond man working at the cash register motioned to Gramps.

As Gramps strode away, Willa realized she'd probably be on her own for hours. When she saw him follow his worker from the store, she sighed.

"Would you like to order ice cream?" the red-haired girl behind the counter asked.

"I'm too full." But Willa did need help. "Do you know if Tim still works at the dry dock?" Tim knew her mother well. But he was like an onion that had to be peeled when it came to sharing details.

"Yup. He's been working long hours since your grandpa got that certified letter about those people coming from Chicago for that old wooden speedboat."

Gramps preferred to call them vintage race boats. "I'm going to go chat with him for a bit. Thanks."

As she exited the building, the crew scrambled to tie off the ropes for a red-and-white yacht being moored.

Willa crossed the street to the dry-dock building. The large sign by it announced the cost of placing one's vessel in there for the year, a substantial amount.

She entered the dry dock. She headed toward the office, its door open. "Hi, Tim. It's me, Willa, Angela's daughter."

Tim still sported his graying mullet. He wore a blue paper facemask. "Great to see you again."

"I'm here for a job at the Grand and came by to see Gramps." And to dig up info on her mom.

"I bet you're here in the dry dock to see that wooden speedboat your mom worked on—before those hotshot owners finally show up from Chicago to claim it."

Willa stilled. She didn't want to lie. "Yes, I'd love to see it." That was the truth, even though she had no clue what he was talking about.

"Come on. I'll show you that handcrafted beauty. Your mom helped with that one—her and those twins."

"Gosh, it must be over thirty years old by now."

"Yeah, we've had that boat here forever—as long as I've been here."

Willa had to hurry to keep up with Tim, who was faster than she'd expected.

"Garrett wasn't too happy to get that letter from the Moores' attorney."

What should she say to that? "No, I imagine not. Who likes hearing from lawyers?"

"Right." Tim sliced his hand through the air. "Least they could have done was to call up here or send their own darned letter. But oh no, they have to almost threaten your grandfather—totally unnecessary."

"Right." She needed to keep Tim talking.

"They paid their dry-dock fee for the past thirty years, so of course Garrett is gonna release their boat to them."

"Uh-huh."

"It's not his fault that boy crashed the other one." Tim stopped walking and turned to face her. "Sorry, I shouldn't have said that."

She remained quiet, hoping he'd continue.

Tim rubbed his jaw. "I mean, your mom and Thad were super close."

Her breath caught in her throat. But she had to ask. "How super close?"

Tim's cheeks reddened. He resumed walking. "Your mom dumped her boyfriend, my best friend, for Thad. She was really impressed by all those awards he'd won for his artwork."

"What did you think of Thad?"

He scratched his head. "Never liked him. But I hate to speak ill of the dead."

From the sad look he gave her, maybe he suspected that Thad was her father.

"But his identical twin was really nice. Quiet. Diligently worked on both boats alongside Angie and his brother."

"They were a matching pair of speedboats?"

"Identical."

A pair. So Thad crashed the other one? "This remaining boat belonged to Thad's twin?"

"Yeah, can't remember his name. But I sorta wonder if it's him coming to get it or his folks. They've gotta be in their eighties by now."

Were they still alive? An ember of hope sprang within her. What if she had yet another set of grandparents?

Tim scratched the back of his neck. "I'm just embarrassed for your grandpa—how they've handled the return. Garrett is the premier vintage wood speedboat designer in the country."

"True."

"He's revived the tradition here, and now we have our summer festivals. Not this year, of course, with COVID. But next year we'll be back if all goes well."

Tim pointed to a spot in the middle of the lower level. The dark interior made it hard to see the boat clearly.

"Let me open these shutters so you can get a look at this beauty." Tim strode to the wall and unclipped two massive shutters that covered exterior windows. Light flooded into the space.

The golden wood of the speedboat gleamed. Someone had kept its glossy finish in immaculate condition. She stood to the side. She'd seen this boat before. She'd ridden on this boat before. There was a picture of an identical boat, if not this boat, at the cottage where she was staying. But the photo hadn't affected her like seeing this in person in all its three-dimensional glory.

"Your grandpa still takes it out on occasion."

"Really?"

"Yup. But its old motor is a concern."

"Did the Moores ask him to keep it running?"

Lines furrowed around Tim's dark eyes. "Nah, I think he poured so much love into making this boat. It's kinda like another kid to him, eh?"

Willa stiffened, unsure of what to make of that comment. "This boat is obviously a work of love—it is simply gorgeous."

"Wish it was mine—just sits here all year. They won't even give us permission to bring it out for the special event every summer." He launched into a tirade about the Moores.

Willa cringed. Obviously, there was no love lost between this man and the owners. "Wish it was happening this year while I'm here."

"You remind me of your mom. Angela loved festivals and all that."

"Yeah?"

Tim nodded. "She was the pride of Hessel. Beautiful, smart—graduated a year ahead of her class—and kind to everyone. She was always checking on neighbors and helping out her mom, your grandma, with church fundraisers."

The door swung open. "Hey! Where's my granddaughter?" Gramps entered the building.

He joined them by the sleek speedboat. He glanced between the two of them and laid a hand on the high-gloss finish of the stern. "I can't believe the owners are finally coming for this, after all these years."

"Why?" If Sue's conjecturing was right—that the Moores owned the cottage that Sue and she occupied—then would the Moore family possibly arrive soon where she and Sue were staying?

"Could be wrong, though, about them showing up. Their attorney didn't exactly say so."

"I wonder what it would feel like to ride this thing across the Straits?"

Chuckling, her grandfather patted her arm. "You must have forgotten the last time. But you just gave me a great idea."

"Yeah?"

"This baby needs to get taken out again. Soon."

"I'm in." She opened her arms wide.

"I'll take you out on it then." Fleeting sorrow danced over his features. "Maybe you'll remember something of the last time."

"I'd like that." She'd like for her nightmares to end, but she wanted nostalgic memories to remain. *Can't I just have that, Lord?*

# CHAPTER ELEVEN

## 1895

*T*onight, an undercurrent of tension crackled within the Grand's opulent music hall, setting Lily's nerves on edge. The guests arriving moved in more fits and starts than usual, with an occasional high-pitched laugh discordant in the general buzz of conversations.

"You have a special request." Clem handed Lily the sheet music for Henry Russell's "Life on the Ocean Wave." "I practiced it earlier."

She cringed. Oftentimes requests for older music were accompanied by further requests, such as for her company, by the men who asked. "What did you tell them?"

"I said I'd ask you—that it's been a while since you've performed it."

"Ages." At the Louisville Music Hall when she was only seventeen.

Clem leaned in. "It's from Mr. Moore, the steel tycoon."

"He's staying here?"

"Your maid says they don't. They own one of them so-called cottages around here, but back in the woods a bit."

"Oh." And how would Alice know that? Mrs. Fox had cautioned Lily that the maids knew all and often told all, so she should keep herself above reproach. Gossip among the servants was supposedly rampant.

Clem winked at her. "Mr. Moore wants it sung for his eldest son, who has just opened a shipping line."

"Some family that must be, my goodness." And her own family—had the brothers, her father and uncle, actually gone to war against one another?

"Is it a go?"

"Not without the lyrics in front of me."

"Stand behind me while I play, then."

"All right."

"That's them coming in now." Clem inclined his head toward the entrance.

The matron of the group, with silver hair arranged in an artful chignon, had a dainty tiara affixed to her head. Her many and varied other jewelry glinted beneath the electric lights.

"American royalty?" Lily quirked an eyebrow at her cousin.

"Reckon they believe so."

Alice appeared in the entryway to the room, clutching her hands at her waist. Behind her, Mr. Williford watched the maid, a quizzical look on his face.

Her neck tightening, Lily whispered to her cousin, "Do you think Alice needs me for something?"

Clem shrugged. "Seems like she's searchin' out someone, but she ain't lookin' up here at you."

Who else would the maid need to find?

Alice's gaze connected with Lily's. If possible, the color from her milky complexion drained even further. She turned on her heel and left. This was her maid's free time. If Alice wished to spend it wandering the hotel, perhaps that was allowed. She'd check with Mrs. Fox just in case. She didn't need to get in trouble with her employers over the servant's behavior.

A short, swarthy man with a stocky build entered the room just as Alice, head down, exited. He was followed by several other men. A chill settled over Lily. She recognized the type by the air they exuded in their sidling swaggers—men who were criminals or involved in illegal activities—but she'd not expected to encounter any at this fancy hotel. "Who's that?" she whispered.

"I don't know, but stay away from them and we'll be all right." Clem took his spot at the piano bench.

A headache began to form at her temple. *Not tonight. Not again.* She'd have to get through this. She went to the back of the room, in the private alcove where she and Clem left their belongings. Lily poured water from the carafe into a glass. She removed a packet of headache powder from her reticule and poured it into her glass. She stirred it as best she could with her index finger.

"You all right?"

"No." She drank the contents of her goblet.

"Another headache?"

"Afraid so."

"Your ma sure suffered with those."

Lily frowned. She was *not* becoming her mother. She'd not succumb to her mother's maladies—especially not with a full contingent of psychiatrists entering the room.

"I'm sorry, Clem, I can't do the song tonight." She dared not fumble in front of this audience. "Please let Mr. Moore know we'll try for another evening very soon."

"Stick to the old standbys?"

As much as she wanted to vary her repertoire, her safety—and her mother's secret—had to be protected. "Yes, you know the ones." Everything she'd sung by heart since she was knee-high to a grasshopper and whose words were so embedded in her subconscious mind that she could probably sing them with her last dying breaths.

*Dying breaths.*

*A single, large, cool hand laid atop hers. The scent of death permeated the still air. A moth-eaten blanket pulled up to her father's neck; his bearded face pale as a Virginia moon in a cloudless sky. "Don't forget me, Lily-belle."*

She sucked in a breath at the memory and pressed her eyes closed. He'd given her the little wooden box that day and told her to always keep it with her. She still had the box and its contents, but she'd almost completely forgotten the man. She'd make up for that. She'd let Robert Swaine and his family fill in her missing remembrances with whatever they had to help her recall the damaged man who'd returned home from the war. But he'd not stopped loving his family—she knew that.

She heard the back door open and footsteps heading toward her. She turned to see Stephen, concern etched on his features. He spoke to Clem, who responded, but she didn't hear their words.

The doctor joined her.

She turned her back to the audience as the seats filled.

Stephen appeared especially handsome when concern flittered in his eyes. Did his lady clients all fall a little in love with him?

"Lily, are you all right? You look a little green around the gills."

"That's quite an image. Not what your Mackinac Songbird should look like." She couldn't help but laugh, despite her blossoming headache.

"No, I guess not." His wide grin made a dimple appear in his cheek.

"Thank you for your concern, but I'll be all right."

Stephen reached for her hand, but she shook her head in caution.

"Let's not give the audience anything to talk about as far as you and me, Dr. DuBlanc."

Regret flitted across his face. "I'm just a lowly doctor here for the season, Miss Swaine. A social outcast because of my profession, and I imagine people consider you very kind to have taken me under your wing."

"Don't be silly."

"I like that moniker—Songbird of Mackinac fits you perfectly." Then he quickly exited.

Clem raised his eyebrow in question, and Lily nodded. He began to play a song that required little concentration on her part. What would she do without Clem? She smiled at him, but he was focused on his playing and didn't look up. Somehow that left her feeling uneasy.

The next day, Lily's headache had improved, and their performances went well. She even sang Mr. Moore's request.

When Lily returned to her room later, she found that Mrs. Moore had sent up a bouquet of mixed roses in appreciation. Lily lowered her head and inhaled the sweet floral scent. She'd spend her break time reading. She settled on the divan just as someone knocked on the door.

Since Alice wasn't present, she rose and went to answer the door. "Who is it?"

"Work crew, ma'am."

When she opened the door, several men stood before her, toolboxes in hand. The worker standing at the front couldn't have looked less like a construction-crew member than did Reverend McWithey, from the island church she attended. With hair cut short and plastered to his cannonball-round head, the stranger stood a half head shorter than Lily. Dark round spectacles perched atop his squat nose. She recognized the other worker with him as a man she'd spied exiting the room on a previous occasion.

Behind the newcomer and the other workman, Garrett Christy waved a hand. "Hope we aren't interrupting your afternoon, Miss Lily."

Yes, yes indeed they were, but Lily wouldn't say so. "I was just thinking"—just now that was—"of taking a walk on the grounds. It's so beautiful today."

Mr. Christy smiled. "That it is."

"And I don't have another performance until later."

The solemn-looking man in the front sported spotless new-looking attire.

Clem's cousin pointed toward the shorter man. "This is Carl Diener. He's new, but he has done great work for us already."

"That's lovely." If only it weren't right now that they'd arrived.

"We wanted to start in Mrs. Stillman's office today, but she asked us to wait. She has several important meetings today."

The assistant housekeeping manager, Mrs. Stillman, had a small office on this floor, directly adjacent to Lily's suite. With Alice's frequent disappearances, Lily had considered approaching the woman for help, but the few times Lily had actually seen Mrs. Stillman, her imperious countenance could have frozen over Lake Huron with a single frosty glance.

Lily opened the door wider. "Come in, gentlemen."

Mr. Diener dipped his chin at her as he entered. Even his fingernails were clean and neat. How did he manage that? All three men trailed into the room, and Lily closed the door behind them.

She turned to face them. "What is Mrs. Stillman having done to her rooms?" Not that it was any of Lily's business.

Garrett frowned and scratched his chin. "Well, her suite of rooms also has access to that long storage room we're trying to partition. We wouldn't want anyone moving from room to room using that space."

Lily blinked at him. She hadn't realized there was an adjoining room.

"That storage room was meant to be divided up, but it never got done. So it still runs through your maid's room and yours."

"Oh." Alarm shot through her. This was a scenario that she and Clem would always have checked out in previous locations. But here on an island, criminals didn't have any easy way to escape back to the mainland. She exhaled a long breath.

"And it will have to be closed off." Garrett inclined his head toward her desk. "That access door over there will probably be papered over."

"And both my maid and Mrs. Stillman have access to that area?"

"Mrs. Stillman has been storing boxes of paperwork in there. The owner wants all that moved off-site. She likely has to remove some personal items from there too before we add that partition wall." Mr. Christy gazed at her expectantly.

Lily went to her dressing table and affixed her hat to her curls. She retrieved her parasol and gloves and a light shawl. "Best wishes, gentlemen, on your work."

Mr. Diener gave her a tight smile. "We are most sorry to disturb you, madam." His formal and clipped speech took her by surprise.

"Thank you."

The tension in the man's face relaxed. "You're very welcome. Have a most felicitous afternoon."

She nodded and left, a niggling of unease working its way down to her buttoned-up boots. Lily spent the afternoon walking along the cliffside, stopping once to stare for a long time at what had surely been her father's home. She knew she shouldn't have gone on her own. But in broad daylight, the rules of social decorum that required someone of her age to be accompanied simply because she was unmarried seemed even more ridiculous than usual.

She skipped dinner since Clem had taken Marie out to a restaurant in town for a quick supper. Lily also wanted to avoid the psychiatrists in the dining hall. If she had to hear one more comment about how women in asylums should not be able to bear children, she'd scream. If her own mother had never been allowed to have Lily, she'd not be here now. Who did these men think they were, speaking of such unmentionable topics in a dining room? At their mealtimes, Stephen had finally given up on trying to redirect conversations by proponents of the eugenics movement. The ornery men would go right back to the topic at first opportunity.

Clem had returned for their early evening performance, face aglow and in good humor. "I think I'm in love, Lil."

"I'm happy for you." And she was.

Her cousin played with particular gusto that night during the romantic songs.

Now, hours later, Lily's stomach growled. The clock chimed nine o'clock, when Lily opened her journal to the front, where she'd written Lily Kerchinsky years earlier. Should she strike through the name and write Lily Swaine instead? Not yet, not until she was sure. But wasn't she? In her heart she was, especially after the meeting she'd had at what surely had been her grandparents' home.

She opened to the first page. She'd bought this journal at a beautiful mercantile in Louisville with some of the first earnings that her parents had allowed her to keep for herself. And she'd kept it all these years. She opened the first page and laughed at her drawing, but then chewed her lip. It was a childish drawing even though she'd been thirteen at the time that she'd drawn it. With no artistic training and just a pencil at her disposal, she'd drawn one of her most vivid memories—that of bedraggled men in dirty uniforms marching sullenly up to their farm and demanding food. Then one of the soldiers, who had only one leg and one arm, had been brought forward.

"Papa," she whispered aloud, tears pricking her eyes.

She turned to the next page. She'd written of her experiences on the stage—how she'd been so terrified but, knowing how badly she and Clem needed the money, had forced herself to perform. In her sometimes wobbly script, she'd written, *"I am so scared up there, but I confess I do love all the flowers afterwards and the candy."* She smiled at the recollection. After every performance, she'd received bouquets of appreciation and sweets from local shops. She and Clem divided the treats, but the flowers they had delivered to the local church where they'd visit if they were still there on Sunday.

She exhaled a sigh, her stomach growling. If she went down to the parlor, perhaps there would still be tea and some cookies. That might hold her until breakfast. Her maid hadn't yet returned.

With determination, Lily headed downstairs. When she reached the ladies' parlor, she heard someone playing the piano. She stood in the hall, listening raptly to the beautiful, haunting music, until someone tapped her on her shoulder.

She whirled around to see Stephen standing there, grinning like a cat who'd found his long-lost bowl of cream.

"Can you believe how Mr. König plays so well? I'd not expect that of a businessman, would you?"

Lily pressed her lips together, considering. This pianist was gifted. From the way the notes flowed, the timing, everything, he was not merely some industrialist stuck in his business ledgers. She shook her head slowly. "That can't be Mr. König."

"I assure you that it is. Follow me."

They both tiptoed slowly toward the entrance. Seated at the piano bench was indeed Mr. König. Lily gaped as he continued to perform like a virtuoso.

"Very strange, if you ask me," Stephen spoke into her ear just loudly enough to be heard over the music.

She nodded.

People had called Lily a musical prodigy with her singing, and she'd grown up in the backwoods and mountains of Kentucky—not that she'd confess such to Stephen.

They stood there a few moments more. Then Stephen took her elbow and pulled her away from the parlor.

Ever since Robert Swaine had told Stephen that there was a Pinkerton agent at the Grand Hotel, Stephen had kept his eyes and ears open. Robert said he believed the private agent was there to investigate the losses to his ships the previous year. Maybe König was the Pinkerton. Stephen was sure the man wasn't who he claimed to be. And Ada Fox was another dodgy sort. Pinkertons were known for hiring women. The new craftsman, Diener, whom Stephen had met that morning, was an odd duck and could be a detective. As a psychiatrist, though, Stephen met many eccentrics who were exactly who they said they were.

As they headed down the hallway, Lily turned to him. "Even an industrialist could be a prodigy. Perhaps his parents encouraged him to play."

Stephen tried to refocus his errant thoughts. "Maybe so."

"Regardless, he's talented."

Stephen cast her a sideways look. "What are you doing down here so late, anyway?"

At least with a Pinkerton around, they may have more protection for guests. The hotel's security detail was lacking in the extreme.

Lily's stomach growled.

He laughed. "Ah, that's right—you weren't at dinner. Didn't you ask the kitchen to send a meal up?"

Lily blinked up at him. "The thought hadn't even occurred to me."

"No?"

She ran her tongue over her full lower lip, her mouth so inviting. Did she even realize how beautiful she was? "I will next time."

Would she kiss him next time he had the notion? He shook his head, needing to quash his impulses. "Come on. I know where to find something for you. Can't have our musical star fainting."

He led her to the main-floor parlor.

When he continued past the stale remnants of cookies and tea service, Lily pulled away. "Aren't we going to stop here?"

"No." He linked his arm through hers and led her to the end of the long room, off of which were several meeting areas. At the final room, he opened the door and ducked his head inside. Seeing the room was empty, he turned and grinned at the lovely woman. "Coast is clear."

Inside, luxurious burgundy leather furniture made the large room seem cozier. At the end of the room, sandwiches were stacked on a plate, a cheese tray with grapes and crackers and apple slices sat untouched, and a round white-frosted cake sat atop a cut-glass cake plate with only a few slices removed.

"This is the men's meeting room."

Lily drew back. "The men's?"

"There's no one here."

She eyed him suspiciously.

Stephen waved his hand over the spread. "Voilà."

He intended to feed her not seduce her in a secluded room. Her cheeks heated. "Why bring in so much food when it doesn't appear to get consumed?"

"Ah, it's our little secret. One of the maids, Sadie, told me that the women's parlor receives only a fraction of what the men get."

Did everyone know Sadie? With the young woman's good looks, it should come as no surprise that men took notice of the maid. But what was she doing working at the Grand when Robert Swaine considered her his lady friend? "Hopefully, the servants are allowed to finish the remains."

"That's probably why none of them complains and this wastage continues." Stephen laughed. "But it serves us well tonight."

"So, it is okay to make up a plate?"

"Yes, but let's take it to the main parlor lest any men actually trail in here tonight. I don't think the psychiatrists' group knows about it, and the regulars here aren't likely to tell them."

"Do any of the men's rooms have a piano?"

"No."

"Ah, so that's why Mr. König was in the women's parlor."

"I suspect so." Stephen jerked his thumb toward the door. "Let's go sit outside on the porch."

"It's still light outside. We can watch the sunset."

He gestured to her plate. "Best eat that first."

She followed him out to the parlor. They took seats near the glass windows looking out onto the porch. Most people were congregating at the end of the porch, facing westward toward Lake Michigan, where the sun would set.

"I'm not sure if I prefer the sunrise over Lake Huron or the sunset over Lake Michigan."

Lily laughed. "It's all one huge lake though, isn't it? I mean it isn't like one ends and the other begins."

"True enough. We're surrounded by Lake Huron here on the island, but in Mackinaw City and in St. Ignace, you can have Lake Huron or Lake Michigan lapping at the shores, depending upon which part of town you are in."

"I liked Mackinaw City very much." She finished her sandwich. Delicious.

"It's beautiful here at the Straits." Stephen leaned forward. "Have you considered settling down in one place, Lily?"

She blinked at him. What was he asking? She was being silly—he was simply asking questions, which was what psychiatrists did. "I must support myself, and that has required ongoing travel."

"What if you didn't have to sing to support yourself?"

Her lips parted, and she pressed them closed again. There was no point in even considering such a tempting dream—and certainly not with this man. If he knew her truth, there would be not even the slightest interest from the doctor.

"There you are, Lil!" Clem's voice boomed out nearby, making Lily jump.

Lily set her plate down.

Clem strode toward her. "Got concerned when you weren't in your room." He shoved his hand back through his hair.

"Why?"

"That's my job." As though just seeing Stephen, he barked out a laugh. "But it looks like Dr. DuBlanc is taking care of you just fine."

Stephen glanced between the two of them, his eyes narrowing. "Does Lily require looking after—I mean when you are at various performances?"

Both she and her cousin looked intently at him.

"There's bad people out there, Doc, and I watch out for Lil." Clem rocked in his shoes then stopped. "Granted this place is so posh that it's got my guard down."

Stephen smiled. "Have no worry. I will be glad to step into the gap."

Clem closed one eye hard, a sign that he didn't understand.

Lily spoke up. "Dr. DuBlanc means that when you're not around, he will look after me, Clem."

Wouldn't it be nice to have someone protect her who also loved her—was in love with her? Her heart beat faster at the thought. Although such a thing could happen for her one day, such would not be with Dr. DuBlanc. *Could not be.*

And she'd not allow herself to continue such fanciful notions.

# CHAPTER TWELVE

*2020*

The sweat breaking out on Michael's brow had nothing to do with sunshine this gorgeous July day and everything to do with the beautiful woman standing six feet away from him. Willa Christy, if that was really her name, given she was a television show host, exuded an air of extreme competence combined with emotional fragility just beneath the surface. She'd been nothing but kind to him since they'd met. He'd like to know more about her.

They stood on the Grand's porch overlooking the gardens and the Straits of Mackinac.

"Sue is walking the Secret Garden with Colton." Willa laughed. "I'm honestly not so sure how that ties in with our design suggestions here at the hotel, but. . ."

He shrugged. "Not sure, either, but it is beautiful there."

Colton had fallen hard and fast for Willa's sidekick. Watching their two assistants working together had been like viewing two super-spreading plants beginning to overtake the other. Maybe like bamboo hybridized with kudzu, although that wasn't an attractive picture.

"Would you like to hear my initial thoughts?" Willa's eyes looked expectant.

"That's why I'm here."

"First of all, guests are blown away by the gorgeous hues of blue in the water. It looks like the Caribbean."

"Or you could say the Caribbean looks like the Straits." Michael chuckled at his lame joke.

Willa stared at him. She probably thought he was a tool. "You know it's so funny that you should say that."

"But not funny ha-ha?"

"No. Not like that. On my first consulting trip to a resort in the Bahamas, that's exactly what I thought."

"That the water was as blue as at the Straits?"

"Yes."

A server brought them the pop he'd ordered earlier. He paid her, including a tip. "Thanks." He gave Willa her drink and sipped his cola.

"Thanks, Michael."

"No problem." He placed a napkin on a nearby side table and set his drink atop it. "So you came up here before?"

She blinked rapidly. "I, uh, I lived here. But I was very young—about three."

"Oh. But you still remembered?"

"I also visited my grandfather up here and stayed the summer I was sixteen."

"On the island?"

She laughed dismissively. "Oh no—in Hessel. Do you know where that is?"

"Yup. Sure I do. Amazing boat show there in the summer, eh?" And he'd had a number of wealthy clients whose homes he'd landscaped there.

"My grandfather builds some of those wooden boats."

"No kidding? Now that's a skill." He snapped his fingers as he made the association. "Garrett Christy is your grandfather?"

She nodded.

"I know him. Duh on me for not connecting that last name with yours. Mr. Christy is the bomb when it comes to crafting vintage wood speedboats." He gave a long whistle.

"Yes, and Gramps gave me my first design job."

"Yeah?"

"At his marina. He gave me free rein to redesign the place."

"I've been there. It's great design and not at all what I'd expected."

"Apparently, my redesign surprised his guests, especially the wealthy yacht owners. That led to some of my first high-ticket redesigns." She shrugged in a self-deprecatory fashion.

"And then you moved on to resort designs?" Her work was right up there with the renowned Australian hotel designer, Estella Davidson. And a few years back, Willa Christy had won the over-the-top Dubai "European" island resorts bid over Estella.

"You've watched my show?" Her cheeks flushed pink.

She looked so gorgeous standing there on the porch, sunlight glinting reddish hues in her hair. He needed to get this conversation back on track. "I have. Aimee had me check out a few shows."

"I hope you liked it."

"Yes." He'd liked watching her, looking at her on the screen, even in those crazy outfits that she wore. "Back to the Hessel marina—did you see my efforts there? And at your grandfather's house?"

"Did you do that wonderful landscaping?"

"I did." He grinned. "A bit under duress."

"How's that?"

Michael shook his head. "Sherry Christy audited all of the Parkers' businesses right before she retired."

"And?" Willa raised an eyebrow.

"Kareen Parker was so relieved with how Sherry handled it, that when your step-grandma retired from the state, the Parkers sent me over to landscape the Christys' place."

Willa frowned. "That seems unusual."

Michael leaned in, keeping his voice low. "Sherry was known as. . ." He dared not use any of the creative, some profane, terms that many Yoopers had used to describe the diligent tax accountant.

"Overly zealous," Willa supplied.

He pointed at her. "That's one way to put it."

Willa raised her palms. "Okay, let's not go there."

"I'd love to go back over. Check on my designs. See how they look now that they've filled in."

The interior decorator's beautiful features tugged in a few different directions, as if she were trying to decide something. "Maybe I'll take you with me sometime." Her face said that she wasn't so sure about that offer.

He'd sweeten the deal. "Okay, I know I haven't been as available or maybe as cooperative as Aimee would like me to be."

"You got that right," she muttered.

"But how's about I dedicate a little more time each day to helping you incorporate your designs in with the landscaping and floral design elements?"

"And in return I take you to Hessel with me?"

He shrugged. "Something like that."

"I really do need to hear more of your thoughts on a redesign."

"Even though I'm only a lowly landscaper?"

She snorted. "If that is your attempt at humility, you can ditch it because I've heard otherwise."

His previously overactive ego threatened to rear its ugly head. His failed relationship with Bianca had punctured his self-esteem. "Oh yeah?"

"You're the go-to guy for all the premier landscaping designs on the island."

He splayed his fingers. "I think you're forgetting about Jack Barnwell."

"Yeah, well, Jack is normally booked through for years for specific projects."

He chuckled. "Which leaves me."

She pointed a finger at him. "But I have it on good authority that you've designed all over the world."

Pride mingled with sadness. "Colton and his big mouth, no doubt."

"Sue told me, but I imagine that Colton was her source."

Michael huffed a laugh. "Those two are what my grandmother would have called 'two peas in a pod.' Anyway, ask away, and I'll try to give helpful input."

Mr. Yooperman was seriously yummy. He wasn't the jerk a lot of people said he was, nor was he emotionally volatile. Michael hadn't exactly been available and cooperative with her, though. When he heard what she had to say, would he think she was clueless? Would he report her initial suggestions, or rather lack of suggestions, to the new management? Would she, like maybe a hundred or so staff members if the rumor was true, be fired?

She ran her tongue over her lower lip. "Okay, like I said, when visitors arrive at the Straits, the color of the water has the potential to overwhelm them." She pointed to the tree line below. "Then you have all this gorgeous. . ." Her thoughts were interrupted by the handsome man beside her. She'd never been this distracted on a job before. Maybe she had COVID-info-overload brain. "Um, fantastic greenery. It's so vibrant."

Michael looked at her in a way that sent a jolt through her nervous system. Since her last relationship, before she left design school, Willa hadn't gotten close enough to any man to have picked up on his attraction to her. But she was sensing it now—big-time.

"Right, that's why we have to landscape in an over-the-top way. We're competing for the view. Yet we have to melt into the setting without disappearing." He leaned back a step away from her, almost as if in retreat.

She exhaled in relief as Michael stared out at the water.

"And there's my problem." Willa pressed her lips together hard.

He stared at her, his eyebrows pressed together in concentration. "How so?"

"I see what Carlton Varney and his mentor, Dorothy Draper, have done inside the hotel and I feel like. . ." She shrugged. "It still works."

He nodded slowly. "I've had the same thought. I wondered how you'd come up with something new that accomplishes that same feeling the old gem has right now."

A trio of seagulls swooped in nearby, squawking, then flew on their way again. Michael glanced at her, and they both laughed.

Willa shrugged. "Even the seagulls want to be here."

"Yup."

"Back to what we were discussing about the setting—it's a huge balancing act."

"As is any design job."

"Agreed."

A ferry horn sounded from the harbor. More arrivals to this beautiful place.

"Okay, so in the Caribbean, Sue and I redesign resorts so they aren't competing with the environment. People are there for the views and the activities."

"Right." Michael rubbed his bristly jaw.

Apparently, he'd forgotten to shave that morning because he'd been clean-shaven the few times she'd seen him thus far. Or maybe he'd been out late on a date and hadn't had time to shave. Willa mentally shook herself. *Stop thinking like that—you have no business wondering about his personal life.*

Michael gave her a quizzical look. "I've landscaped several big projects on St. Lucia, and the owners wanted me to bring in pops of color but nothing that would distract from the view. That was a little frustrating."

"Yeah, I'm not a fan of being limited, but that's part of doing a job for someone—knowing their parameters and what works for them."

"Part of the deal."

"It applies to our situation here too. With this place being on the National Registry, it's also a destination unto itself."

"With the grounds and landscaping, we're all well aware of that. Staying at this hotel has to be a stellar experience, and everything has to be, well, grand enough for the guests to feel they've gotten special treatment." He smiled broadly, revealing his white, even teeth.

He truly was gorgeous. If she were designing his wardrobe, what would she put on him that could compete with that handsome face and muscular build? Willa forced herself to stop gawking at him. "The landscaping works with the bright, even gaudy, colors in this place. I'm not sure I'd be asking you to do anything differently." Not that Aimee had actually permitted Sue and Willa to make landscaping suggestions.

"That's a relief." He pretended to wipe sweat from his brow and shake it off.

"Don't you see that makes me basically useless?"

"Makes you smart."

She gave a curt laugh. "I doubt the new owners will see it that way." Especially after what they'd paid her and Sue to consult with them.

"I could help you." He sipped his soda.

Why would he do that? What did he mean? And why did her heart leap at the thought? "How so?"

"I can make more time available to you. After work, if you want to." He slacked his hip and leaned against the porch rail. "If you want some more ideas, I could be with you after I finish up my assignments for the day and make some suggestions off the clock."

"Why?" The word slipped out of her mouth before she could stop it. When her ex-almost-fiancé had offered to help her on a project, he'd ended up stealing her ideas and passing them off as his own.

"Then you wouldn't have to leave so soon if they sack you."

"I, um...Right." She'd never been fired from a job. Ever. Nor had her partner. "Sue really needs this job, and I do too."

"Wouldn't hurt for Colton to spend more time with Sue." His secretive grin suggested he too had noticed the attraction between their two coworkers.

So, this was really about helping the two fledgling lovebirds. "Right. There's that to consider." And was there anything more? Why did she feel so overjoyed at the thought of spending time with this man and staying longer at a job where she truly hadn't come up with any great plans? *I'm running on dry right now.*

"All right. Today after three."

"Three? Are you off the clock at three?"

"When you start at the crack of dawn you are." His face became serious.

"Hadn't thought about that."

"I could meet you down at Sadie's Ice Cream Shoppe."

"I'll pay."

"It's free for you, isn't it?" He chuckled. "One of the perks of the job?"

She cocked an eyebrow at him. "A lady never tells." Oh my goodness, she was flirting with him. Willa really had just flirted. And her head hadn't exploded. COVID brain. That had to be it.

But the hours until that ice-cream appointment couldn't pass soon enough.

After touring the hotel's massive main parlor, Willa stopped at the far wall. She cringed as she examined what appeared to be a Colonial or Early American mural. Completely out of place. While one might expect a plantation scene at some Virginia resorts, it seemed weird and insensitive to have one here. She sighed then sipped some extremely potent espresso and nibbled on a thin, vanilla-and-pear tart. Those images seriously needed to go. A minimalist mix of summer flowers or a mural of the Secret Garden at the Grand would be much more appropriate. She'd make a note.

She sat down on one of the many vibrant sofas nearby and placed her espresso cup and plate on a cherrywood table. Willa pulled out her iPhone and checked her emails. About a dozen from Dubai. She compressed her lips. She'd sit down later and answer those when her head was clear.

She opened the new St. Ignace newspaper email and clicked the link to see if the ad she'd worked up for Gramps had gotten in there. She logged into her newspaper account, then scrolled down toward the bottom. The history column caught her eye:

> July 1895: The Grand Hotel's new singing sensation continues to draw in crowds. Miss Lily Swaine and her pianist have breathed new life into the repertoire. They offer new popular music, as well as many of the old favorites. Miss Swaine will entertain guests through the remainder of the season.

Suddenly, Lily seemed real. Reading the historical note in the newspaper flipped a switch, fully connecting her current project with a woman who had lived there over 120 years earlier.

Willa's text message indicator chimed, and she checked her phone.

Can you come up and look at Lily's rooms? I could use a little help, Sue had texted.

Willa jabbed at the Y, shorthand for yes, and headed up to their project room. What had they gotten themselves into? If Sue was also having issues, maybe they both needed to reconsider what they were going to do. But Sue was so close to achieving her dream of her own show, a failure on something like this could really discourage her.

The door to their makeover room stood open. A well-muscled guy with skin the shade of Pantone's Iced Coffee exited. Dressed in cream-colored coveralls, he pushed a dolly piled high with boxes of debris from the room. He turned. It was David Williford, a well-known disc jockey in the area. She'd met the love interest of their boss, Aimee, the day before.

Willa cocked her head at the man. "You are a man of many talents."

He paused in his efforts. "What Aimee wants, Aimee gets." He waggled his eyebrows. "And today she needed a construction bum. She knows I used to do that kind of work in Detroit."

"Seriously?"

"That was before I got my DJ company set up here at the Straits."

"That's an interesting switch. Was someone in your family involved in music?"

Sadness flickered over his strong features. "I'm afraid I'm the family disappointment."

*Oops, TMI.* "Oh—"

He looked at her stricken face and shook his head. "Nothing bad like that. I'm the only Williford in generations who wasn't in law enforcement."

"Really?"

"Yeah. In fact, one of my ancestors from way back worked here at the hotel before he moved to Detroit and met my great-great—many greats anyway—grandmother. She was a singer."

"You're following in your many-greats-grandmother's footsteps?"

His face brightened. "Yeah, I guess you could look at it like that. I do it all, and I heard she played piano, sang, and composed music too."

"That's a nice legacy."

"Sure thing, but my dad always pictured me in a cherry-top cop car chasing criminals down the interstate." He shrugged.

"What do you enjoy most?"

"Right now, I'm diggin' being with the most amazing woman I've ever met." If there could be literal stars shining in someone's eyes, they'd be glowing in David's big brown eyes right now. "It'll be chill, working on this project to help Aimee."

Attired in a gauzy retro tie-dyed kaftan with a matching face mask, Sue emerged from the adjacent room, holding several swaths of fabric. "If I were you, I'd have asked Aimee for more than just dinner at the Woods. Why not demand that a little plaque be put up in here with your name on it?" Sue set the cloth down.

"I'll stick with the dinner." David pushed the dolly forward toward the door. "Have a good afternoon, ladies." He sang a line from the Weeknd's single "Blinding Lights" as he headed out.

Willa shook her head. "He has it *bad* for Aimee."

"Yup." Sue rolled her eyes.

Willa scanned the room. "Looks like things are moving right along."

The construction site was remarkably clean too.

Sue waved her forward. "We've gotten a lot done." She pointed to the wall, now stripped of wallpaper, where the desk had been. "And I wanted to get your opinion."

Willa took a few steps forward. This wall was wood-paneled behind the paper. "That must have been a heavy wallpaper to have covered all those grooves in the boards."

"It was a pain to remove too, yes, and surprisingly thick. But look a little closer. I wanted you to be with me when we opened this. I know you love finding little hidey holes in places." Sue bent and touched the wall.

"Oh, I see it now—that cut could have a false wall, maybe an opening behind it."

"Ready to find out?" Sue turned and picked up a pry bar. "I know if you were redesigning this room, you'd probably add another little secret space for the new occupants, but that's not really my thing."

Sue's words had been kind, but Willa hadn't realized that her sidekick wasn't a fan of her penchant for those secret hideaway spots. "This is your project now, Sue, and you should do it the way you think is best."

Angling the bar in, her friend pushed behind the gap and began prying the wood loose. It gave easily. "This thing is hinged I think, but maybe from the inside." Sue pushed, and the secret door opened.

"What's in there?" Willa held her iPhone near her lips. "Flashlight on!" she told Siri, and the light on her phone turned on. She held it out toward the wall.

Willa got down on her knees and pointed the phone's light toward the opening. Something glittered, and she reached inside to pull out a chipped bowl with an assortment of jewelry. Most were so dusty it was impossible to judge whether they were costume jewelry or the real thing. "I'll dip these in ammonia later at the house and see what they are."

"Should we be taking things off-site?"

Willa chewed her lower lip. "Good point."

"I've got a small bottle here." Sue gestured to a small utility cart stocked with multiple cleaners.

"All right. Let me see what else there is." She set the dusty bowl aside and looked again. "There's something wrapped with a pillowcase or some cloth."

"Don't touch it. It could be evidence from that murder."

"Girlfriend, you've been watching too many murder mysteries on Netflix. They said someone died. People die all the time." Willa exhaled loudly, stirring up dust. She sneezed.

Sue shrugged. "You never know."

"If it is evidence, that crime took place over a hundred years ago."

"Still, it could be something really gross."

"Yeah, it is—this sheet looks disgusting. Hand me that old cane."

Sue turned and pulled the slim ebony cane from the wall and gingerly handed it to her.

"Thanks." Willa patted at the bundle. "It's something hard. Maybe a book or a box."

"Could have a dead person's heart inside the box."

"Oh my. You are becoming a drama queen." Willa pulled the cloth-wrapped bundle toward her with the cane. "It's smallish and rectangular—not heart-shaped."

"Yeah, but after all this time, wouldn't a heart be all dried up and hard?"

Willa exhaled loudly as she unwrapped the item.

"Looks like a book," Sue's disappointment infused her words.

The battered brown-leather book had a broken spine. Willa ran her finger over the crackled leather. "Maybe an old-fashioned journal?"

"Should we look inside?"

"It belongs to the new owners, doesn't it? I don't want us getting in trouble." Willa clenched her jaw, thinking about the lawsuit filed against the owners of the hotel for property that the previous designer said was from his own personal collections, on loan, and not belonging to the Grand.

"Doesn't mean we can't look at it, right?"

Willa flipped to the first page and read. *Property of Lily Kerchinsky.* "Oh my goodness! I read an article in the historical section of the newspaper about a suspected arsonist named Lily Jones or Kerchinsky."

"Really?"

"Yes. Wow." Willa's heartbeat picked up. "And the picture on the wall of my bedroom shows a Lily Swaine, who was the singer here in 1895."

"That's got to be the same woman."

Willa flipped the pages. "Why would she change her name again unless she really was guilty of something?"

Sue playfully punched her shoulder. "Excuse me, Willa, but you don't use your legal name either."

"True. And a performer might well use a stage name. But I'll show you that article—I kept it—where it talks about a Pinkerton following a Lily Jones, who also went by Kerchinsky, a singer suspected of torching the tavern where she'd performed and then hastily departed."

"Yikes. So maybe our Lily did kill someone up here." Sue rubbed her cheek. "I bet with her last name of Kerchinsky, we could probably find her info on the internet pretty easily."

Willa turned to the next page of the journal, where a childish drawing of a farm with broken fences and a line of stick-figure men with almost triangular arms elicited the sense of despair the child artist must have felt. Flocks of scribbled birds clustered over a barn in one corner. Sketchy rain clouds loomed close over the heads of the stick people.

"Oh my." Sue pointed to the triangles. "I think those are arms holding guns and those are stick-figure soldiers."

The bottom of the picture had Ladysmith, Virginia, written on it and 1863 with a question mark after it.

"Maybe so."

"I wonder why the question mark after the date."

"Maybe it's a memory, and she wasn't sure." Willa had the same thing happen to her, when she reconsidered a fleeting memory with her mother. She'd estimate the years and guess when it might have happened.

"Maybe Lily was the daughter of a Confederate soldier?"

"Maybe. Or maybe soldiers occupied her family's farm." Dr. Svendsen would likely have an opinion as to what the childish drawing meant. The psychologist had looked at some of Willa's early drawings and had told her adoptive mother that Willa had known for some time that she had another home, another mother. Dr. Svendsen also said privately to Willa that her parents should have told her much earlier than they had.

Sue adjusted her face mask. "As much as I'd like to know more about Miss Kerchinsky, or whatever her name is, I've got my work crew coming back in about ten minutes."

Willa stood, holding the journal to her chest. "Agreed." But as to the rest of it, Willa was going to head back to the parlor and Google Lily Kerchinsky's name as soon as she sat down.

# CHAPTER THIRTEEN

*1895*

"Sorry I let our performance go so much over tonight." Clem gathered his sheet music.

Although her cousin knew most of their songs by heart, the pieces requested by guests this summer had to be pulled from Clem's trunk and rehearsed. Between the extra practice time and now this lengthy performance, Lily was quite spent. "We need to keep better watch in the future."

"Right. Except for we don't know where our next venue will be, and we want to keep these folks happy, don't we?" Clem's tone was curt.

She flinched. Her mild-mannered cousin must be overtired too, but he had a point. "The new opera houses in the Upper Peninsula will be open this winter, and we've already gathered some interest."

"Despite you not being an opera singer and in case you hadn't noticed—I'm not an orchestra."

"I did describe what we do, though." What they'd done for years together. They descended the stage's back stairs and stepped out into the hallway.

Clem grunted in response.

"Several have said they'd be interested in our act and that we could perform popular music and some of the old favorites." She left out the part of how one had cautioned that they mustn't perform dancehall-type music. "I'm grateful our act supported us all—my mother, while she was yet alive, and your family too."

"My mother's remarried and don't need help now, she says."

"Really? That's good." But fear shimmied through her.

"And I don't have my own family." Clem sighed. "But it seems you've found your rightful kin here on the island."

All the air seemed sucked out of her. What would she do without Clem? She needed him to continue her musical career. But now that he didn't have to support his mother, he could start his own family. He deserved to be loved and cherished. "What are you thinking?"

Clem shrugged. "I might want to stick around here for a while."

They'd never been separated. In truth, Clem was more like a brother than cousin. "What do you mean?"

He patted his auburn hair, a habit he'd broken once he'd begun dressing his wavy locks with hair oil, but now the old gesture had returned. "I want to be where Marie is."

Lily blinked up at him as the lights in the hall reflected his tense features. "Couldn't she come with us?"

"She won't."

"Why?"

"Her family is on the mainland and stays there with the tribe come winter."

"But—" If Clem wasn't with her, then she had no act, could sign no contracts.

Clem raised his wide palm. "She's pigheaded like your ma was, and there'll be no changin' her mind."

Stephen approached them from the far end of the hallway. Willa and Clem walked toward him, both deep in their own thoughts.

"Wonderful performance tonight—as usual." Stephen's smile faded as he glanced between the two of them. "Is everything all right?"

"Fine." Clem jerked his thumb toward the other end of the hall. "I'm gonna head up to my room. Do ya mind watchin' over Lil for me?"

"A pleasure." Stephen turned and offered her his arm as Clem strode off from them. "Bee in his bonnet? Or rather under his bowler hat?"

Lily drew in a slow breath. "He's in love." And that could change everything for her.

*So am I.* Stephen wished he could keep Lily at his side forever. "And why is that a problem?"

Lily yawned. "Sorry, I'm overtired."

"That was a long performance tonight. But the crowd was pleased. You should have heard all the praise." Except from the Chicago businessman, Hans Butler. The sharp-eyed man had been ushered out of the men's parlor the previous night when he'd been caught cheating at cards. Butler's friend, or maybe a bodyguard, named Parker had exploded at the accuser and came near to fisticuffs. Had any of the men there reported the behavior to the hotel's owners, he'd no doubt Butler and Parker would have been put out. As it was, both men remained.

Stephen leaned in. "Would you like to go for a stroll on the porch? Look at the stars in the sky?"

"I wish I could, but I'm near to keeling over." The accent he'd noticed in Lily's voice when she was unguarded, and now when fatigued, sounded more Appalachian to him than Virginian.

"I'll walk you up to your room."

She cast him a cautionary glance.

"Trust me, I'm a complete gentleman."

Even her laugh held a musical quality. "With Clem up the hall, I would expect so."

But as they walked through the parlor toward the stairs, he spied the back of Clem as he headed toward the exit onto the porch—or to walk away from the Grand. "Is he in love with Marie then?"

"Yes." She sighed. "And he may be breaking up our act."

"Haven't you been together for over a decade?"

"And then some with our music."

He had to help. "You should ask König to play for you if Clem departs."

She stared at him in astonishment. "Why would a wealthy industrialist want to play for me?"

He shrugged. "To indulge his talent? He's a virtuoso, and it can't be easy stifling that ability."

She rolled her eyes upward as though irritated with him.

"All right, it was merely a suggestion." He patted her hand, nestled on his arm.

"If I don't have a pianist of Clem's quality, I don't know if I can find a position after this one ends."

He could find her a situation—as his wife. With the offer of work at the Newberry Asylum, he could afford to start his career in earnest and begin a new life out from beneath the cloud of his father's disaster in Kentucky. For surely his father had been guilty. Stephen knew it in his heart. Yet they'd blamed it on that poor woman—Kerchief or some other such name that sounded like it. "I believe they have a new music house in Newberry."

"Isn't that where you want to go?"

"It's where I shall be working." He patted his breast pocket, where the letter offering him employment still rested against his heart. "After the season ends here."

"I see."

As they continued walking to Lily's room, he shared about the burgeoning town in the eastern Upper Peninsula. By the time he stood before her door, he'd run out of superlatives.

"Isn't it dreadful cold in the winter, though?" Lily stepped free from him.

"Yes, but if you enjoy winter activities—"

"I don't."

"I could keep you warm." He looked down at her, longing to pull her into his arms and kiss her right there.

Lily fished her key from her reticule.

"I meant if you were my wife, Lily."

She cast him a dismissive look. "You barely know me."

"I know what I feel."

The warmth blooming in her eyes told him she may hold affection for him too. He had hope. "I pray that one day you will hold me in the same esteem in which I hold you."

But if she ever learned what his father had done, would she? Shame exhaled loudly on the flame of hope, snuffing it out.

Rousing herself from a fitful sleep full of Confederate soldiers missing one or more of their limbs, Lily awoke to the sounds of someone opening a nearby door. Mama must have gone out for more firewood. She inhaled, expecting the scent of ash in the fireplace and stale meat odors. Instead, a fresh breeze carried roses, geraniums, and lilies—bringing her back to the present.

She sat up in bed. Alice stood by the wardrobe. She pulled out a blouse, skirt, jacket, and hat and hung them on the hooks inside the armoire door.

The servant turned toward her. "Miss Lily, good to see you waking up."

"Oh? Why?"

"You're supposed to be at breakfast at the Moores' table in only a half hour." She chewed her lower lip. "I didn't want to wake you. But they've come over special from their cottage to visit with you."

Lily stretched, frowning. "I don't remember agreeing to that."

Alice stared down at the thick wool carpet. "I, um, I might have forgotten, miss. Mr. Mace asked me to tell you."

"What?" Lily tossed off her covers. She really had to speak with Mrs. Fox—soon. When she rose, she felt a little dizzy.

"You know I can't write, or I'd have left you a note." The maid sounded so contrite that Lily bit back the urge to fuss at her.

It wasn't Alice's fault that she'd not been educated. If Lily's own mother hadn't been taught to read and write in Virginia, then neither she nor Clem would have been able to do so. Mama had taught Lily, and she in turn had taught her cousin.

Alice helped Lily to wash then dress and finally fixed her hair. Still woozy, Lily sat at the vanity table and pulled a pair of gold and pearl earrings from their velvet case. These earrings had been a gift from an admirer, but Clem had made sure the man understood that her acceptance of them didn't mean she'd be granting him any favors. "Do you know why exactly the Moores wish to breakfast with me?"

When there was no response, Lily glanced at the girl's image in the mirror and saw Alice shrug. A look of disapproval danced over her small features. Perhaps Alice was reading too much into this breakfast request.

Would she have this opportunity for a fine breakfast with high-society people at her next venue? The opera house she'd applied to, at the western edge of the Upper Peninsula, would be frequented by miners, mine owners, lumberjacks, and other local people. Would it be a rough place? Could she even consider employment there if Clem didn't go with her?

"Be careful what you say to Mr. and Mrs. Moore." Alice took two steps back from the vanity.

Lily rose and turned. Alice's face appeared years older as some dark emotion flitted across her small features. "What makes you say that?"

"You said they'd already asked you the favor of a song."

"Yes."

"Then they sent you flowers."

"And they are lovely and generous."

Alice clasped her hands at her waist. "I only meant that. . ."

"Yes? Please feel free to tell me."

"Sometimes folks keep asking you for favors. They start small and then ask for more." Hard green eyes locked on Lily.

A shiver coursed through her. Obviously, the girl spoke from experience. What favors had been asked of young Alice?

Later, throughout what could have been a delightful morning meal with the enthusiastic couple from Chicago, Lily couldn't stop thinking of what might have happened to Alice. The Moores' conversation consisted of small talk and pleasantries.

*So far so good.* It looked like Alice was wrong.

"Did we tell you that we have another son about your age, Lily?" Mrs. Moore's eyes sparkled. "Still unwed."

Husband and wife exchanged a knowing glance. Mr. Moore set his china coffee cup down, and a white-suited waiter immediately refilled it. He didn't thank the worker, but Lily had observed that few of the guests ever acknowledged the servants.

"Thaddeus is a gifted engineer, but we worry that he spends too much time poring over his designs and may never marry."

Lily sipped her coffee, which she'd loaded with sugar and cream. She set the cup down but held the handle. "Not all of us are meant to marry." *Some of us have shameful secrets that chain us.* How ironic that at her age she should have Dr. DuBlanc mention his wish for her to consider being his wife and now here was a society matron seemingly wanting to shove Lily off on her unmarried son.

Mrs. Moore pulled a small *carte de visite* from her reticule and handed it to Lily. "Isn't he handsome?"

Lily accepted the photographic card. Thaddeus Moore was indeed a striking man. "Yes, you are not merely speaking from a mother's heart." She smiled and handed the card back.

Lily considered Alice's comments about things not being as they seemed. Lily was with this wealthy young man's parents, who appeared motivated to interest her in an introduction—which Lily would never allow. But would a servant in a home like the Moores' have had to stave off the unwanted advances of her employers' sons? As difficult as Lily's life had been, she'd been given the gift of song, and that had propelled her out of a life of poverty and possible servitude.

"Thad will be arriving this week." Mr. Moore sipped his coffee.

Mrs. Moore returned the picture to her reticule. "We're hoping to introduce the two of you."

Lily tried to smile, but her lips seemed to furl in on themselves.

"More coffee, miss?"

She looked up into the waiter's knowing, kind eyes and released the handle of the cup. Her fingers felt stiff, she'd clutched it so hard. "Yes, please."

He expertly poured the coffee.

"Thank you."

"You're welcome, miss."

Mr. and Mrs. Moore again exchanged a look. They were not from her world. Nor would their son be. If this one little exchange helped them see that, then so be it.

Mrs. Fox strode through the dining room, heading straight for their table. When she arrived, she greeted the Moores warmly.

Mr. Moore narrowed his eyes at the newcomer. "Don't I know you?"

"I'm the housekeeping manager. You've no doubt seen me here at the hotel."

Unlikely. Ada Fox rarely left her office. She possessed catlike stealth and could show up without notice, startling her workers. "I apologize for the interruption, but could I speak with Miss Swaine privately for a moment?"

Lily pushed away from the table. "I'm finished with my lovely breakfast with Mr. and Mrs. Moore." She smiled at the couple. "Thank you for the invitation."

Mrs. Fox frowned. "I didn't mean to disturb you."

"Oh, you're not," Lily replied before the Moores could.

"Thank you." Ada skittishly glanced around the breakfast room. "Let's converse elsewhere."

Lily directed her attention briefly to the pair at the table. "Good day to you both." Then she followed Mrs. Fox as she strode out of the room. She was surprised when the woman continued into the parlor, turned a corner, and kept moving down the hall. She didn't stop until she reached her office. "Come in."

They entered a small, empty waiting room and then the woman's private office.

"Take a seat, please."

Lily sat, her nerves jangling.

Ada steepled her fingers together. "I have a few things I need to tell you in private. The main thing is about Alice and the other is about me."

Relaxing, Lily pushed back in her chair. "What is it about Alice?" Was now the time to discuss her smoking?

Ada exhaled loudly. "The police have come to me. Someone has alleged that Alice may have set the fire that burned the mercantile down this summer."

Lily's jaw dropped open. She briefly compressed her lips back together. "I heard about that."

"Your uncle Robert saved Sadie from being injured in it. And her sisters could have been killed had they been inside."

"Why do you suspect Alice?" She shuddered. Did her maid suffer from the same malady that had killed Lily's mother and many at the asylum?

"The police said that someone wrote an anonymous letter to them, pointing the finger at her. But since there was no name, no address of the accuser, they aren't doing a full investigation. Still, since she is your maid, I thought I'd ask you if you would keep an eye on her."

Lily huffed a laugh. "I would if I knew where she was most of the time. I have smelled smoke on her, and I've chastised her."

Mrs. Fox waved her hand dismissively. "She's a smoker. What a horrid habit. I've caught her numerous times sneaking a cigarette out back."

"Can't you get her to stop? Threaten her?"

"For some reason, Mrs. Stillman has taken Alice's cause up for protection. When I've talked with her about Alice, Stillman reminds me that she's technically in charge of Alice. She wants to keep her on—seems to be a favorite of hers."

Lily stared at the older woman. "Other than a curt nod of her head toward Alice, I've never seen Mrs. Stillman utter one word to her."

It was Mrs. Fox's turn to gape. "Isn't that something?"

"Yes." Lily clasped her hands in her lap. "Very odd. I'll keep an eye out both for Stillman and Alice."

"Also I wanted to let you know something else. You could well encounter me on one of your visits with the Swaines and Wellings."

"Oh?" Maybe it shouldn't have been such a surprise, since Sadie, a lowly maid, also was friends of the family.

"Yes, Peter Welling and I are old friends." The rosy color in her cheeks suggested a closer relationship.

"How nice."

Mrs. Fox glanced up at the clock on her wall. "Oh, before I forget, the work crew will be in your quarters most of today. I'm sorry for such late notice, but I only just heard myself."

"Thanks for informing me."

The housekeeping manager pushed back in her chair and then rose. "Thank you for your understanding—and your discretion."

Understanding the dismissal, Lily stood too.

The afternoon flew by, and her performance resulted in much applause, pleasing her. Lily had been relieved that the Moores hadn't attended that one, but she felt a little guilty about it.

Clem gathered his music. "I'm headin' down to see Marie real quick."

"See you at dinner?"

"Not until tonight's performance." He appeared awfully sullen for someone going to see his sweetheart.

Maybe Clem was struggling as much as she with the notion of the two of them ending their act.

"All right then."

Lily returned to her suite and unlocked the door. She sneezed as she stepped inside. She'd have to speak with Garrett Christy about the sawdust the workmen had tracked around. She locked her door. Where was Alice anyway? Her maid's door was open, which was unusual.

"Alice?" She stepped toward the maid's room, but there was no sign of her.

Lily retrieved a worn towel and dipped it into her wash basin, which hadn't yet been dumped. After wringing out the towel, Lily dropped it on the floor and used her foot to push it along over the dusty footprints left by the men. Soon she had set things to rights.

Thoughts of Stephen pushed her to record a little memory in her journal. She'd need to be on her own again at some point. She couldn't form an attachment with him. She sat at her desk and pulled the journal from the drawer.

She opened it, the leather-bound book seeming different. Although she'd done nothing to it, the leather seemed cleaner, shinier even. She opened the first page. But instead of her childish drawings, script scrawled across the filled lines. Startled, Lily pushed back in her chair, almost knocking herself over. She read the words—ramblings that sounded so much like her mother's own rants.

Shaking, Lily stared at the handwriting, which very much resembled her own, except there was a waver in the script, as if the writer's hands had been shaking: *"I've done some terrible bad things. God will never forgive me. I fear others have figured out my sins and there will be an accounting. I'll be an outcast forever."*

Had she put these words down? Had she stepped into her mother's shoes as she'd always feared? No, how could that be? Alice couldn't read nor write, so she'd have not been able to do this. Lily closed the journal, her hands trembling. She must be careful—more vigilant than she'd ever been. She tucked the journal into a different drawer and covered it with her Bible. None of the drawers locked.

*My fears cannot be coming true. I cannot be unraveling as Mama did.* Was the dizziness she'd felt that morning like that her mother experienced during her episodes? If the psychiatrists who'd spoken at the hotel, those who espoused the eugenics movement, were correct, it was only a matter of time until her mother's defect could be visited upon her.

*Lord, may those pompous men be wrong.*

# CHAPTER FOURTEEN

## 2020

*W*illa exited the taxi at the Grand and paid the driver. *Worth every penny.* If only they had an IV of coffee set up on the porch...

"Good morning, Miss Christy." The kind-eyed employee at the foot of the steps greeted her warmly.

"Good morning." Since she'd never actually slept, it seemed odd giving that greeting.

If Willa's new redesign plans of the high-end suites at the hotel didn't impress Aimee today, then tonight would be another all-nighter reworking the design. Willa had incorporated a fresh minimalist approach crossed with the Grand's signature geranium flowers. She'd restyled the rooms with a focal wall featuring various types of geranium floral images, mostly a single massive bloom, centered in a white or dark gray wall. She'd kept the colors limited to a palate of white, black, gray, red, and deep green. The serene retreats she'd hoped to achieve would begin with the areas only recently remodeled by Carlton Varney. Aimee and the new owners might not get on board with that approach, due to both the expense and the current legal battle in which Varney was alleging ageism in no longer requiring his services and looking for a younger designer.

She headed up the stairs to the porch. Waiters carried trays of tea cups and coffee mugs to patrons already seated at this early hour.

A waitress, who reminded Willa of her sister, Clare, paused. "Would you like me to bring you some coffee?"

"I'd love that. Thanks." She'd like an entire carafe of coffee, but she didn't have time.

Willa settled in a chair to wait for Aimee, then opened her iPad. She logged onto the hotel's Wi-Fi. Immediately, she opened the St. Ignace newspaper link, hoping to see if the new history column had anything more about Lily. There it was:

> 1895, News from Mackinac Island
>
> Miss Lily Swaine has indeed made a triumph at the Grand Hotel and has been coined "the Songbird of Mackinac" by her devotees. Mr. Clem Christy, her pianist who is a relation of the Grand Hotel's master craftsman, Mr. Garrett Christy, was recently feted at the Christy Tea Shop on Market Street, along with Miss Swaine. A good crowd turned out, including notables Dr. Stephen DuBlanc, psychiatrist; Miss Laura Williams, the renowned actress; industrialist Mr. Charles Bobay and his fiancée, Miss Lyndsey; and the Moore family of Chicago, who reside on West Bluff during the season.

Blinking fast, Willa reread the paragraph. The singer, whose journal she now possessed, had been accompanied by someone who was kin to Willa. Gramps's namesake, the first Garrett Christy, was also prominent for his workmanship. A flutter in her heart affirmed her connection both to the present and the past.

"Deep in thought?" Michael called out to Willa as he jogged toward her across the Grand Hotel's front porch.

She slid the iPad into her bag. She'd give Gramps a call later and read him that historical note. And at an opportune time, she'd ask Michael if Dr. Stephen DuBlanc was a relation of his.

Michael reached her side with not one drop of sweat on his tanned brow. "You got the message too?"

"Meet me for a breakfast meeting at seven on the porch." Willa attempted to imitate Aimee's lyrical French accent.

"That's an epic fail." Michael laughed. "Good thing she's too far away to hear you."

Willa turned to spy Aimee LaFerier gliding toward them, her couture navy-and-white suit emphasizing her enviable figure. Willa swallowed hard. If Aimee nixed her initial suggestions, she wasn't sure what else she could go with. Willa would have to get her creative juices flowing. For now she'd just listen. She and Sue agreed that paying attention to the client was one of a designer's most necessary skills.

"*Bon matin.*"

"Good morning to you too, Boss Lady."

Willa's eyes widened at Michael's comment.

Aimee laughed. "Let's walk down to your *belle jardins.*"

Michael pressed his hand to the center of his broad chest. "My beautiful gardens? I think they're yours."

Aimee hurried past them toward the red-carpeted stairs that led down to the drive. They crossed to the sidewalk and entered another set of stairs that led down to the grounds, the pool, and the gardens.

Halfway down, Willa heard the unmistakable sound of a man's hard footsteps tearing down the stairs behind them. They turned.

Aimee sighed loudly as David Williford's muscular form came into view.

"David!" She pronounced her boyfriend's name like *Dayveed.*

He joined Aimee and gave her a quick kiss.

Once they all reached the bottom, which was at the edge of a huge green area, Michael and Willa moved to one side of a bed of roses and Aimee and David to the other.

David pointed to an area about ten feet away. "I say instead of letting folks play croquet and other games right here, we should put up a statue in honor of my ancestor who worked here." His playful tone left no doubt that he was teasing.

Aimee scowled. "There is no Williford listed in those employee ledger books that Mr. Tagatz gave me to look at."

"Did you look through all the 1890s, *mon amour?*"

Aimee put her hands on her hips. "Yes, I did, like I promised you."

Lovers' quarrel? Willa angled her body away from the couple and Michael did the same.

She covered her eyes against the sun and peered to where the adorable horse and carriage formed from evergreen bushes stood. "That's amazing."

Standing beside the gorgeous designer, Michael fought the urge to let down his guard. He'd wanted to tell Willa that he thought she was amazing too. Instead he said, "I'd like to have more topiaries, especially in the Secret Garden. But with all the craziness due to COVID and the sale of the hotel, I'm not about to ask for more."

Nor would he ask for more from this famous woman. He'd had enough of the high-profile life to last him a lifetime.

They walked with David and Aimee through the gardens. Then they moved on to the Esther Williams swimming pool, a favorite place for visitors to relax on a hot afternoon.

"The pool will be redesigned and ready for the 2021 season."

Willa arched an eyebrow. "Oh, I didn't realize that."

"*Oui*. It is time to move forward on our vision for the future."

What did Michael's future include? Would he even have a contract here next year? He'd lost Bianca, who he'd thought was the love of his life; the home he occupied belonged to his parents; he'd released his Mackinac Island landscaping business over to the Parkers; and he struggled with recurring bouts of feeling lousy. Add to that, he sensed from his recent limited contacts with his boss that something beyond the death of her daughter-in-law was troubling Kareen. He didn't know where Kareen Parker had picked up her emotional baggage, but she had something in there that weighed heavier than bricks. And she observed him like a hawk whenever they met.

Willa was talking about minimalism design. He'd missed the first part of what she'd said. *Focus.*

Aimee wrinkled her nose. "I'm, as you Americans say, not a fan of that movement."

But wasn't that one of the Willa Christy hallmarks? *Minimalism with flare* was one of their themes. Why would Aimee have brought Willa here then?

Willa pulled a sketchbook from her slim messenger bag and handed it to Aimee. "These are some initial thoughts of how those rooms with the best garden view would look."

David leaned in next to Aimee. "Different."

"Maybe a little too different." Aimee shook her head. "Give me something else that I can take to the board next week."

The way Aimee parsed her words, Michael heard a hidden threat.

The French woman handed the sketchpad back to Willa, whose red cheeks revealed her discomfort. Michael wanted to wrap his arm around her and reassure her that everything would be all right.

He glanced as the simple but stunning sketches before Willa returned them to her bag. If the Grand didn't want them, maybe the Parkers would. They were looking to redesign their East Bluff luxury hotel. If that would keep Willa on the island longer, then he would approach the hoteliers and ask.

But what was he doing, thinking of ways to keep Willa Christy here? He knew she was on borrowed time on Mackinac. But he needed more time with this amazing woman—before they went their separate ways.

After a long nap at the cottage, Willa joined Sue in the living room. Outside, rain pattered down on the woods and plants surrounding the home.

Sue sat in an overstuffed chair, working on her iPad. She looked up. "I saw your sketches for the Grand's best rooms and they're amazing. Oh my goodness, I love the clean color palate."

"Thank you. Too bad that Aimee hates minimalism."

"Ouch!"

"Yup." Maybe Willa shouldn't have said anything to her partner about it. She didn't want her to worry. "I'll work on something again tonight, but for right now I'm on vegetate mode."

Sue nodded and looked at her tablet.

Willa settled on the couch and grabbed Lily's journal. She turned the page and spotted a familiar name.

"Ohmygoodness!" Willa's words all ran together. "My great-great-grandfather's name is in this book!" She held the journal aloft so her friend could see it. "It matches up with what I read earlier in the historical section of the newspaper."

Sue dropped her iPad onto her lap. "No way."

"Yes way, and according to the journal, he's the one who made or fixed that wall for that secret room."

"What's his name?"

"Garrett Christy. But that space wasn't meant to be a secret compartment."

"No?"

"No. Lily writes it is supposed to be a compartmentalized storage room."

"Are you sure it's your great-great-grandfather?"

"I don't know how many greats he is." Willa rolled her eyes at her friend. "Let's put it this way—my grandfather is Garrett Christy the third."

"Oh. Sorry." Sue made a face of contrition. "And who was the first Garrett?"

"A craftsman here at the Grand."

"Wait! That's right." Sue pretended to lick her finger and make a mark in the air. "Score one for me. A little late, but I remember now. I took the history tour with Colton, and I saw some of Garrett's work. Those columns in the dining room with the angels and those ornate fruit-and-vine massive buffet servers in the parlor are only a couple of his designs. I forgot to ask you if there was a connection."

"Wow. I didn't know that." She'd definitely have to call Gramps. "I think my grandfather, who designs the boats, inherited some of his talent."

"And you too." Sue frowned. "Didn't you know about him?"

She gave a curt laugh. "My adoptive mother wouldn't talk about my birth mother—do you really think she'd discuss our ancestors?"

Outside, the wind gusted debris against the house.

Sue flinched. "Probably not."

Willa didn't even know who her biological father was. That was a closed topic with her adoptive parents, who didn't seem to have a clue anyway. And Gramps claimed that her mother would never tell him. Tim, though, seemed to think Willa's mom and Thad Moore might have been involved with each other. Maybe Thad could be her father. But he'd died so young.

"What about your grandfather?"

"I think he would if I asked."

"That is so cool. I hope he has some juicy stuff." Sue waggled her fingertips together as if in anticipation.

Willa gave her friend the side eye. "Hopefully nothing nefarious. I guess I'll see." She returned to reading the journal.

Willa flipped the book over, curious if there was anything recorded in the back. Inside, script very similar to Lily's covered the page, albeit in a more erratic fashion. "Check this out." She held the journal aloft for Sue to see.

Her friend leaned in. "Looks like our Lily either was overcaffeinated or something."

"It looks a lot like her other writing, but as if she had tremors."

"That's what happens to me if I drink a grande mocha espresso from Lucky Bean in downtown Mackinac Island." Sue laughed. "That's why Colton swears he is going to decaffeinate me."

"It'll never happen."

Sue laughed. "Never say never."

Her business partner was a bona fide caffeine addict.

Sue pointed to her iPad. "That's why this little baby is so handy—you can't tell what's happened to my handwriting."

Willa scratched her cheek. "I think I'm gonna do some online research on Lily, and I may put a call in to the newspaper to see what they have in their files."

"I love a good mystery, my friend, but you do recollect that we're here to do a job?"

"Yessss." Willa drew the word out long because if she didn't stop herself, she'd make up a load of excuses for why she needed to find out more about Lily Swaine.

"Tell you what. There's no television at this place, so I can't watch my mystery shows, and you can't watch remodeling and destination shows. Maybe we could allow ourselves to do a little sleuthing when we're off the clock at night. Deal?"

"Deal. And we'll start this evening." Willa was not up for another redesign attempt tonight.

"Right. As soon as you come up with one more pitch for Aimee that isn't with a minimalist style." Sue arched an eyebrow at her.

Willa scrunched up her nose and made a grumpy face at her friend. "Spoilsport."

"It's a carrot and not a stick."

Willa laughed. "When did you start getting all parental on me?"

Sue's face became more serious. "Maybe after I finally listened to you." The rain outside poured down, forming rivulets on the windows. Lightning split the sky, and Willa flinched, but Sue simply stared, wide-eyed.

These past few years, with Sue at her side, had been some of the best years of her professional career. The younger woman made work easier. Her positive attitude spurred Willa on.

"You've listened to me?"

"Yeah, you've been a great help to me. I've learned so much from you." A muscle twitched in Sue's cheek.

Maybe Sue wasn't overcaffeinated but instead nervous. Willa drew her eyebrows together. "You make it sound like past tense. What's going on?"

"Willa, I've been wanting to tell you." Sue chewed her lower lip. "My agent got an offer for my own HGTV show today. And she wants me to seriously consider it."

"So, you'd be leaving me?" A rush of mixed feelings cascaded over Willa. Joy for her friend and business partner, fear about what this meant for her own show and brand, and relief that she could make decisions that she'd been putting off for far too long.

"I've loved being with you. But yes, I'd have to go on set in September."

That wasn't even six weeks away. She'd be on her own again. Panic bubbled up.

*Where do I go from here, Lord?*

# CHAPTER FIFTEEN

*July 1895*

Lily's hand trembled as she opened her journal and flipped it to the back. Were the ramblings written there a trick to make her believe she'd gone mad? No. Even having such thoughts was madness. She'd slept on the decision of whether to ask about the workmen, and today she would do so.

There was a rap at the door, the staccato cadence the signal for Alice. "Come in," Lily called.

The door lock turned and her maid stepped in, carrying with her the scent of smoke.

Lily pointed to the door. "Take that dreadful odor out of here."

"What, miss?" Alice cast her eyes downward.

"You've been smoking again, haven't you?"

"No, ma'am." She flexed her reddened hands. "That is, yes, Miss Lily, I'm sorry but I did. It's a dreadful fearsome habit to give up."

"Don't let me smell that on you again, or I'll report you to Mrs. Stillman." Lily's words came out harsher than she intended. If she invoked Stillman's name rather than Mrs. Fox's, would she have better results? This would also give her an excuse to speak with the assistant housekeeping manager. There was something about Mrs. Stillman that sent prickles through Lily every time she spied the sour-faced woman.

Color bled from Alice's cheeks. "No, miss. It won't happen again."

Lily waved a hand to shoo the girl away. "Go back outside and get some fresh air. When you return, you may spray some of my vanilla scent on your clothing to get the last of that out."

"Yes, miss." Alice bobbed a curtsy and departed.

Lily tipped her head back, stretching her tight neck muscles. *Dear Lord, what am I going to do?* Alice was beginning to feel more like a liability than a help. And someone was writing in Lily's journal—either that or she was slipping down the slope to madness as her mother had done.

Inhaling deeply, Lily lowered her chin. She'd start first with Clem's cousin Garrett. Perhaps one of the men was messing about with her journal. That Mr. Diener made her feel distinctly uneasy, despite his good manners. She went downstairs and rapped at the craftsman's workroom door. The sound of something heavy being set down carried from within. In a moment, the sturdy man opened the door.

Garrett smiled benevolently at her. "Lily, what brings you here?"

"I. . ." Two of his crew members stood bent over a wooden desk, carving a ship's likeness on the top. Clearly that piece would require glass to be set atop it in order to be useful.

"James and Mr. Diener, please give us a moment." Garrett gestured for them to leave, and the two men passed by Lily, removing their cloth work caps. Mr. Diener respectfully averted his gaze, but still her skin prickled as he neared.

When they left, she stepped inside, angling herself so she could view the small entrance hall and the longer one leading to hotel rooms. "I fear someone may have gotten into my desk recently."

"Oh?" A line formed between the man's dark eyebrows.

"Yes, my journal has been tampered with."

"I'm sorry to hear that."

"Could you tell me about your work crew?"

"My workers? I can't imagine any of the fellas doing that."

*How foolish I am.* Her cheeks flushed.

Garrett continued, "I only have a few men on your project, and you just met the main ones. James is a local and handy with any tool. And Mr. Diener—"

"Why do you call him Mr. Diener instead of by his first name?" The man was no older than Garrett, who was in his early thirties. He might even be younger.

The craftsman shrugged. "Diener is old-school. Talented. Requested we keep things a little more formal, and I agreed."

Lily exhaled a long sigh. What had she been thinking? Why would any of the workers want to write crazy ramblings in her journal?

"Sit down." Garrett pulled a sturdy oak chair over for her, and she sat. "Diener has strong recommendations from many patrons in Chicago. Proven to be especially talented as an artist. Renderings are exquisite."

How could she accuse Mr. Diener of writing in her book? Because if she didn't find any other reason, she'd have to face the fact that she was descending into the insanity that had befallen her mother.

Garrett grabbed a sheet of artist's paper and held it before her. "This here is his idea for your room's mural."

An ethereal red-haired woman, attired in a seafoam green gown, was sketched gazing out to the water.

"It's beautiful."

"True. But management prefers wallpaper in this next project. Mr. Diener is disappointed. Too much of a gentleman to protest. He'll put up that floral wallpaper and pretend he's glad about it."

She had planned to go to Ada Fox next but reconsidered. The woman would think Lily to be absurd or mad—which she just might be. No. She'd ask Alice and Clem to keep watch over the room. She'd not tell Clem what was happening in her journal. If he believed that she was going down her mother's path to insanity, would he take her to the asylum? No, surely not. Tears pricked her eyes at the thought of Stephen finding her there at the hospital at Newberry—in her cell, a madwoman.

"Are you all right?" Garrett handed her a clean handkerchief. "Was something of value taken?"

Her peace of mind was indeed of great value.

Lily shook her head. "Not exactly."

"Ask Clem to keep watch, and I'll remind my men to not touch anything personal in the room."

"Thank you."

"Miss Lily, don't forget to take your troubles to the Lord too."

"I will." She smiled at him. "I'm planning to attend church tomorrow with the Swaines."

"That's good. They're a wonderful family, although they've had their trials."

"I can't imagine how my grandmother, Jacqueline, must have felt to have her sons fight on either side of the War between the States."

"Happened with a great many families. Mostly folks from the neutral states having kin fighting against each other when they joined up on opposite sides."

"I wonder how many of them had two sons in the same family die like that, on opposite sides of the war."

Garrett shook his head slowly. "I don't rightly know how I'd feel if any of my children grew up to do that. But I trust the good Lord would get me through."

"Yes, of course. That's where we must put our confidence." She needed to remember that.

"Tomorrow you can take one of the hotel's carriages and go listen to Reverend McWithey. He's a fine orator."

"Clem and I were told that on Sunday mornings the carriages were reserved for the paying guests."

"Will Clem attend with you?"

She sighed. "Truth be told, Clem is often down at the settlement as soon as the sun rises on Sundays, so no."

"He and Marie will probably be married and parents by this time next year." Garrett rested his hand atop a small console that was partially carved with acorn clusters beneath its edges.

Was he right? Clem deserved his own family.

"What about Dr. DuBlanc?"

Lily's cheeks heated. Did he mean she and Dr. DuBlanc would be married too? "What?"

"Mightn't he attend with you?"

"Oh, I don't think so." She pressed her hand against her collar.

"He's had his own family troubles."

"Oh?"

Garrett drew in a deep breath and exhaled. "Till about three years ago, the elder Dr. DuBlanc was one of Michigan's top psychiatrists. Then something happened. His wife died, Stephen's mother, and Dr. DuBlanc headed down South."

"To Kentucky?" A boulder seemed to have dropped into her stomach.

"Yes, to direct a big new asylum there."

"Oh?" she squeaked out.

"But there was a fire. The place was built of wood and went up like a tinderbox. Dr. DuBlanc died when he ran inside to help rescue the patients."

Lily stared at Garrett for a long moment. Surely Clem hadn't told his cousin about her mother. "Do you remember the name of the place?"

"No." Garrett frowned. "But all that to say Stephen has suffered the loss of both of his parents in the past few years. You could be a comfort to him, Miss Lily. Keep praying for him."

"I. . .um. . .yes, thank you." Lily dipped her chin and left the room, shaking like a leaf.

A comfort? Her mother had caused the death of Stephen's father and of many others. Yes, she'd pray, but she should keep well away from Dr. Stephen DuBlanc lest she bring him further pain. Yet how could she do that when everything within her longed to know him better?

How could a loving God be so cruel?

Although Lily couldn't have asked for a prettier Sunday morning in July, her sorrow over learning that Stephen's father was one of her mother's victims ruined her enjoyment. She'd ended up walking alone on her way to church, which was on the village's far end. As she moved along the boardwalk, it seemed that Lake Huron should be as tumultuous as her feelings, with whitecaps and turbulence. Instead the mighty lake lay calm, with gentle waves lapping at the shore, its striations of turquoise and sapphire colors as beautiful as ever this sunny day.

"Yoo-hoo!" Sadie, her blond hair pinned into a chignon, waved at Lily from her seat as Robert pulled his carriage to a stop.

Lily's young uncle, who was driving the carriage this morning, wore a perplexed look on his handsome face. "If I'd known one of the Grand's drivers wasn't bringing you to the church, I'd have stopped to get you."

Lily waved a hand dismissively. "It's no trouble." She'd worn her old low-heeled boots for the walk.

"Hop in." Sadie opened the carriage door and moved over. Across from her in the open carriage sat three young girls attired in dresses of various pastel shades. "These are my sisters."

Sadie introduced the girls as Lily climbed in beside her. "Opal is my youngest sister, Garnet is the next youngest, and then Bea." Each girl nodded in turn.

The eldest girl, who appeared to be in her late teen years, had sharp, knowing eyes that made Lily uneasy. Still, Lily managed a polite greeting. "Nice to meet you all."

"The Cadotte pew is gonna be crammed today," Opal asserted.

Garnet leaned forward. "Guess what? Did you know that Maude Welling's fiancé isn't named Friedrich König?"

Lily frowned. She didn't know that Maude was engaged, much less to the industrialist from the hotel.

"We all had a big dinner last night up at the Canary with him." Bea smirked. "Mr. König's real name is Ben Steffan."

Lily made her face a mask, despite her disappointment. She'd not been invited to celebrate with the family. "I'd heard Ben Steffan was an important newspaper reporter. Why was he passing as a German industrialist?"

Bea sneered. "You should ask Maude."

Garnet smiled shyly. "I dressed up in a fancy gown."

"How nice," Lily managed to say.

"Maude and Ben will be married soon I bet." Bea nodded firmly, as though agreeing with herself.

But Lily had been left out of the celebrations. Hurt coursed through her. She'd grown up an only child, with Clem more like a brother than a cousin. But now he'd gone off with Marie in most of his free time. And Lily's newfound family members were also excluding her. She pushed back against the carriage seat as Robert directed the horses to move on again.

Sadie covered Lily's hand. "Maude's father has been having some heart issues. And he's been anxious over a number of situations that have nothing to do with you. Robert and Maude have been waiting for a time to speak with Mr. Welling about you being part of the Swaine family. I'm sorry we didn't feel we could invite you to the dinner without having to cause Mr. Welling possible further distress."

The *clip-clop* of the horses' hooves sounded in the street, reminding

Lily of how many carriage rides in cities she'd had over her career. Often the rides were only as she arrived in town or when she was leaving the venue to return home once again. In the countryside where she'd grown up, they'd owned no horses or carriages to take them anywhere.

Bea leaned forward. "Did you know that Maude was fired from the Grand Hotel?"

"Yes, I'd heard from Alice a little while ago." What a surprise it had been to learn that the clumsy maid had been Lily's cousin, Maude. "But her family owns the Winds of Mackinac, right?" Cousin Jack had told Lily that one day when he'd popped by her room to leave an adorable home-made card for her.

Sadie fussed with the broach at her neck. "It's complicated, and Robert's trying to work things out so that Mr. Welling will be okay."

With the knowledge that Mama had caused Stephen to lose his father already on her mind, Lily didn't need more complexities in her life. "I see."

Lily didn't want to learn more about what her Swaine and Welling family members were working out. Perhaps, as it was with Stephen, her newly found kin would be better off with her gone. The thought of being totally alone, without even Clem, made her heart ache.

They finally arrived at a lovely white, wood-sided church and were seated in a pew marked Cadotte. This had to be one of the fanciest churches she'd ever been inside. At home, they'd often had sermons delivered outside beneath a canopy of trees. In bad weather, they'd have service inside the small schoolhouse in the clearing.

The preacher was a fine orator. He had a zeal for Christ and a heart for the lost. His deep voice carried conviction.

Afterward, as they left the pew, Robert asked her opinion of the preaching.

"Reverend McWithey's sermon was indeed a balm to my soul."

A smile of satisfaction crossed his face. "Good."

They all departed the church and headed out to where the carriage was parked.

"Will you join us for lunch?" Robert asked Lily, as he assisted each of them up into the carriage.

"Picnic by Arch Rock." Sadie set her youngest sister on her lap.

Soon they were all seated and on their way.

Lily tugged at her gloves. "I've never been to the Arch Rock. I've heard it is lovely."

"Oh, it is." Garnet bounced in her seat. "And if Jack comes, maybe he'll walk across the top for you."

"Garnet!" Sadie glared at her younger sister. "That's not safe."

"He's done it all his life," Bea muttered.

When Robert parked near the vast limestone rock formation, Lily was aghast that the girls would think it was fine for a child to clamber across the top of the massive stone arch. Then again, look at all the things that mountain children were allowed to do in the hills of Kentucky. Some boys were convinced by a stump preacher that they could handle rattlesnakes. That usually resulted in the preachers being run off by the boys' parents.

They settled on two large quilts spread on the grass—the Duvall girls on one and the adults on the other.

Sadie fixed Robert and Lily each a plate of food and handed it to them. Bea came and took the hamper to their spot. Robert spoke a brief prayer of thanks for the meal. When Lily looked up, he fixed his gaze on her.

"It's only fair to share a bit of our dirty laundry, Lily."

Sadie shook her head. "That's not a very nice way to put it, Robert."

"It's not very nice what my mother did all those years ago." He pressed one eye closed shut.

"I'm sure she had her reasons." Sadie took a bite of her sandwich and angled her body toward her siblings.

A breeze stirred and pulled at Lily's hat, but her pins kept it secured. "What did Jacqueline do?"

Robert swept a few crumbs from his vest. "She added a codicil to her will that is now disrupting lives."

"I'm sorry to hear that." Lily took a small bite of a strawberry. She winced. A little tart.

"And her heirs have limitations on what they inherit." Robert rattled off the names of a half-dozen businesses on the island. "Poor Peter Welling, Jack and Maude's father, has been kept from claiming as his own that at which he has worked so hard. He never knew that, under the will, only his wife and her descendants inherited."

"That doesn't seem fair." Did Mr. Welling then see Lily as a threat to what his children might inherit? Lily had little to call her own, but what she did have, she thanked God for daily.

"Not only that, but my mother put a codicil in her will so that her heirs would have to remain living on the island to keep their inheritance."

Lily frowned. "Aren't you a ship captain and gone from here most of the time?"

"I am, and I lived off the island last year after my sister's death." He gestured to Sadie. "But we're planning on living here after we marry. We've got her sisters to think about, and we don't wish to uproot them. Their father was injured in a logging accident, a brain injury, and he's at the asylum in Newberry."

Lily's hands shook. Just hearing about the asylum made her jittery. "I'm sorry."

"They can go and visit him and if he ever recovers. . ."

Sadie turned toward them. "There's always hope that my father will eventually be well."

"Yes," Robert and Lily said in unison.

"I feel my mother tried to exert her control after losing her sons, both on opposing sides of the Civil War, by putting these untenable terms in her will."

"If your mother hadn't been so distressed by losing her sons, though, you wouldn't be here." Sadie touched his arm gently.

He gave a curt laugh. "Yes, I'm the replacement child."

Sadness cloaked Lily. This man before her, her uncle yet near her age, was a completely different kind of man than her father had been. Her birth father had left his home in the North and joined the Confederate army. But her uncle had been born almost a generation later. "You're not a replacement, Robert. You are your own person."

They all picked up their sandwiches and ate. The Duvall sisters laughed and chased a group of butterflies away from their quilt. Overhead, clouds piled up, shutting out the brilliant sun. Birdsong filled the air as robins and other songbirds flitted overhead.

"What do you remember about your father, Lily?" Robert wiped his mouth with a napkin and set it aside.

"He loved me." Tears pricked her eyes. "He loved Virginia and my grandparents and my mother." But there were two sets of fragmented memories. One of a young father who'd ridden off whole, a happy person. And another of the poor mutilated soldier who'd been returned to their plantation.

Sadie pulled her wrap more closely around her. "If your father hadn't left here to fight for the South, then you wouldn't be here either, Lily."

"No." She wiped her tears away. "Yet he must have loved this place to have kept the box and the paintings all those years and to have made sure that I had them. He must have wanted me to know about this place. And I can see why." She gestured around to the beauty surrounding them.

"It's a great place, but as a performer, would you want to live here?"

"Oh no, I have to travel to my venues." She saw where they were leading this conversation.

Sadie settled a little closer to Robert. "But you could keep a place on the island."

Lily frowned. "How would I do that?"

The couple exchanged a long glance.

Heat singed her cheeks. They believed that she intended to ask for part of an inheritance. If her grandmother knew that her father had survived the war and had descendants, Jacqueline surely would have omitted him from the will as well. "My father made his choices, and I feel guilty about what that did to this family—"

"But it's not your fault." Robert exhaled loudly. "And we do want to welcome you into our family."

Lily nibbled on her sandwich, which began to taste like sawdust.

"We just thought you might want to understand some of what's going on right now." Sadie's plaintive voice didn't move Lily to respond.

Bea joined them, handing the hamper back to her sister. "Did you tell her about Mr. Steffan and what he was doing at the hotel?"

"We'll tell her more about that some other time." Sadie cast Bea a hard glare.

The girl returned to her sisters and pulled them up from the quilt. They all ran off toward another carriage that had just arrived.

"There's Maude and Ben now, with Jack." Sadie stood and waved.

Lily gathered up the plates. "I'll congratulate the happy couple, but then I'd better return to the hotel."

Robert looked at her askance. "I'll give you a ride back and then return for all my Duvall girls."

"Thank you. I'm sorry to put you out." She wasn't up to remaining and hearing anything more about her new extended family today. If they pushed her harder, would she slip and reveal the truth about her mother? She needed to keep that to herself.

Lily returned to the hotel and went straight to her room. She rubbed the tension out of her neck. After bathing and enjoying some rosewater scent that soothed her nerves, Lily dressed and went to the desk. She set up her ink and pen and then opened her journal and began to write all about her picnic with her cousins.

Then she added:

> *I feel a terrible headache building and I will sleep soon, now that I took the powders that Alice gave me. I'm afraid, though, of what I might find written in this journal when I awake. Is it me, Lord? Please don't let me become what my mother was. I don't know how I could live like that.*

> *What kind of God allows me to fall in love with a man I can never marry? If Stephen knew the truth about my mother, he'd hate me. So I'll make my plans to move on to my next venue.*

> *I will force myself to cut out of my life the one man I've ever really loved.*

# CHAPTER SIXTEEN

## *2020*

Willa had a few days to process Sue's announcement. As she stepped outside of the cottage, where the yard appeared almost Alpine green, elation for her friend prevailed in her mixed feelings. The selfish part of her wanted to keep her business partner nearby. But since Willa had been encouraging Sue to take flight and launch her own career, how could she allow herself to be upset? The answer was simple—she couldn't.

Willa moved toward Sue and Colton, who sat on a metal loveseat covered with preppy navy and hot pink padded cushions. "You two look comfy."

"Yeah, these are great." Colton pointed to the cushions.

"Your lady friend there designed them." Willa pointed at Sue.

The brawny man beamed at Sue. "Good job."

Her business partner's cheeks bloomed a pink almost as bright as the azaleas in the cushions' fabric print.

"It's no mystery, Colton. I do design things, you know."

"And soon you'll be showcasing your talent on your new show." Willa prayed the contract would come through.

"If it gets picked up." Sue pushed her bangs back off her forehead.

"Of course it will." Colton nudged Sue.

"Speaking of mysteries." Willa was still digesting what Sue had told her earlier. "Let me get this straight. Colton, you have a friend who investigates unsolved murder mysteries?"

"Not exactly." Colton took Sue's hand. "Ronnie has been producing shows in Michigan for about a decade, but this is his first murder mystery series."

Willa set Lily's journal down on a side table, along with her drink. She lowered into one of the Adirondack-style lawn chairs across from the lovebirds. "And he wants to feature an episode on Mackinac Island?"

"Right." Sue and Colton echoed.

"And he's the one who gave Sue's pitch to HGTV a little extra shine, right?"

"Yup." Colton squeezed Sue's hand.

Sue took a sip of her iced coffee. "He reviewed everything you'd already helped me with and then he added on some more elements from a producer's angle."

"That's awesome. I'm so happy for you." Willa lifted her sweetened iced tea to her lips. If she was perfectly honest with herself, she really didn't want to resume their HGTV show. And with the pandemic, the choice might well be out of her hands. Lately Willa longed for a break. Some time to figure out what was next in her career.

Colton leaned forward. "Did you know my buddy was actually considering reinvestigating a race-boat crash from the eighties? I knew from Sue that your grandpa built that boat, so I kind of persuaded him to look elsewhere. Didn't want to upset your grandfather."

Instead, he'd just upset her by revealing this. Willa narrowed her eyes. "They thought it was a murder?" Another tie-in with the mysterious Moore family. But who would want the young man, who might be her father, to die? Her mouth went dry.

"When the producers looked over the paperwork, the police had been thorough." Colton shrugged. "A rich teenaged kid, drunk, and speeding into the harbor."

"And the Moores and that teenager—it turns out they *did* live in this house." Sue set her coffee down on the nearby table.

"They still own it." Colton turned to look first at Sue and then at Willa. "Aimee told me."

"Really?" That meant she could be living in her own father's home. Her mouth went dry. "Are the parents still alive?"

"Not sure." Sun burst from beneath billowing cumulous clouds overhead, making Colton's blond hair almost glow.

Sue chewed her lower lip. "Instead, we're pretty sure Ronnie is going to do a show about our Lily's maid. And he said he's been lining up sus-pects, including a member of the Moore family."

"Seriously?" Willa frowned.

"Mrs. Parker told me that the Moores have owned this cottage since the 1890s." Colton popped the top on his beer can. "But they haven't stayed here at all since the time their son died in the 1980s."

Willa considered this information. Part of her was emotionally trapped in the past as well. "That explains why this cottage looks like it's stuck back in time."

"Nah, that's how most of the houses are here. It's impossible getting stuff off the island. That's why a lot of old houses look like museums inside." Colton shrugged. "That's island life. What comes here stays here. So expensive getting stuff out again that it isn't worth it. Islanders were repurposing stuff long before it was the thing to do."

"It feels like no one has actually lived here in maybe thirty years or so." Willa leaned her head back toward the house. "But we can tell that someone has made improvements."

"They started sending work crews over about two years ago. The younger Mr. Moore—he's a Chicago media hotshot—he paid for the landscaping and upkeep. That's what Mrs. Parker said. She's good buds with the family."

Willa lifted her iPhone from her pocket and googled "Moore Media Chicago" for the search terms. A ton of links pulled up. "Looks like the owner, or their son Chad, has a media design business. And his stuff looks pretty good." She opened a page that was full of logos that made her gape. The design, the colors, the unique fonts all spoke of excellence in creative design.

"Rich, like most of the people up here on the bluff." Colton wrinkled his nose and took a swig of his local craft beer.

Willa closed out the open page on her phone. Now wasn't the time for cyberstalking the Moore family, even if they might possibly share the same DNA. "Let's get back to looking at Lily's journal. But we can't let Ronnie know what's in here. He needs to do his own research." Willa cast a stern glance at the happy-go-lucky landscaper. "I really don't want a lawsuit if Aimee finds out I took this from the premises."

"Gotcha." Colton pretended to unwind a roll of duct tape, rip off a piece, and slap it over his mouth.

Sue stirred her iced coffee. "Let's hear some more of what's in that journal."

"It's bizarre, because there are front and back entries. I'll start with one that she wrote in the front."

Willa read it aloud:

> Some days I believe I am going mad. How could a just God allow my crazy mother to do the things she did? And I was left to deal with the mess. I thought I'd escaped the past, but now I end up here where I'm confronted with the one man who could ruin everything for me. I don't know if I have the strength to go on, now that C has a sweetheart and will be quitting. Before, I could count on him to look out for me, but now I'll truly be alone.

"Sounds like a bummer." Colton put his arm around Sue. "Is the stuff in the back any better?"

"Nope. Here's what's scrawled in the back."

> When I think of the mess I've made of things, of how I had to seek out my own way in the world, the disaster it became, I lose all hope and want to die. If C wasn't here, I'd have done it already after I learned about what I was up against. Darkness encroaches like a giant shroud ready to wrap me up and toss me into the abyss. I see the images on my ceiling in the night, and they threaten me. They'll take me back to that hell from where they came.

Sue's eyebrows rose. "Yikes. That sounds way darker than what she wrote up front."

"Right. I wonder if when she feels really bad, she flips the journal over and unloads on those back pages?"

"Maybe." Sue frowned.

Colton's brow puckered. "But then again, maybe someone else wrote it. The handwriting looks kind of messed up."

"She certainly sounds distraught." Sue patted Colton's hand. "And sometimes people's hands shake then."

He shrugged. "She sounds an awful lot like Michael when he's on one of his downward spirals. Up one day, then the next, and maybe for a week he's a complete downer. I keep wondering if he has bipolar or something."

"Bipolar disorder is a serious condition." Willa knew how frightening that diagnosis could be. Her dad, Dr. Joseph Forbes, always worried about his patients who struggled with it. "You have to really stay on top of bipolar and manage it. If you don't, you can get the 'kindling effect' is what Dad called it. You have repeat episodes that get worse and worse, and you end up in and out of the hospital and then medication can't control it."

Poor Michael. Was he really struggling with a psychiatric problem?

Colton drained the rest of his beer and crunched the can. "I don't think it's gotten any worse. He's been like this for a few years. Even before that Bianca chick."

"Do you think that's why she dumped him?" Sue's eyes widened.

He gave a curt laugh. "She only used him to get back at her husband. There was no real dumping to be had. Bianca never considered herself in any kind of relationship with Michael. But he was really into her, and he loved those girls. He still sends them gifts once in a while."

"I can't imagine that kind of betrayal." Sue inhaled deeply.

A light breeze swayed the old-fashioned hollyhocks and gladiolas in the nearby garden.

"It's not something you ever get over." Willa knew that from experience. But the wall that she'd built around her heart was beginning to feel less like cement and more like an evergreen hedgerow. And those could be trimmed and even cut down.

Michael breathed a sigh of relief to catch Kareen Parker in her office. His eyes hurt so bad that he was barely able to tolerate the sunshine outside, where he was tending the Parkers' perennial garden. Even now, he had to leave his sunglasses on to keep the overhead lights from bothering him.

When he knocked on the doorframe, she looked up from where she was standing by her window. Kareen's frown and piercing gaze could have frosted the hardiest of the gladiolas that Michael had been tending.

"I need to go home early."

"Will you need another day off?" Her curt voice screamed disapproval.

Michael took a step forward, yard debris from his pants scattering to the floor. He wished he'd brushed his muddy knees off. "Sorry."

Kareen glared at him.

If she said one more thing accusing him of alcohol abuse, he'd yell at her for sure.

"Do you need to go?"

If he didn't get his mood under control, he'd burst. "Yeah, I need to rest." He turned away and feigned a cough.

The older woman took two steps back and pulled on her face mask. "Do you feel sick?"

He pulled his own mask up so she wouldn't see the guilty expression he was sure that he wore. God would forgive his white lie with the cough. It was true, though, for different reasons that he felt unwell. "I don't feel good."

She made waving motions with her slim, age-spotted hands. "All right then. Go home. But if you end up with that cough continuing, get down to the clinic for the COVID test."

"I'll be fine tomorrow, I bet."

She narrowed her eyes at him as if considering. "You're not drinking are you? Doing drugs?" Her voice was harsh.

*I will not yell. I will maintain control.*

"Nope." He raised his hands in mock surrender. "I know what that has done in your family."

"Darned right you do." Kareen crossed her arms over her chest, her multiple gold necklaces swinging as she did so. "My husband thinks our daughter-in-law, Amanda, was self-medicating some infernal mood disorder or something, but I still think she was selfish whether she was crazy or not."

A bucket of thick mulch could have been thrown on him. He'd never heard his employer speak so strongly or negatively about mental health issues before.

"It's hard enough what with my grandson's health problems." She bit her lip. "Never mind, that's not your concern. You go get some rest and we'll see you tomorrow."

"Thanks for understanding." But she didn't really understand. And if Kareen discovered that he struggled with mental health problems, would she pull the rug out from under him? He'd made it home riding his bike at full tilt and keeping his eyes closed into almost slits. Finally, he unlocked his front door, went into the house, and collapsed onto his bed, dirty clothes and all.

Sometime later, his cell phone woke him. He pulled his phone out, which was still in his pocket instead of on the side table. He accepted the call.

"Are you doing okay? We missed you today." Willa's sweet voice cut through Michael's brain fog.

He sat up and peered at his clock. After two in the afternoon. "Sorry I didn't call."

"It's all right." It sounded like she was sipping something—probably that tea she preferred in the afternoon. "I did want to catch up with you and tell you more about what's in Lily's journal."

"Oh?"

"Yeah, I found some scary stuff in there."

"Yeah?" He rubbed his eyes. He should get up and try to do something, but his whole body ached with this episode of depression.

"It looks like she may have suffered from some kind of mental health problem, like her mother did."

"Her mother?"

"Oh, I'm sorry, I should have told you. Sue and I found out that her mother burned down an asylum in Kentucky. Can you believe that?"

Michael swallowed hard, the information triggering a memory of weird family lore. He needed to get hold of that journal. He would ask his dad about his island ancestors. "If that was the case, why would anyone have hired her back then?" He shoved a hand back through his messy hair. "I mean, they were seriously freaky about that stuff."

Willa was silent for a moment. "It might be why she was so afraid that the hotel doctor, who by the way shares your last name, would find out about her secret."

"I'd like to look through it on my own."

"I don't know."

"I thought you wanted to show this journal to me."

"I did. I do. But it might be the property of the hotel."

If this Lily was an ancestor of his and Kareen Parker got wind of this, who knew what might happen. This was a small island, especially when all the tourists went home. "Why don't you bring it to me tomorrow at work so I can just see it." His voice was raspy. His eyes burned like fire. Michael wanted to crawl back under the covers and stay in bed for a week, not go back to work.

"At work?" Her voice held another question. Probably one questioning whether she'd see him socially.

They normally did meet-ups in the evening, walking on the boardwalk, swinging like kids down at the school, sitting behind the library and watching the ferries come and go. They'd discuss work at the Grand, but mostly he'd just enjoyed being with this beautiful woman. And that was almost scarier than how he felt right now.

He sure didn't need Willa catching him like this. "Yeah, I'm not up to going out tonight." What an understatement.

"All right." Her cold voice ensured that she'd gotten his point. "Sue and I have some things to work on."

He should feel disappointed, but he couldn't even summon up the energy to feel much of anything right now.

"I hope you're feeling better tomorrow."

"Thanks."

He rose from his bed and went to the bathroom to splash some water on his face. He flipped on the light and almost threw up. Blinding pain shot through his eyes. Quickly, he turned off the light and sank onto the bathroom floor. Now not only was he depressed, but his anxiety over seeing that journal had brought about a massive psychosomatic response.

He pressed his back against the bathroom wall and tried to keep his breathing even. His ex, if he could even call Bianca that since there had never been a real relationship, had constantly been on him about any little issue he had. Everything was a physical manifestation of some inner turmoil, according to her. He'd loved Bianca so much, so desperately, that he'd overlooked all the signs that she was a self-serving narcissist of the highest caliber.

At first Michael had wondered the same about Willa Christy. But she'd proven to be kind, thoughtful, and not at all the diva persona that she tried to project on her show.

He called his dad's cell phone. No surprise when he didn't answer. Michael left a message asking him to call back.

The last time he'd felt this truly awful was when Bianca dumped him. Then he'd lost high-dollar contracts because owners didn't want any negative publicity coming their way.

After Bianca's rejection, he'd crawled home to the island and had holed up here in his small house in Harrisonville. Then family friend Hampy Parker had knocked on his door one day, his grandson Carter at his side. He'd informed Michael that he should take his grandson under his wing and show him the ropes or Hampy would let everyone know that Mike was too much of a sad sack to keep his island contracts for the following season. Hampy had a few other choice words, but Michael knew the elderly man was being harsh to get his attention.

Michael let Hampy Parker commandeer the resuscitation of his career on Mackinac Island. But now Parker's wife, Kareen, had taken over the landscaping business. Although she'd offered to give the reins back to Michael when he was ready, if she thought he was "mental," she'd likely cut him off and let her grandson run things.

Michael's body began to stiffen like wet concrete drying as he sat for what seemed like hours. He finally got up and flipped on the light. His eyes were swollen, bloodshot, and still painful. He pulled his cell phone out and held down the right button to get help from Siri. "Call Dr. David Buck."

"Calling Dr. David Buck, work," Siri repeated.

He waited as the phone rang.

"Straits Optometry."

"Hi, this is Michael DuBlanc. Dr. Buck said I should come right in if I had another one of these weird—"

"Can you hold for a moment, please?"

"Sure." He didn't want to, but he would.

He listened for a long while to Michael Bublé's background music and was about to give up when the receptionist came back on. "Sorry, it's crazy around here. You said this is Mike DuBlanc?"

"Yes, and Dr. Buck told me the next time my eyes got all wonky I was supposed to take the next ferry over to see him."

He could hear the woman sucking in air. "Oh, well, that was before everything, ya know?"

"COVID."

"Now we're looking at two weeks out, Mike."

"Two weeks?" What would he do if this lasted two weeks? It hadn't last time—only a night. "But he wanted to see what was happening with my eyes right when I have this going on."

"Sorry, we're only by appointment."

"What about emergencies?"

She sighed even more dramatically than Bianca used to do. "Go to the ER in St. Ignace and have them request Dr. Buck see you."

He didn't want to do that and take a chance on Dad seeing him like this.

"You still there?"

"Yeah, give me that next appointment then."

"You sure?"

"Yes." He was sure that COVID was making everything harder.

He made the appointment and had just hung up when his father called. "Dad?" Tears stung his eyes. He sniffed and swiped at the wetness on his cheeks. Men didn't cry. . .like he was doing now.

"Michael?"

He couldn't answer. He just tried to breathe.

"Are you there, Son?"

"Yeah," he managed. He reached for the nearby roll of toilet paper and pulled some off, then blew his nose.

"You sick?"

Michael made a noise of agreement.

"I'm just off the clock. There's a ferry in. . .looks like I'd have twenty minutes to get down there. I'll call a taxi on the ferry on the way there, and I'll come directly to the house."

*I'm broken. I can't be fixed. Oh God help me.*

"Michael, just get back in bed. I've got my key. Don't do anything stupid, Son. Your mom and I love you."

Was his father afraid he'd hurt himself?

He blew his nose again. Is this what it was going to take to finally get help?

"Do you hear me? Just say yes." His father was shuffling something around.

"Yes."

The knock on her bedroom door startled Willa. She opened it to find Sue hoisting fabric samples aloft.

"Voilà! We got them in finally."

"That's great." Willa waved her in.

"Definitely not minimalist." Sue laid the vibrant fabric swaths out on Willa's queen-sized bed. "Have you heard from Michael today?"

"Nope." She'd only met the man weeks earlier, and already it seemed that each day should include Michael in it.

"Colton says he's lying low and that the Parkers are getting a little worried."

"Oh?" Her gut clenched.

"Yeah, he got like that after Bianca Rossi dumped him. Colton thinks that Michael seems to struggle with depression. Maybe it's a familial thing." Sue stared pointedly at where Lily's journal lay on the bureau.

Willa gave a curt laugh. "This is 2020 not 1895. So what if his ancestors had mental health issues? We have treatment options." She'd benefited so much from Dr. Svendsen helping her work through her own adoption issues. But she had to admit therapy could only take her so far—it couldn't recover her memories for her. Dr. Svendsen had been encouraging her for some time to return to the area and dig deep. That was one big reason she had accepted this job. To quiet her own recurring nightmares and to get answers. She really needed to get together with Gramps again soon and dig for more info.

"Burning down an asylum kinda puts that old Eulala in her own special category, dontcha think?"

Willa exhaled hard. "Yeah, I guess so." Was Michael really struggling with mental health problems? He always seemed pretty upbeat—but then again so was Lily in the journal, at least part of the time when her inner demons hadn't taken over.

Willa's phone buzzed, and she turned it over on the desk. "A text from Michael."

"Really?"

Willa read the message. "He's in St. Ignace and ran into my grandfather."

"That's so cool."

"Grampa Christy is giving him a ride back over to the island on one of his speedboats."

"Even more cool." Sue's blond eyebrows shot up to her bangs. "When can we get a ride?"

"I'll ask." Willa texted a message back to Michael.

"Speaking of speedboats, Colton's friend Ronnie says the beauty your Gramps made for Thad Moore was perfect."

"The one he crashed?" If her sister, Clare, who was Thad's age when he'd died, perished in something like that, she'd be devastated. She'd want to track down anything that would explain why it happened. Now, having learned that he may have been her father, she wanted to know more about Thad.

"As far as a story—just a drunk kid speeding in the Straits." Sue sighed dramatically. "No mysterious death there."

Still, Willa felt there was more she wanted to know about what happened that night.

Her phone vibrated. She read the next message. "Michael says Gramps will bring the Moores' boat down soon for a trial run before they take possession of it."

Sue's eyes grew even wider. "Same family?"

"Almost the same boat."

"As in a duplicate?"

"It's the twin of the one that crashed."

"I'm in!" Sue squealed. "I want a ride too."

Willa rolled her eyes and texted back. "SUE AND I WANT A RIDE."

Whatever Sue was saying to her faded out as an old memory overtook Willa.

*Willa and Gramps rode the waves, the shiny wooden boat so fast—faster than anything she'd ever been in. Faster even than the Ski-Doo snowmobile that Mom liked to ride, with Willa seated behind holding onto her for dear life.*

*Willa and Gramps had just walked up the driveway when Mom burst out of the house, her braids bouncing against her bright yellow shirt.*

"How could you, Dad?" Mommy shook her pink hairbrush at Gramps. She looked like she might hit him with it if he got too close. "How could you take that boat out and how could you take Willa with you?"

Willa covered her ears and began to cry. Mommy had never shouted like that before. She must be really, really mad.

Mommy ran to her and dropped on her knees. "I'm sorry." She didn't hold the hairbrush anymore. She pulled Willa into her arms and held her so tight that she almost couldn't breathe.

When her mother finally released her, tears still streamed down her face. Willa patted her cheek. "You'll be okay," she told her pretty young mom. That was what Mommy always said to her when Willa had a boo-boo. Mommy's lips parted, and she looked at Willa for a long time.

"You're right, Willa my girl. We'll be okay."

Then Gramps helped Mommy up and gave her a bear hug. "I'm sorry. Won't happen again."

"Willa? Willa, did you hear me?" Sue cocked her head at Willa.

"Huh?"

"Your grandfather said I get to go too."

"That's great." Willa wiped at the tears pouring from her eyes.

"Are you all right?"

"Yeah." She forced a smile, just like her teen mom had always done. "Everything's gonna be all right."

# CHAPTER SEVENTEEN

## 1895

*A*ugust had finally arrived, and soon Lily would need to be on her way. She sang the last bar of the Stephen Foster song "Was My Brother in the Battle" and bowed as the audience clapped loudly. She swiveled around swiftly, wiping away errant tears and regretting that she'd sung the requested song. Now that she knew how her father's brother, her uncle, had died in the Union army, the song more powerfully resonated with her.

She followed Clem as he left the stage, pressing her handkerchief against her cheeks. Outside, Dr. DuBlanc waited for them in the hallway.

"Another wonderful performance, Lily." Stephen leaned in and brushed a soft kiss against her damp cheek.

Warmth spread through her and the desire for something more.

She was besotted with this man, but it would never work out—not in several lifetimes. He'd want a wife who would give him perfect sons and daughters. His colleagues, those who were caught up in the eugenics movement, if they ever discovered her history would ostracize him. She cared about him too much to jeopardize his career, which he was only just starting. How strange to think that she, close to his age, had begun a professional singing career almost two decades earlier, yet he was only now charting the course of his profession as a psychiatrist.

"Lily?"

Exhaustion overwhelmed her. She'd not let her good sense be overcome by the temptation to kiss him back as Clem lumbered off away from them. At the other end of the hallway, Alice headed toward them.

Stephen followed her gaze. "Is your maid always out and about so late?"

Lily exhaled a long breath. "She's a smoker, and I'd much rather she did that outside than to try to do so in our quarters."

Stephen's eyes widened. "I dare say so. The habit is dreadful enough in a man, my own father—" He ceased speaking and ran his hand along his jaw.

"What happened to your father?"

"His smoking killed him."

His smoking? It had been her mother's fascination with fire that caused him to perish. "I'm sorry." Why did Stephen say this?

"Could you come on a jaunt with me tomorrow? A ride around the island in a beautiful open carriage?"

"I'd love that." Why had she agreed when she knew this flirtation must end?

When Alice drew near, Lily offered her maid a thin smile. "Alice, I need you to accompany me and Dr. DuBlanc tomorrow on an outing."

The younger woman's eyes darkened for a moment as she dipped a curtsy. "Yes, miss. What time?"

It should be any time that Lily deemed fitting, but she'd not say so. She looked up into Stephen's dark eyes. "After luncheon then?"

"I'd need to make it after two o'clock—my last appointment."

Lily glanced expectantly at Alice, whose features seemed to have softened.

"Aye, miss, that'd be grand."

"Two thirty then. I'll meet you ladies on the porch."

"All right. Have a restful sleep, Dr. DuBlanc." They parted ways, and she and her maid continued upstairs.

Once she and Alice were inside the room, she waited as Alice poured water into the wash bowl and retrieved fresh washcloths and towels for Lily.

She reached into her reticule for her Fisherman's Friend lozenges. *Gone.* "Oh no. I must have left them on the piano." She'd offered one to Clem earlier because of his sore throat. Until she had more delivered from the mainland, which could be up to a week, that little tin had to hold her. "I'm going back to get something I forgot on the stage."

"Yes, miss." Alice went to the wardrobe and pulled out Lily's night-gown and laid it on the bed.

"I can do that, you know." Lily touched the girl's arm lightly, and Alice jumped.

"Oh, I'm sorry, miss. I don't know why I'm so excitable tonight."

Alice had been even more twitchy in the past several days than she normally was. "I'm sorry I startled you. I'll be back in a few minutes." Something made her want to bring one of her old longtime friends with her. She moved toward the bureau and pulled open the drawer, which housed her stash of weapons. She selected a small, leather-sheathed knife and surreptitiously tucked it into her pocket before leaving the room.

No one was in the hallway except the elderly couple from Detroit, who were entering their suite. The maids were off duty now, so no carts cluttered the long expanse as they sometimes did during the daylight hours. With their shifts beginning around four o'clock in the morning, most housekeeping staff members were long asleep.

Once she reached the main floor, Lily heard every little sound. A couple laughing in the parlor. The sound of a clock's muted chime marking the hour. The creaking of a door opening and closing on protesting hinges. She exhaled a sigh as she began to hear her own heartbeat in her ears. This was ridiculous. No, this was the first time she'd ever been alone, truly alone, in the longest time. If Clem abandoned her, she'd continue to be on her own. How would she protect herself?

Footsteps sounded behind her, and Lily reached into her pocket for her knife.

"Good evening, Miss Lily. Beautiful performance." Mr. Williford offered her a tight smile.

"Thank you."

"What are you doing down here by yourself?" The assistant manager was often seen strolling through the hotel, checking on things.

"Forgot my throat lozenges down on the stage, and I do depend upon them when I'm performing."

Clem, though, had said that he thought it was all in her mind and not that her throat needed soothing. But Clem didn't sing, at least not for hours on end.

"I'll walk you down and then back to the parlor, Miss Lily, but then I believe I'll call it a day."

"A very long day from what I've seen of you."

"Ah, but it's a very short season here." His eyes looked unfocused for a moment and he blinked. "Workers at the Grand Hotel will have the winter to rest."

His words gave her pause. Odd that he would speak about the employees, almost as if not including himself.

"True. Thank you for accompanying me." She'd never had any staff offer to escort her in the past, but then again she'd never walked around on her own at night. Still, this place was safe, a place for gentlemen and women. She was overtired, and the story she'd heard of recent gambling and resulting fisticuffs at the Grand had brought up all those fears she'd had over the years of traveling around the South performing.

Soon she'd scrambled up on stage and grabbed her tin. "Thank you, Mr. Williford, for coming with me."

When she turned, she was surprised to see the man looking behind the curtains.

"You're very welcome, Miss Swaine." He caught her eye and blushed beneath her scrutiny. "Can't be too careful. I've been asked to be even more vigilant than usual."

Vigilant? Weren't assistant managers supposed to be more concerned about pleasing the guests and accomplishing certain tasks? Maybe she was overtired. "That's not a word I'd expect to be used at such a lovely hotel as this."

His lips twisted. "You'd be surprised at what some of these rich folks get up to."

For some reason that struck Lily as funny, and she began to laugh. Soon Williford was laughing too.

She shook her head. "I don't think I want to know."

His eyebrows rose. "Trust me, you're right."

"Well, we better get you back to the parlor, sir, so you can head off to get your rest for the night. Then you can be vigilant again tomorrow."

Soon they'd parted ways, and Lily headed upstairs to her room. As she reached the top step of the stairs and entered the hallway, she smelled something oily. She drew in a short breath. Yes, that was the distinct odor of Macassar, which was so popular among the younger men. Perhaps Clem had overdone his hair preparations and snuck off to see Marie. As much as Lily didn't condone late-night activities, it was one of the few times her cousin wasn't working or chaperoning her.

She continued down the hall.

"Hey you," a man's voice hissed behind her.

Lily cringed. A gentleman didn't address a lady in such a manner. She hurried toward her door, glancing around to see if there might be anyone to help. There was no one, and none of the doors were open. How could she get to her door and unlock it if the stranger overtook her?

The man's hurried heavy steps indicated he'd soon be upon her. She couldn't get her key out and unlock the door and hold her knife at the same time. She opted for the latter, removing the sharp knife from its sheath. Lily wheeled around as she reached her door.

Gus Parker, Mr. Butler's buddy, stood only a few feet back from her. Those men were supposed to have been evicted from the hotel. Parker raised his hands as she pointed the blade at him. "Hey, I just wanta talk to you." His words were slurred as though he'd been drinking.

"Go away." She grasped the knife's handle tight.

"You've got something I want."

She had an idea what that might be, despite the lack of lust in his eyes. But to some men, it wasn't about desire but about hurting a woman. "I can filet just about any part of you that gets too close to me, so don't try it."

She thought she heard movement behind her door. Was Alice standing there?

"Let me in." He wobbled a bit.

Straightening, Lily had to stand her ground. A door down the hall opened. Lily moved to the side, into the center of the hallway, hoping that the occupants would see her and Gus.

He narrowed his eyes at her. "I'll take care of this later." He turned and left as Lily, hands shaking, slipped the blade back into its case.

She felt for her key as she watched Parker greet the older couple as he passed them. From the odd looks on their faces, they weren't acquainted with him.

Once inside her room, Lily locked the door from the inside and leaned against it, breathing hard. Had she imagined it, or had Alice's door closed just as she'd come inside?

She'd need to tell Mr. Williford in the morning. Regardless, from now on, she'd have to keep herself protected and not take any chances. Her collection of friends would be put back in play once again.

Clem sat across from Lily in the small parlor in her suite. He twisted his soft felt cap so hard Lily was sure he was about to crush its shape forever.

"I'm awfully sorry, Lil." He ran his tongue over his upper lip. "You're gonna have to be extra careful."

She narrowed her gaze on him. "But can you help me?"

"I would if I was gonna be here."

"What do you mean? We have a contract."

Outside their door, the maids' carts rumbled up the hallway.

"I know, but me and Marie, well, she wants to go home sooner."

Lily stiffened. "She can go, and then you can join her later."

"She thinks it's best for me to go with her when she leaves."

"But Clem." She'd not make a scene. The workmen should be there any moment, and they didn't need to hear them arguing.

"I've never felt like this before. I've been tellin' ya about it. I need to start my own life. You've got Dr. DuBlanc, and the opera house in Newberry wants you. Can't you find another piano player here until your next job starts?"

She shook her head slowly, so angry with her normally sweet-natured and supportive cousin that she couldn't see straight. If she said anything more right now, she'd ruin their relationship, possibly forever.

"What about that Mr. König? Can he help you?"

"His name is actually Ben Steffan, and I guess I could ask him."

"What was he doin' calling himself König?"

"He was writing an undercover story for the *Detroit Post*, but now he's quit that job."

"Thunder and tarnation. That's really something, Lily."

"And he's marrying my cousin Maude Welling."

A lopsided grin slid onto his face. "Well, since he'll be kin, go on and ask him to play for you."

She might have no other choice. Clem was abandoning her, and if she told Stephen about the thug, what would he do? Maybe she should try to get out of her contract, but she'd already been warned of the penalties. "We only have a short while left on our contract. Can you at least wait out the season?"

He shrugged. "I'll ask Marie. And you talk to Mr. Williford too. He keeps a keen eye out, I've noticed."

Too bad he wasn't there when she needed him.

An hour later, Lily shared with Mr. Williford about the altercation with Gus Parker. Williford's dark eyes blazed. They stood in an alcove not far from Mrs. Fox's office.

"I'll take care of that buffoon, but you'll have to be patient."

"Patient?" What cause could there be to wait?

"Things aren't exactly as they seem here. I'm wrapping up a few loose ends on another situation." He stepped away from the alcove. "Don't take any chances, Miss Lily," he said as he walked away.

She patted the pistol in her deep pocket. During all her years as a performer, she'd never had to actually use the gun. Who'd have thought that it might need to be called into action at a place so fine as this one?

She moved out of the alcove as Stephen strode up the hallway toward her.

"I got your note. Do you have time to talk now?" Stephen leaned in to kiss her cheek, but she backed away from him.

This infatuation had to end today. She had the possibility of two other job offers at venues in the Upper Peninsula, she needed to be safe, and she couldn't live with this issue between her and the one man she wanted to give her heart to but couldn't. "Yes. Let's walk down toward the Canary. It's lovely out."

"All right." He extended his arm, and she took it.

They walked alongside one another, greeting guests as they strolled down through the grand parlor and out the side door. Seagulls squawked overhead. Brilliant blue skies blazed with sunshine. The rose garden offered up its heavenly scents as they passed. Stephen bent and broke off a single pink rose and offered it to her.

"Lily, I have to tell you something about myself."

She almost laughed, because his news certainly couldn't be as grave as hers, despite his solemn tone.

"And I have something to tell you too." If she could get it out.

"You go first."

She drew in a shuddering breath, the cool air suddenly clammy on her bare arms. Autumn would soon be upon them. "I have recently learned that Dr. Étienne DuBlanc was your father."

His dark eyebrows drew high. "Yes, that's true. Étienne means Stephen in French."

"And he was a psychiatrist like you." She swallowed hard. "I'm very sorry for your loss."

"Thank you." He shoved his hand through his hair. "It's been a difficult time with losing both my mother and my father within a short time."

"I'm very sorry." She'd at least had the benefit of a number of years between her biological father's death, her stepfather's death, and finally her mother's. Time to allow the grief to dissipate before another round began.

They continued walking.

"You said recently that your father died from his smoking habit." Acid filled Lily's gut. "But Garrett Christy said your father perished in a fire in a Kentucky asylum."

How could she tell him what her mother had done? How would he accept her? This was absurd—she shouldn't tell him. She should go on her way to a new music hall and begin anew. But the gist of Garrett's words from when they'd chatted earlier that day echoed in her mind. "Sometimes you have to speak the truth in love and let the cards fall where they may—as God wills."

She drew in a fortifying breath. "My mother was an inmate at that asylum."

Seagulls squawked and dove to the ground nearby. What had it been like for her mother to have lived in that place? The one time that she and Clem had been able to visit, the cacophony of shrieks and moans within the place sounded far worse than the squawks of those seagulls.

The color seemed to drain from Stephen's face. He grasped her hands and ran his thumb over her knuckles, head bent. "I can't tell you how deeply saddened I am."

He acted as though he had some control over the tragedy. She pulled her hands away. "But it's not your fault—it's my mother's own doing."

Stephen lifted his face, confusion dancing on his handsome features. "How so?"

This was the hardest thing she'd ever have to confess. *Lord, help me.*

"Eulala Kerchinsky was my mother." She let the words stand between them.

"The woman accused of burning the asylum down?"

"Yes."

How deeply it must grieve him to do what he'd have to do next, for surely no self-respecting psychiatrist could continue in a relationship with such a woman as Lily, whose mother had accomplished the unspeakable.

When he didn't respond, she said, "It's what I was told."

"What you were told," Stephen repeated.

"And what the newspapers all reported."

A carriage rolled by, and guests from the Grand waved at them. Although she didn't feel like doing so, she waved back as she and Stephen continued walking.

He rubbed his chin. "What was said in the press may not be the truth."

Lily's deepest desire had been that there had been a mistake. But when newspaper after newspaper printed the same large headlines about her mother, she'd finally accepted what had happened. "Witnesses said she was Dr. DuBlanc's last patient that day."

"Yes, that matches his appointment book."

"So there you have it. The fire broke out soon afterward. And he. . ." Lily couldn't bring herself to say that the man had died trying to save her mother. So many people had died in the inferno.

A hot brick seemed to be pressing against her chest. This man could have been her one true love—something she'd always believed could happen. That was before her mother's misdeeds, though. Was God so cruel to do this to the two of them?

"Lily, I need to tell you something." He stopped walking and faced her.

When she opened her mouth to protest, he pressed one warm finger against her lips.

"I've always believed that my father was responsible for my own mother's death."

"What?" *How horrible.*

"The house burned down. My mother was always reminding Dad that he shouldn't leave his pipe lying around. She was always afraid that with all the papers in his office and how forgetful he was becoming that he'd start a conflagration."

"Was he so forgetful?" Thoughts swirled in her head. Her mother had been fascinated by fire. But could it be possible that the blaze was from inattention?

"Yes. And I believe that is exactly what happened to my mother. But both Dad and I were so stuck in our grief at first that I didn't push the investigators too hard when they deemed it an accidental fire possibly caused by cooking."

"Could it have been?"

"I don't think so. That next year whenever I visited with Dad from medical school, I'd stay on him too about his smoking. It finally got to where I wouldn't come home because I was afraid to go to sleep in our rental house, which was constructed of wood like our home had been. Dad smoked his pipe even while seeing patients."

"And you think he may have been smoking when he saw my mother?"

Stephen shrugged. "I've felt in my spirit that Dad caused that horrible asylum fire. I am so very sorry. I think he probably left his pipe in your mother's room."

"If he had, I'm fairly sure what she'd have done with it." They'd called her disease pyromania.

He took her hands. "Regardless of whether his pipe accidentally started the fire or your mother used it, it's still his responsibility. How else could she have gotten something flammable?"

Tears slipped down Lily's cheeks. This terrible thing, these deadly secrets, no longer lay between them.

"Lily, can you set that aside? Could you forgive my father? Or will the tragedy he caused always be a wall between us?"

She stepped into his arms right there by the street. Sunshine on her back, the warmth of the man she loved in her arms, and the sound of a thousand bricks falling away from her heart.

# CHAPTER EIGHTEEN

## *2020*

Standing in front of the Island House, nerves buzzing, Willa waited for Michael. She'd missed him the few days he'd been out—like a hole-in-her-heart kind of ache. And that scared her.

What that anxiety meant was that the obsessive behavior that had launched her in the design world had morphed out of control. Her dogged pursuit tracing the connections in Lily's journal gave evidence of where Willa's emotions were going—out of whack.

Willa bent to admire the late-blooming white peonies in the nearby semicircular garden. The peonies' large creamy petals provided a stunning contrast to the multicolored annuals and daylilies that nestled around them.

"That's my work," Michael called out.

Willa swiveled to face him. Her heartbeat accelerated. "Beautiful job."

His skin appeared flushed, and his eyes red.

"Are you all right?" She knew he'd been off of work because he wasn't feeling well. In her experience, though, that could mean many things. At design school in Savannah, friends' "sicknesses" were often hangovers.

"Kinda hot right now."

Yes, he was. But he didn't mean that kind of hot. "Nothing compared to Virginia."

He closed one eye and pointed his index finger at her. "You score on that one."

*Men. Always making stuff be about sports.*

He pulled his sunglasses on, as a couple strode past them hand-in-hand.

"They're gonna take our spot." He patted his stomach.

Willa laughed.

"Follow me." He pointed to the steep uphill driveway to the left of the building. "It's back behind here."

As they made the incline together, Willa drew in a deep breath and inhaled the smoky and savory scents wafting toward them. Her stomach growled in anticipation. "If their food tastes anything like it smells, then this is a great idea, Michael."

"Glad you accepted my invitation."

Invitation? She'd thought this was a meeting to catch up on plans for the Grand, although her goal was to talk to him about the journal. Willa tapped her fingers against Lily's journal, which was nestled in her tote alongside a packet of employee lists from the summer of 1895 that Aimee had loaned her. If what she'd read was true, and if Sue's research was correct, then Michael may be Lily's descendant. But if she brought this up with him, pushed too hard, she feared she'd upset him.

She stole a glance at him. A tiny smile of satisfaction tugged at his lips.

He pointed to the lush landscaping alongside the drive. "Like the rest of the island, there aren't many spots without flowers."

She relaxed a little. So maybe he wasn't thinking of this as a date. "Those peonies out front really are to die for—one of my favorite flowers." Good to be focusing on their duties. "I'd love to change the Grand Hotel's signature geraniums over to peonies. But Aimee already nixed that idea."

"Aimee nixes most ideas." He pointed to some raspberry-colored flowers. "Chose those specific peonies myself at a show."

"Don't you love those trade fairs?" Except when men hit on her at those places, and she'd had to brush them off.

"Yup. You can find some great stuff. But I kept to the regular vendors for the bulbs and bushes that I used on the outside patio." He gestured to the left.

Lush greenery and flowers encircled every small seating area. "I like how the design gives some privacy at each table."

"Exactly. Like you suggested for the Grand Hotel's front porch."

"If I can get more people in front of that fabulous view, enjoying their evening dinners, the happier they'll be."

"Agreed. Rolling planters with trees and floral arrangements is genius. We could move the landscaping decorative features once dinner is over, for the sunset crowd."

Willa's cheeks heated as she imagined strolling hand-in-hand with Michael on the porch, watching the sun descend over the Straits of Mackinac in vivid oranges and pinks. "Thank you."

"Even in wild rainstorms, you have little chance of getting wet on the porch."

"We'll see what Aimee says, given the budgetary restrictions." Which could send Willa packing earlier than she had planned. Another good reason to stop imagining a relationship with Michael.

"She's more open-minded than her predecessors."

Predecessors. Ancestors. Willa needed to get this conversation going in the right direction.

"Let's tell them we're here." Michael pointed to the hostess's stand.

"Sure." The bag that held the journal suddenly weighed heavily on her.

What if he got upset with her? She didn't want to take a chance at messing up their business arrangement, but she really wanted to know more about the people in the journal.

They both donned their face masks.

"Reservation for DuBlanc," Michael told the hostess.

"Gotcha. Good thing because we don't have anything else available until ten o'clock."

"Seriously?" Willa was glad she had on her mask or her grumpy face would have shown.

"Totally. It's crazy busy." Not too busy for the slim blond to be thoroughly checking out Michael.

A family of four, standing six feet behind them, must have heard the hostess because they left.

Soon they'd been seated and placed their order for brisket nachos, with sweet iced tea for Willa and craft root beer for him. The waitress departed, leaving the single paper menu on their table.

"I guess they throw these out."

"Yup." Michael crumpled it into a ball. "Way better than when restaurants ask you to scan a code to see their menu online."

"Especially since you never know, on this island, when you're going to be in a dead zone."

"You got that right."

She had to make sure this conversation with Michael about Lily and Stephen didn't end up in the dead zone.

Despite Willa's odd questions about his ancestors, Michael found the buzz of chatter, laughter, and the clinking of dishes and utensils soothed him tonight. It sounded like a semblance of "normal" in an anything but normal world right now.

Willa reached for her big leopard-printed bag and pulled a leather-bound book from it. "I brought the journal."

"I'd love to hear what's in it." He'd listen to her read *War and Peace* if it meant she was with him.

Apprehension touched her pretty features, stirring unease in him.

"So your great-great-grandfather was Dr. Stephen DuBlanc?"

He gave a curt laugh. "Yeah, I'm from a long line of late progenitors or whatever. He ought to be many more 'greats' removed, but most of the DuBlanc men didn't have sons until they were over forty."

"Did they have multiple wives?" Willa asked wryly.

"Nope. The DuBlanc men have had one wife each. That's why with Bianca, I really wanted to be certain before we made any commitment." He gave a harsh laugh. "Till I learned I was just a bit of entertainment for her viewers." Would Willa try to rope him into some episodes on her show when it resumed? She'd not yet asked, but he figured she might.

"Okay, well, Dr. Stephen DuBlanc married Lily Swaine, right?"

"Sounds right. I'm distantly related to all these Swaines and Wellings on the island." He drank some of his root beer. Sweet, a little smoky, and perfect light vanilla accents on the tongue. Bianca probably was right about accusing him of being a foodie—one accusation that was true. "Pretty much most year-rounders on the island are related to half of the other islanders."

Willa's perfect lips twitched. "But Lily didn't always go by the name Swaine."

Michael set his drink down. "Why not?"

Willa opened the brown leather journal and placed it before him. "Her name is written as Lily Kerchinsky in the front."

Michael stared at the childish handwriting and flipped the page. Inside were sketches of rows of stick people holding something.

"Do you see that?" Willa pointed to where Ladysmith, Virginia, was written. "I grew up not far from there, a few hours away. People are big into their Civil War history and visiting the battlefields in Virginia."

He pointed to the corner, where the year 1863 with a question mark after it was scrawled. "Maybe a drawing from her early years?"

"Perhaps where she'd lived. The lines in the arms of those stick figures could be guns." Willa exhaled loudly.

Michael shut one eye hard, considering. "News to me if I had ancestors who fought in the Civil War."

"Sue and I spent some time on this."

"Really?" He bit back the urge to ask why.

"It looks like Lily's father fought for the Confederacy."

He scowled at her. "What? No way."

She nodded slowly. "We found his record of enlistment online. And his grandfather owned a farm in Ladysmith."

"But he lived on the island. I remember hearing that. Born and raised here. We've had Swaines here forever." Defensiveness loosened his lips.

"Not quite forever. The first Swaine married Jacqueline Cadotte."

"That's one my dad found on the family tree too." Dad hadn't said where that first Swaine was from. But then again, what Michigander would be running their mouth about having a Confederate soldier in their closet?

His mouth suddenly felt dry. He caught their server's attention. "We need some refills, please."

"In the journal, Lily talks about her mother." Willa turned the pages ahead and pointed.

> *Whenever I am with Dr. Stephen DuBlanc, I feel a connection like I've never known before—except for that of the love my father showed to me.*

*If Stephen knew that my mother was Eulala Kerchinsky,*
*who burned down the asylum in Kentucky, killing his*
*father, he'd never have anything to do with me again. Or*
*even worse, he could destroy the career I've begun here. I*
*can't imagine that he'd do such a thing, but this secret is*
*eating me up inside.*

The dizziness Michael had been battling returned. He rubbed his forehead. "Why did you show this to me?" With all he had going on, he didn't need this right now.

Regret immediately smacked Willa, as Michael pushed back in his chair. "I have so many questions about this journal. About why it was hidden. About who Lily was. I was hoping you could help answer those."

"I know I had an ancestor who'd had an amazing singing career. She did a bunch of things for the arts around here."

"Must be Lily." She'd hold off on telling him about the Pinkerton article and Lily Kerchinsky/Jones. There was nothing she'd read in the journal so far that suggested Lily had committed arson.

"Nosy people have asked me if she was part of some unsolved mystery on the island. But I just brushed that off." Michael scooted closer to the table.

Willa exhaled in relief as Michael's posture relaxed. "Oh?"

"Locals who love to tell tall tales."

"So what's the tall tale?"

"First, realize these stories usually get started at Horns after a few boilermakers get tossed back." Michael tapped his fingers on the oak tabletop.

"That's the bar that's so popular with old-timers, right?"

"Yup. Anyway, a few times they've spun this story that a singer at the Grand murdered a poor young maid."

"Yikes." She seriously needed to read through the rest of the journal. Michael was not keeping this tonight. She pulled the journal back.

"Don't I get to see it?"

"When I'm done reading it."

"But that was my great-great-grandmother's, right?"

"Yes, if she was Lily Swaine the singer who met Dr. DuBlanc at the Grand."

"Then it should be mine."

"Maybe. But more than likely the Grand owns it."

"And you're afraid of them?" Michael crossed his arms. "They weren't the ones who initiated a lawsuit."

"Good point, but let's work that out later. Let me show you these records from Aimee."

"The ones she and David argued about?"

"Yes. There's no Williford showing for the summer of 1895." She pointed to the employee's register. "Not in here and not on the contract employees' list."

"How about Dr. DuBlanc?"

"An employee. Lily Swaine was under contracted employees, as singer with Clem Christy as pianist."

"No way. Another Christy?"

"Yes. Clem is probably super-distant kin to me. There are hundreds of Christys around here."

Michael swigged his root beer. "Like I've said, half the island is related."

"And the other half may be kin to people around the Straits." If not for COVID, she'd have seen at least a dozen of her extended family members. Maybe next summer. Was she really thinking about coming back?

The waitress returned and set the brisket nachos on the table. "Here's a pile of napkins."

"Thanks, we'll need those." Michael pushed several toward Willa and grabbed some for himself.

"Messy but good," the waitress called as she departed.

Willa moved the paperwork from Aimee away from the food.

Michael tapped the old registry. "I wonder if anyone else Lily named in her journal shows up."

"I've only looked at the first bit. There's still Alice the maid to find."

Michael flipped to the page where maids were listed by hiring and departure date. "She arrived in early June."

Seeing the maid's name on the page brought the journal to life. "And she's listed as only fifteen. Too young to be on her own."

"Maybe not back then." Michael moved a pile of nachos onto his plate and ate several bites.

"Maybe." But she couldn't imagine Clare on her own when she was fifteen.

He pointed to the empty spot where a date should be listed for Alice's end date. Empty. "Wonder what the deal is with that?"

"Strange. Everyone else has a date entered." She inhaled the scent of the nachos but wanted to wait a bit to avoid making a mess on the borrowed papers. "Look, there's a maid named Maude Welling. That's Lily's cousin—she mentioned her in the journal. There's her start date and, whoa, look at that—about three weeks later she's gone."

"If she was anything like her brother, old Jack Welling, then who knows what antics she got up to." Michael sipped his root beer. "The first Jack Welling, Jack Junior, and Jack the third all have long-running stories told about them on this island."

"You'll have to tell me someday." Their gazes locked. She was already imagining somedays with this man, which was ridiculous.

"Right beneath her name is Sadie Duvall's. Like Alice and Maude, she was another latecomer to the hotel maid staff."

Willa looked at the registry dates. "The rest of the maids started in May."

"The housekeeping manager and assistant housekeeping manager should have come on a little earlier." Michael frowned. "But they didn't."

Willa pointed to Mrs. Fox and Mrs. Stillman's names, entered within days of one another. "The other supervisors arrived in April. And the general hotel manager and assistant hotel manager arrived even earlier, in late March."

Michael continued to eat his nachos. She couldn't quite see his eyes, still hidden behind his sunglasses. "Can you imagine how cold that crossing would have been?"

Willa feigned a shudder. "Brrrr. No, thanks."

She read sections from Michael's great-great-grandmother's diary to him as he finished his soda. Mostly, Lily wrote upbeat entries about her performances and all the fun things she'd done on the island. But she also periodically included sad reminiscences.

"Back to what Lily wrote about her mother." Michael looked around the restaurant and leaned in. "There are a lot of nicknames people on the island get—kinda like our own branding up here. But you're never gonna hear a Crazy Joe or anything like that, at least not in public. We don't deal too well with our locals having mental health problems."

*Much less killing someone, as Lily wrote that her mother had done in burning down the asylum.* Willa chose to not bring that up again. "Maybe it's better on the mainland."

"Definitely. My grandfather and his father before him had something to do with that. But on the island, only the tourists get to have mental health issues."

Was Michael trying to tell her something? "I believe emotional problems are an 'equal opportunity' affliction."

"Ya know, my own father can be described as cranky, which some people might see as mild depression. I think it's due to his workaholism as an ER doctor. Which has him more stressed right now."

With COVID. "I understand. My father is a physician in Virginia in private practice."

Michael bobbed his head slightly. "Then you know how they can get after a too-busy day."

She finally gave in to the nachos, loading up her small plate with them. "A 'cranky pass' should be allowed when we've worked too hard all day." Or stayed up all night like she'd done. Thankfully, though, she was holding up okay, at least for now.

His lips quirked into a smile.

She took a bite of the brisket nachos, savoring the taste. "Oh my goodness, these really are the best."

"Would I lead you astray?" Michael scooped up two chips dripping with cheese, sour cream, chili, and a thick layer of brisket and popped them in his mouth.

She took another meat-laden chip and closed her eyes. *Pure heaven.*

Someone jostled her chair as they walked past, surprising her. So much for the six-foot distance rule implemented for COVID safety.

Willa looked up at the older woman whose cool eyes examined her and Michael.

The older woman bent closer and sniffed Michael's drink. He simply sat there.

"Excuse me?" Outrage shot through Willa along with a healthy dose of fear. People were acting so strange during this pandemic.

Michael appeared surprisingly calm. "Mrs. Parker, what are you doing here?"

"I've been eating at this establishment since before you were in diapers." The petite woman's nostrils flared. "I suppose you'll be drinking here all night?"

*Oh, no.* So, Michael might have an alcohol problem. But he was only consuming root beer tonight.

Michael raised his hands in surrender. "Now, Mrs. Parker, we've had this convo numerous times."

"Convo?"

"Conversation."

The well-dressed woman sniffed. "I've heard all manner of lies in my lifetime, Mike."

From the muscle jumping in his cheek, Michael must be biting his tongue big-time. She extended her hand. "I'm Willa Christy." This was one of the times she'd love to disclose that, yes, indeed, she was the host of that popular HGTV show.

The woman gaped. "Garrett's granddaughter?"

"Yesss." She didn't realize that she'd drawn out the word in irritation until Michael shook his head gently in warning.

"You're Jaycie's cousin?"

Willa nodded.

"My dear, we must talk soon. Come up to my hotel and visit." She fished a business card out of her beige clutch and handed it to Willa. "My husband, Hampy, is fishing today with your grandfather, Garrett, and with Jaycie's grandfather, Jim."

"Oh."

Mrs. Parker gave Michael a pointed look. "That's the reason I'm here eating by myself, since Hampy isn't home to cook dinner."

"You should make Carter grill for you." Michael's voice sounded falsely cheerful. "He makes a mean blackened salmon."

The older woman cringed. "*Heartburn delight*, I'm sure." She departed without a good-bye.

"I'm not granting her a pass for her grumpiness." Willa shook her head. "Mrs. Parker's behavior well exceeds the cranky-pants stage."

Michael slumped back into his chair. "Maybe I should order something stronger."

Willa chuckled. "Me too."

"In fairness to Kareen Parker, she's had to deal with some heavy personal losses—from addiction and all that."

"Oh." Hadn't Jaycie mentioned something about an overdose in the family that she'd married into? "Was that Mrs. Parker's daughter-in-law who died?"

"Yup. Amanda Parker was a hard case, though." He tapped his index finger on the tabletop. "I don't know who could have saved her from herself. Sometimes, that's just how it is."

He refilled his plate and began eating. They sat and consumed their nachos in silence for a few minutes. This was a companionable silence, something he'd never had with Bianca.

"My dad has said the same thing about some patients. Mom, however, believed she could save anyone if she tried hard enough. But. . .she couldn't save her own sister."

Tears filled Willa's eyes. "I just had some insight. Maybe Mom is trying to deal with not being able to save her own sister, her only sibling, by being Superwoman to other people and causes."

"Your adoptive mom was the older sister?"

She nodded and swiped at her tears.

"Yeah, that makes sense." Michael didn't want to embarrass her by pushing the conversation further in public.

She sniffed. "I understand big-sister stuff. I spent an hour last night on the phone with my baby sister, talking about her options for college in the fall since things are so wonky right now."

"I bet she appreciated that."

"I think she did." Willa smiled, and his heart melted. She was so lovely. So sweet and caring.

A few families were seated in the next row from them. A breeze stirred leaves on nearby oak trees and the hydrangea bushes blooming nearby. The sun was still high overhead, as it was normally during a Michigan summer.

"Resuming our discussion, after that interruption from Kareen, my family has some who shouldn't be given a 'cranky pass' as you call it."

"Mine too."

"Grandpa was a cantankerous old cuss, but he still ran his medical practice full-out until he dropped dead on the job. That was only five years ago."

"Really?"

"He was cussing up a blue streak at his computer screen. Managed care's requirement that Grandpa enter his notes on the computer was what put him in the grave." He gave a curt laugh. "Given all the mess I've gone through these past couple of days with insurance issues, medical appointments, and lab work, maybe there's a diagnosis for medical cranky-pants. Or there should be."

Willa stared at him for a long moment. Her beautiful pink lips parted, but she didn't ask anything.

He had to test the waters. If they had any kind of honest relationship at all, any kind of friendship, part of that was disclosing difficult stuff like this latest blow.

"My dad thinks I have lupus." Just hearing the words leave his lips sickened him.

"Oh, no." Compassion filled her words.

"We're waiting on the test results." He tapped his eyeglasses. "Lupus can attack your eyes. I'm on a bucketload of steroids including drops for my eyes, and they're getting better."

"Lupus is a pretty serious condition."

"It can be." Michael wasn't ready to look this thing in the face too hard. Not yet.

"Pretty scary." Willa sipped her drink slowly.

"You know the only good thing about this?" He recalled all the psychobabble that Bianca had used when describing what he now understood were symptoms related to an autoimmune disease.

"No. What? I can't imagine anything good about it."

Here was another woman who could reject him. But he had to take charge of this illness before it took charge of him. "I'm not a crank. I'm not difficult. I'm not moody or a dozen or more other negative attributes I've been given. I'm told that those down times with lupus are called 'flares,' and they make you feel like roadkill."

To his surprise, Willa laughed. "Will they call you 'Flary Michael' when you're like that? Or Roadkill Mike?"

He cringed then laughed. "Given that I may have an ancestor who burned down an entire asylum full of people, I think not. Flare, fire, ya know, eh?"

"How do you feel about this info about your ancestor?" She leaned in across the table.

Was she expecting him to do the same? Was she wanting a kiss? The same longing in her eyes reflected what he felt inside. She gazed intently at him.

"You know what, Michael?" She gently touched his face, and he leaned in over the nachos.

"What?" he managed, his breathing slowing. He closed his eyes as she stroked his cheeks.

"I think I can see the butterfly on your face." Willa lowered her hand.

"Huh?" *What the heck?*

"You have a lupus butterfly rash on your face." She gestured by bringing her fingertips to the bridge of her nose and then fanning them out over her cheeks. "That's a classic autoimmune rash, especially prevalent in lupus patients."

That was their tender moment? He chuckled. But with that gentle touch, she'd given him hope that the two of them had a chance. He wasn't a kid, and he knew what he wanted. *Willa.*

# CHAPTER NINETEEN

*August 1895*

*L*ily strolled the Grand Hotel's porch, waiting for Alice. On the grounds in the distance below, several couples played croquet while others clustered on the badminton courts. If only she knew how to engage in those sports, she could be out there too. Perhaps if they began offering a game of wood chopping and carrying water as sports, she might excel. Mama and Pa had made sure she knew how to accomplish those tasks lickety-split.

"Good day, Miss Swaine." Mr. Williford's dark eyes briefly met hers as he strolled past.

"Good afternoon, Mr. Williford." But he was already gone.

Nearby, two people played a game of checkers. Mrs. Moore looked up. "Oh, my dear Miss Swaine. Do come over." She waved Lily toward their table.

Lily affixed a polite smile to her face and joined the matron.

"This is my son, Thaddeus." Mrs. Moore gestured toward a young man still gazing at the checkerboard.

When Thaddeus lifted his gaze to Lily's, she bit back a gasp of admiration. His brooding dark good looks were only further enhanced by his most unusual eyes. He had three different colors—blue, green, and amber—that encircled his pupils. When he caught her staring, a slow smile tilted his lips upward. He pushed away from the table and stood.

"Thad, this is Miss Lily Swaine, the singer I told you about."

Thaddeus bowed and reached for Lily's hand. "Delighted to meet you, Miss Swaine."

Although he was undeniably one of the most handsome men Lily had ever met, she didn't feel the little rush of excitement that she did whenever she saw Stephen. "I'm glad to meet the son of such a lovely lady."

Lily turned and smiled warmly at Mrs. Moore. The woman, however, was staring beyond Lily, her expression perplexed.

"I, uh. . ." Mrs. Moore's complexion paled. "Are you expecting someone?"

Lily swiveled to see Alice skulking by the wall near the porch exit. "Oh, yes, my maid is accompanying Dr. DuBlanc and me on an outing."

Thaddeus narrowed his fine eyes and followed Lily's gaze. "Alice? She's here?"

"She was our maid. In Chicago." Mrs. Moore reached for her coffee cup and took a long drink.

"Before you drove her off." There was no mistaking the anger in Thaddeus Moore's voice. "And then you allowed that fifteen-year-old child to be placed in one of the clubs of that horrid man, Butler."

"Thaddeus, you forget yourself!" Mrs. Moore set her cup down in its saucer hard. "Alice is obviously doing fine. Mr. Diener must have sent her here instead."

"Mr. Diener?" That was the name of the artistic handyman.

Thaddeus's eyes hardened. "He's known for helping remove and place difficult servants—"

"Or incompetent ones." Mrs. Moore frowned at her son, an imperceptible warning in her tone.

"In his half-brother, Mr. Butler's, establishments—some of which are not reputable."

"But many of which are," his mother asserted.

When Alice lingered by the door, Lily realized the servant wouldn't approach them. Was Thaddeus the man to whom Alice had vaguely referred to as having bothered her?

Stephen strode up the steps to the porch and waved at her. Young Jack Welling bounded up behind him and tapped on Stephen's shoulder.

"If you'll excuse me, I'd better go." She looked back up at Moore, but he was staring fixedly at Alice.

"We hope to watch your performance tomorrow night, Miss Lily." Mrs. Moore's tone was light, even friendly, but with a tremulous vibrato.

Lily turned and left.

"Sit down, Thaddeus," Mrs. Moore scolded. "And stop gawking at that girl."

Lily forced her expression to remain relaxed. Jack and Stephen were still talking. Stephen said the Grand was supposed to be off-limits for the child, per his father's request. Jack had a bad habit of running off with bikes. She sighed and headed toward her maid.

When she reached Alice, the stench of smoke again cloaked the young woman. Lily pressed her eyes tightly closed. Through gritted teeth, she asked, "What have I told you about smoking?" Not only could Lily not tolerate the odor, but Stephen too was troubled by it due to his mother's death and his father's.

"I don't care!" Alice's voice rose. A few hotel guests turned to look at them. "I'm old enough to have a cigarette if I wish." Gone were all traces of her Irish accent. Had that all been an act? And if so, why?

"Alice, keep your voice down." Lily reached to touch Alice's shoulder, but she swatted her hand away.

"I'm not a child." Her voice rose even louder. "Don't speak to me as if I am." The girl turned on her heel and ran off.

When Lily turned around, still gaping at what had happened, she spotted Thaddeus Moore with a shocked look on his face that surely mirrored her own. Hadn't he called Alice a child? Only fifteen. Maybe her message had been meant more for him than for Lily.

Stephen hurried toward her. "What was that about?"

Lily shook her head, aware of the many eyes upon them. "I don't know. But let's go."

"Certainly." He looped her arm through his and accompanied her across the porch as her cheeks burned in embarrassment over Alice's outburst. "I think I know who could chaperone."

"Oh? Who would that be?"

As they descended the steps, Jack Welling popped out of the bushes. When Lily startled, Stephen held her arm tightly.

"Jack, your initiative has been rewarded." Stephen smiled at the boy. "You may join us on the ride."

Jack hooted and tossed his blue-and-white-striped cap in the air. When it came back down, it landed atop Stephen's hat. He left it there.

"Do I look jaunty?" Stephen winked at Lily.

Jack scowled. "Ya just look silly, so give it back."

Lily reached up and retrieved the cap. "Here you go, Cousin Jack."

The boy's expression transformed into one of intense happiness. "I'm so glad you're my cousin."

"I am too."

"You remind me of my mom." To her surprise, the boy threw himself at her, hugging her so tightly that she almost toppled over.

The warmth, the love that she felt, that need to be connected, anchored her to the spot where they stood. What would it be like to have children to love? To hold them like this?

Jack pulled away. "I don't care what the rest of them say about you, I know I can trust you."

"Jack!" Stephen waved the boy to move down the walkway. "Let's not be repeating unkind things."

Jack hurried ahead then turned. "Why not, if they're true?"

"Come along, Lily." Stephen offered his arm.

Her newly found family members weren't sure they could trust her?

Jack circled back. "Let me hold my cousin's arm."

Stephen frowned but allowed Jack to take his place.

Lily slipped into her Kentucky accent. "Boy, in them thar hills where I come from, ain't nobody trust nobody, lessun they try and pull a fast one on ya. Not even yer kinfolk. Always have yer shotgun ready to greet folks when they come, if'n they ain't welcome."

Jack's eyebrows lifted. "If that don't beat all! I guess I can say ain't around you as much as I want. Ain't that right?"

Stephen sighed as he led them to their conveyance.

Lily pointed to the carriage. "Now you git on up thar with us and be real proper-like. Ain't that right, Dr. DuBlanc?"

The psychiatrist cast her a quizzical look.

What would Stephen think if he'd met her hauling wood and water, her bare feet dirty, wearing an old cotton dress that stopped midcalf? If not for the singing voice that God had given her, that would have been her life. God had blessed her. He'd allowed her poor father to suffer and die, but the Lord had brought her full circle to a new home. She could feel it in her heart.

# CHAPTER TWENTY

## *2020*

*T*he heavenly scent of lemon bars baking and whitefish frying in butter made Willa's mouth water. "Too bad this isn't for me."

Sue whirled around from the nearby stove. "I made plenty."

"I thought this was date night for you and Colton."

Peeking around Sue's aproned form, Willa gasped as she counted eight large whitefish fillets, all nestled in the massive frying pan. "Are you expecting an army?"

Sue pressed her lips together hard and shrugged. "I've been telling you for the past hour that you might want to freshen up a little."

Willa raised her arms, but she wasn't surrendering. "Oh no. Hold on here a minute. You didn't invite Michael, did you?"

"Nope." Her friend placed a bowl of green beans in the microwave. "Colton invited him."

"This was supposed to be my work-free night." Which meant no Michael.

Willa had found love letters from her mother to Thad Moore in a drawer upstairs. She'd begun reading them. Strange that Gramps and Gran had never found anything like that in Mom's belongings. Maybe she'd burned any letters from him after he'd died.

"Colton thinks you two are dating." A sassy smile danced on Sue's lips.

"Huh?" From the letters, it sounded like Thad and Angela weren't dating, just sneaking around together, something Gramps had confirmed they must have been doing. He didn't know anything about the two going out together. "We're not dating."

Since the Ice House meet-up, she and Michael had daily consultations with vendors, scheduled by the owners. Every night they'd eaten someplace different—always, though, discussing work and the journal.

"I can't just uninvite him." Sue cocked her hip. "Colton says he's crazy about you."

"*Your* new boyfriend is crazy about *me?*"

Sue snapped a kitchen towel at her. "No, that's not what I meant."

"Maybe Michael is just crazy and won't admit it." Willa laughed.

Sue was staring past Willa.

She turned. Colton carried a bag of groceries into the kitchen while Michael stood there, a cold expression of hurt on his handsome features.

Resisting the urge to make an excuse and leave, Michael forced a half-smile onto his face. He wasn't crazy, even if he sometimes felt like it. His labs had come back showing clearly that he had a diagnosis of lupus. His mother had been pretty distraught, but Dad must have said something to her, because her last call was very upbeat. Now he had Willa making cracks about him behind his back, even though she knew what was wrong with him.

Willa's hair was clipped up in a plastic thing, but half of her mass of curls had broken free. She was wearing a fluffy bathrobe over knit pajamas. With no makeup on, she looked younger—and more vulnerable.

He rubbed his chin. "You didn't know Colton invited me."

Willa cinched her bathrobe tighter. "Nope."

"Ah." He wished he hadn't said anything. Now she looked as self-conscious as he felt. "I should leave."

"No. Stay." Sue waved a metal turner at him. "I've paid top dollar at Doud's to get these fillets, and you're going to eat some."

"Yeah." Colton winked at him before turning to kiss Sue's cheek. "Fish does not keep well, so you need to stay, dude."

Willa headed out of the kitchen. "Let me put on some real clothes."

"No leopard print," Sue called after her as Willa departed.

"Normal people stuff," Colton added.

"This is awkward." Michael crossed his arms and leaned against the far wall. "And who says I'm crazy?"

Sue and Colton exchanged a long glance.

"I'm crazy about Sue is what I said earlier." Colton pulled Sue into a quick hug. "Not that you were crazy, Mike."

"Thin line there, my friend." Michael took in the kitchen decor and the high-dollar stove. "Falling in love and being a little crazy are pretty much the same thing, aren't they? You saw what happened to me last year." And what was happening to him now.

When the twosome began kissing, Michael went to the living room.

He glanced at the St. Ignace paper on the cocktail table. The headline read "Vandalism at Cemetery—Much Damage." He frowned. Mom had said some developer had really messed up and had disinterred a bunch of graves at a private cemetery outside of town. Someone was gonna get sued big-time.

Did it bother Willa that the Grand's longtime designer was suing the Grand Hotel? She'd said that she'd never encountered this challenge in the past, so maybe so. And she had seemed concerned about whether the journal officially belonged to the hotel. Still, he was going to get hold of Lily's journal and read the whole thing through for himself.

As the dinner went on, all of Willa's attempts to resist her heart's urging failed. Michael's smile, his quips, even just the way he looked at her did something to her insides that was like butter slowly being melted for a rich caramel sauce. As he worked beside her after the meal, cleaning up the kitchen, she was aware of his every movement. The almost-touch of his elbow against hers. The heat of his body alongside hers. The way he shifted on his feet when he tossed a towel over his shoulder. How ridiculous that all those little gestures should make her want to throw herself into his arms.

It had been so long since she'd dated anyone, she began to wonder if maybe she and Michael were actually doing just that.

When they'd finished the dishes, she looked up into his blue eyes. "Cleanup went well."

"We're a good team." He grinned.

Her knees wobbled. That had never happened before, but it must be a real thing.

"Yes." She turned away and placed the last dinner plate onto the stack and closed the cabinet door.

"Hello?" someone called through the front screen, and Willa startled, bumping into Michael.

He grabbed her shoulders. "You expecting anyone?"

"No."

Colton stepped into the kitchen, frowning. "There's a carriage out back."

"Let us guys check on this, ladies." Michael left the kitchen, followed by Colton.

From the other room, Colton's voice boomed, "Can we help you?"

Willa edged toward the front rooms.

"I'm Rick Moore, and this is my wife, Beverly. The owners of this cottage. And who are you?"

"The owners?" Colton repeated dumbly.

What were the owners doing here? Willa clamped her lips shut, moved near the guys, and awaited an explanation. She peered around Michael's broad shoulder.

"Didn't you get our message that we'd be arriving today?" The woman pushed her way into the house, and the three of them stepped aside.

Attired in expensive but casual boutique clothing, Mrs. Moore had immaculately coiffed and highlighted hair. The diamond on her engagement ring appeared to be at least five carats. A Marco Bicego three-strand, eighteen karat necklace, worth well over fifteen thousand dollars, circled the woman's slender neck. Willa had been offered one like it to wear on her show but had declined—afraid she'd lose it and be responsible for the cost.

The older man wore a navy blazer and an open-collared white dress shirt beneath. His khakis, expertly tailored, and his expensive leather boat shoes were trying to shout that he was being casual but failed.

Behind the two, a tall, athletically built man with some silver in his dark wavy hair wore one of the saddest expressions that Willa had ever seen. He glanced toward the staircase, where the family pictures were displayed.

If her suspicions were right, this man could be her father's twin brother. A little shiver went through her. Would her own biological father have looked just like the man standing there now?

They stepped farther into the living room.

The couple's son locked eyes with her. The light still streaming through the windows, even at this hour, revealed that his eyes were identical to hers—gold and green in the center with wide navy rings around them.

Willa pressed a hand to her throat, her breath sticking there. No one that she'd ever met had irises like hers. If this man's identical twin brother was her father, as she suspected, then they shared the same unique eyes as she had. *Weird eyes*, a lot of her childhood classmates had called them.

*Dear God, is this one of Your answers to my prayers?*

Heart pounding, she watched as the younger Moore's lips parted, but then he pressed them together.

Had he noticed? This was a media designer, and he no doubt could quote the new Pantone color chart names by heart.

"I'm Chad Moore, and I'm sorry that our message didn't get to you." He rubbed his jaw.

His mother arched an eyebrow. "We had our luggage brought up with us, and they're unloading it now."

"If I run out back, I can likely catch them." Chad glanced at his parents. "And we can work something else out."

"Aimee told us they have rooms for us at the hotel. We'll go there," Willa offered.

Chad's forehead crinkled. "How about we use those tonight and swap out tomorrow?"

"That's fine," Mr. Moore agreed.

"I'll call Aimee and let her know," Michael offered.

"I'll need to take my overnight case with me, as will you and your father." Beverly waved at her son as if shooing a fly. "Go tell the carriage driver to wait."

Chad dipped his chin in acknowledgment and moved with the grace of an athlete back out the door and past Colton, who stepped aside.

Michael pulled out his cell phone and stepped into the nearby hallway. The older couple glanced around the room, examining the place.

Thank goodness she and Sue had cleaned the place thoroughly that day. She'd not known then that the big cleanup had been in anticipation of Colton and Michael's dinner invitation.

Mr. Moore sniffed appreciatively. "Do I smell whitefish?"

Sue grinned at him. "Do you want some? I've got a couple of fillets left, and they won't keep."

The man actually smiled, a full-blown grin, while his wife looked like someone had slipped a lemon wedge into her mouth. "I'd love that. Honey, how about you?"

He turned to his wife, but she shook her head.

Michael ducked back into the room. "You're all set for the Grand."

"Thanks." Willa knew she could count on him and Colton to transfer her belongings and Sue's the next day. Wouldn't it be nice to have someone to rely upon every day?

Colton clapped his hands. "Dinnertime, folks."

Sue and Colton led Rick into the dining room, Michael following.

"Go ahead without me," Willa called after them. She needed time to talk with Beverly alone and with Chad when he returned. Would this be her only chance?

Beverly exhaled sharply, her facial features relaxing. Instead of a disapproving socialite, her facial expression was vulnerable and sad. "We've not been back in a long time."

She walked to where family pictures occupied a wall and wiped at her eyes.

Willa couldn't help herself. She stepped alongside the woman, her own eyes dampening, as she tried to hold back her secret. "I'm sorry for your loss."

Beverly gave her a sideways glance. "Who told you?"

She had to stick with the truth but not reveal too much. "My assistant recognized the artwork on the wall as that of Thaddeus Moore. I knew that he'd died very young. And then when we saw some pictures upstairs of him, we thought he might have lived here."

Beverly averted her gaze. "My boy was so talented, such a marvel." She touched the picture frame. "An artistic prodigy."

Chills worked through Willa. People had said the same about her design abilities. Had she inherited that from Thad? "It must be hard coming back here."

"Yes." The word came out as a whisper, and Beverly drew in a shuddering breath.

The door swung open again, and Chad, who likely was her uncle, returned to the room.

Laughter echoed from the dining room.

"Your father is consuming his favorite food," Beverly offered dryly. "I'd best go grab him if we're leaving."

"Do you mind if we leave the luggage on the back porch?" Those eyes, which matched her own, searched Willa's face.

"No problem."

"So we have a few minutes?" Beverly cocked her head.

"Tell Dad ten minutes max."

"All right." Mrs. Moore—or should she think of her as Grand-mother—left them alone in the room.

Willa rubbed her arms, suddenly feeling shy.

"I didn't catch your name. We just knew that a designer consulting at the Grand was staying here. We'd heard Vern Yip was consulting."

Vern Yip? She'd not seen him. But that didn't bode well for her. "Willa Christy." She needed to focus on this moment and not get distracted by this information about the former HGTV star.

Color seemed to drain from his face. "Are you from around here?"

"I live in Virginia—that's where I grew up and keep my home and business. My father has his medical practice there."

"Ah." Relief washed over his handsome features.

"But I was born near here—in Hessel—and spent my first three years there." Had she really just blurted that out? What had made her do that? Heat singed her cheeks.

His gaze swept over her face feature by feature. "You're Garrett Christy's granddaughter, aren't you?"

"Yes."

"And your mother?" The man looked like he was holding his breath.

"Arlene Forbes." It was the truth. That was her adoptive and psycho-logical mother's name—but she wasn't being fully honest.

He puffed out a long breath. "I met her only once, when my brother and my boats were being built by your grandfather."

"My grandfather is an amazing man. He and my grandma helped with me my first years—before my mother died."

He ran his tongue over his full lower lip. His lips were like hers too, she realized, which meant his identical twin's had been too.

Chad's brow furrowed. "Arlene died? I'm sorry."

"No. She's fine." Her heart beat more rapidly at the notion that she was looking at a carbon copy of what her father might look like.

"Oh?" Confusion flickered over his strong features. "You said your mother died."

"Arlene is my adoptive mother. My mom's older sister."

"And your mother was the younger sister?" He ran his hand along his jaw.

"Yes, her name was Angela." Gramps used to say she was his angel. "She died." And if Willa had been in the car with her, she'd have died too.

His shoulders slumped. "My brother, Thad, and I knew Angie well."

He knew. This man, her uncle no doubt, knew that Willa was his brother's child. Would he let it go? Would he want to know more? Willa fisted and unfisted her damp palms.

Mrs. Moore, smiling, moved back into the room with such grace and quietness that Willa hadn't heard her footsteps until she was mere feet away. "Who did you and your brother know?"

"My mother and aunt," Willa supplied.

"And don't forget your grandfather—Garrett Christy." Chad crossed his arms over his chest.

His body language said that he was distancing himself from her. Sadness washed through Willa.

"Oh yes, when your father took you and Thad over to the marina." Mrs. Moore pulled out a silver-plated box and held it aloft. "Haven't smoked in years, but carrying that memento around brings me comfort for some crazy reason." She pulled the engraved rectangular box free and clutched it in her left hand.

Chad leaned in toward Willa. "Do you know what happened to my brother?"

"I know about the crash in Gramps's boat. I'm so sorry." She'd never know the man who had been her father and who may have given her the artistic bent she had. Of course, that could have been from Gramps's side too.

"In my husband's boat, you mean." Beverly flipped the cover of the antique box open. "It was after all *he* who insisted on having those speedboats built."

"My grandfather recently told me that you were coming to retrieve the other boat."

"My husband hasn't been able to bring himself to unload that albatross."

*An albatross?*

"That blasted wooden boat." Beverly shook her head. "Like the one that splintered into a million pieces."

And killed her father. Willa blinked back tears.

"Are you all right?" Chad cradled her elbow with his palm.

"My grandpa took me out in your boat the summer before my mom died. It's one of the few memories I have of her."

Beverly clutched her cigarette case tightly. "So you've suffered a terrible loss too. How old was she?"

"Almost twenty and in nursing school—on track to become an RN."

"When was that?" Chad asked softly.

Willa named the year.

"Only a few years after Thaddeus left us." Beverly stared down at her cigarettes but didn't pull one out.

Chad drew in a slow breath as once more he scanned Willa's face. "An interesting way to put it, Mother. Thad took the boat without permission."

"True." Beverly's mouth quirked to the side.

"Thad planned to bring Angie, Willa's mother, to a party on the island. He got drunk and crashed into the pier."

Willa cringed at the way her uncle, for he had to be, factually stated the event. This tragedy had upended her entire life. If Thad hadn't died, maybe her mother would still be here too. If she'd not run up and down the road to nursing school, she'd have not been killed in that blizzard. If only. . .

Beverly's eyes widened. "You state those facts so coldly, Chad."

As far as facts, Willa had read the one newspaper article she could find, and very little had been mentioned. Thaddeus Moore hadn't been a local, so the regional newspapers didn't have in-depth coverage.

"You don't understand." Beverly pulled a cigarette free from the case, hands shaking. "You don't have children so you couldn't possibly. . ."

Chad's features hardened.

"I'm sorry, I shouldn't have said that. It wasn't your fault that I'm not a grandmother."

Willa resisted the strong urge to tell this woman that, yes, she had a granddaughter standing right in front of her.

Had Thad sped off because her mother, Angela, was pregnant? No, he couldn't have known. By Willa's calculations based on the date of the accident and her own birth, her teen mom had gotten pregnant shortly before the time of the accident.

Mr. Moore joined them, patting his trim stomach. "Delicious."

"Get me a light, Rick." Beverly held her cigarette aloft.

"What?" In two swift long-legged steps, the older man snatched the cigarette from her hand and crumpled it in his. Then he went to the door and tossed it out onto the ground.

Willa didn't know what to say. She certainly wasn't going to get involved in a domestic issue, even if they were likely her grandparents.

Chad touched her arm. "I'd love to talk with you some more, Willa, about your mother."

"I'd like that," she managed to get out, her voice catching.

He pulled a business card from his wallet. "You can reach me on my cell."

She stepped away to the desk and retrieved one of her cards and handed it to him.

"Colorful."

"That's me." She grinned. "I have them changed out every season to fit my latest persona."

"I work with artsy people in my business, and I've noticed that kind of thing often."

"Come on, Chadwick, we need to go." Mr. Moore called over his shoulder.

"Willa. . ." The way he said her name, so gently, made her want to please him. To console him. He'd lost a twin brother, and she'd lost her father and mother. "Call me soon."

"I will." And she would.

Finally, after all these years, she may be able to find the truth about her mother—and stop the nightmares once and for all.

# CHAPTER TWENTY-ONE

*1895*

After a beautiful afternoon with the love of his life, Stephen clutched Lily's arm tightly inside the crook of his elbow. When they'd returned to the hotel, a message had been waiting, asking them to go to the Swaine home for the evening. The trembling in Lily's body increased with every step closer to the bright yellow house on the cliffside. He opened the ornate gate and led her up the pathway, ever closer to a life that could take her away from him. If the Swaine family accepted her, if she was included in the division of the family's inheritance, Lily would have to remain on Mackinac Island. And she'd be a woman of means. Stephen still needed to continue his work, and that meant a relocation for him. Her place in the Swaine family would not be decided tonight, but this visit was a step in that process.

A light breeze ruffled the strands of hair wisping around Lily's lovely face. She looked a decade younger than he knew her to be. Vulnerability and hope danced across her expressive features.

"It will be all right, my love." He couldn't take back the last two words. They were already out of his mouth.

Lily looked up at him, eyes wide. But before she could say anything, the front door opened, and the Duvall girls spilled out.

"Miss Lily, you're here!" Opal ran toward them and pulled Lily away from him.

Bea rolled her eyes at her younger sister. Garnet grabbed Lily's other arm and helped propel her toward the house.

Jack Welling ran from the house scowling. "Get away from my cousin and let her be." He made shooing motions as he chased after the girls.

Beside Stephen, Lily laughed.

Robert Swaine and his sweetheart, Sadie, emerged onto the porch, followed by Maude Welling.

The adults streamed back inside.

Jack strutted up to the porch, arms akimbo. He looked just like a banty rooster.

Peter Welling stood in the entryway, shaking his head at his son. Jack sprinted off after the girls. "Welcome. Lily, you come with me, and Stephen, my fiancée wants to see you."

"Your fiancée?" Lily moved forward, next to Peter.

"Ada Fox will be Jack's new stepmother." Peter craned his neck to watch as Jack raced by the house again. "And not a moment too soon."

If anyone had a chance at bringing Jack under control, it would be Mrs. Fox.

They entered the home, a fragrant arrangement of garden flowers overflowing their vase on the center console table. Peter led Lily to the right.

Ada stood by an open door to the left of the stairs. "Dr. DuBlanc, do you have a minute?" Ada's words, while soft, indicated that Stephen *should* have a moment for her.

Stephen followed her inside Robert Swaine's dark masculine room. Several maps of the Great Lakes covered one wall. Ambrotypes and tintype images of people, presumably family members, clustered along a nearby shelf.

Stephen was aware of Mrs. Fox's concerns about Mrs. Stillman and her negative behavior toward the servants. Stillman also appeared to be jockeying for Ada's position. Not that Mrs. Fox needed the position. Her true reason for coming to Mackinac Island likely was to reunite with Peter now that he was widowed.

Mrs. Fox closed the door behind her. "I paid for a Pinkerton to investigate Stillman. There's something off about her." Her stiff demeanor and failure to suggest they sit down concerned him.

"Really?"

"Yes. When I told Robert about it, he shared that he had put in a Pinkerton inquiry about Lily."

His breath constricted. "And what did he find?"

"The Pinkerton learned that Lily and Clem were present when the venue they'd been performing at, near Detroit, burned."

"Really?" Surely Lily hadn't been involved in setting fire to the building. He swallowed hard. "What did he discover?"

"Absolutely nothing linking Lily to the inferno." She sighed. "Someday every business establishment will have protective water sprinklers to stop fires—like they demonstrated at the World's Fair in Chicago."

"Change takes time." Too late for his father and Lily's mother and those patients in the Kentucky asylum, though. "Maybe one day."

"I pray so. Also, the same Pinkerton was investigating both Robert and Stillman." She raised her eyebrows high, her lips pulled tight.

Heat singed his cheeks. "I confess—I knew about a Pinkerton being here for Robert's ship fires." He tapped the toe of his brown brogans.

"And you didn't tell us." Irritation edged her words.

He shrugged. "I'm a psychiatrist. I keep all manner of secrets. In fact, it's so inbred with me, that I'd dare not repeat what someone had for a meal, much less something of this nature."

She stared hard at him but then laughed, covering her mouth with a lace-gloved hand. "We have something in common then."

"Perhaps so."

"My contact said the Pinkerton determined that Robert's character is sterling."

"And Lily's?"

"Her situation is more complicated." Ada averted her gaze toward the bookcase, which held several rows of nautical books. "Ben Steffan has also been investigating, and she is indeed the daughter of Terrance Swaine. That's what they're discussing tonight."

He frowned. "I didn't think that was in doubt. So now Lily would be part of the descendant's group."

"But the Pinkerton overheard her telling her cousin Clem that she won't accept anything from the family."

"I imagine she'll tell them that tonight then."

"And she intends to move on to a venue about four hundred miles northwest of here."

His mouth went dry. She was leaving him? "Oh." Lily hadn't said anything about it on their drive.

Laughter pealed from a nearby room. Ada cracked the door open. "Good, Jack's not hiding out there. He's got a habit of listening in."

"As to Stillman." She took a seat across from him and straightened her skirts. "Early in the hiring season, a gentleman from Chicago paid for Pinkertons to investigate her."

Stephen rubbed his forehead. "Who would have known that we have so much detective work going on at the Grand?"

"It's not unusual in large organizations to have all manner of investigations underway. It's a sole Pinkerton agent who is also following several other people who are in the area for the summer, but my contact wouldn't say who they were. Not for any price." She huffed a laugh.

"What about Stillman?"

"He said Stillman had been a madam at a brothel in Traverse City before she was hired at the Grand."

"What?" Stephen couldn't help his shock.

"Yes. Her references are genuine, though." Ada arched an eyebrow at him. "From very well-to-do and high-up men who claimed she had the business acumen to serve well at the Grand."

"Which meant she'd likely blackmailed them for the recommendations."

Ada nodded. "Doctor, I wonder if that poor young Alice may have been one of Stillman's 'girls' in Traverse City."

"Lily's maid?" Alice was so young.

"Yes. One of her work references was from Stillman."

"Alice can't be more than sixteen or so."

"Fifteen."

"Lily learned today that the Moores had employed her in their home."

Ada Fox frowned. "So a Chicago connection."

"Mrs. Moore's son reacted strongly to seeing Alice here."

Her eyes lit up. "What happened?"

Stephen briefly summarized what he'd seen.

"Strange."

"I wonder how a young girl like that was in Chicago, then possibly a brothel, and then somehow up here."

Mrs. Fox shook her head. "I don't know. I can tell you this—Alice didn't come here with Mrs. Stillman straightaway. Perhaps she knew her somehow in Chicago. I don't know. And there was ongoing tension between the two of them, which didn't make sense since Stillman gave her a reference. As did the owner of Chicago Service Placements."

"Who was that?"

Ada frowned. "I don't remember. But the letter appeared to be legitimate."

Jack's tawny head popped up from behind a low sofa. "I like Alice. She never tells on me when I borrow a bike from the Grand. She just keeps talking to her friend."

"Jack!" Ada's flummoxed expression cast doubt upon just how well she might bring the boy into line. "I can't believe you are eavesdropping."

The boy shrugged.

"Were you taking bikes from the hotel?" Ada crossed her arms.

"Yeah, Alice would come out for a smoke and keep an eye out for me. They've got lots of models I'd never tried before."

Ada wagged her finger. "No more of that."

"Alice is from Wisconsin. From a farm. But she can't go home."

Stephen took a step closer to the boy. "Oh?"

"Yup. But she's got a friend, maybe more like an uncle, lookin' after her here." Jack rolled his eyes. "Yeah, he looks real old, maybe thirty."

Stephen almost laughed. Thirty was really old?

"She always made me scat when he came out." Jack scratched his cheek. "What's a brothel?"

"Let me get your father." Ada marched out of the room.

Jack opened a candy jar on the desk. "What did I say wrong?"

*Out of the mouths of babes.*

# CHAPTER TWENTY-TWO

*St. Ignace, 2020*

"*I* can't believe we took a ferry over here, only to turn around and catch a boat ride back." Willa clutched a Michigan cherry latte in her hands, purchased at the mainland coffee shop.

Sue sipped her mocha frappe. "It was worth it just for the coffee from that café."

Willa laughed. "Our ride on the speedboat will be even better than the coffee."

"Maybe." Sue drank some more. "But this stuff is epic."

They headed to the marina to wait.

Fifteen minutes later, Willa tapped her navy boat shoes. They matched the retro sailor girl outfit she'd pulled together for the trip on Gramps's boat, or rather on the Moores' boat. Grandpa Moore's boat? She laughed at the thought of the austere gentleman being called grandpa.

She turned to her soon-to-be-former business partner. "How do I look?"

"Awesome. How about me?" Sue wore a coral-and-yellow sundress with crocheted lace around the V-neck collar. Her retro straw sunhat sported a wide peach ribbon.

"Beautiful."

Seagulls squawked and flew overhead, the skies a brilliant blue this morning. From the harbor, a ferry boat blasted its horn.

"Oh, there it is!" Sue pointed to the glossy wood speedboat being commandeered into the marina by Gramps.

Willa waved. Chad Moore, quite likely her uncle and seated beside

Gramps, waved back. "That's weird. I thought we were riding from here so that we got a trip in it before the Moores received it." Gramps was supposed to deliver the vintage speedboat to them on the island.

Sue shrugged. "As long as we still get to go."

In a few minutes, Gramps moored the watercraft.

Willa and Sue hurried to the slip.

"Welcome aboard, ladies." Chad greeted them warmly. "I've not been on my boat in decades, but she runs like a charm."

*His boat. That's right.* "This one was made for you?"

Gramps nodded. "Yup." His facial features looked hard this morning. He didn't even offer her a hug, but then again, he was driving.

After Sue got in, Willa followed, with Chad offering her a hand. It was strange but pretty cool, knowing that behind those Ray-Bans were a pair of eyes that matched hers.

They hurriedly donned their life jackets and took their seats.

"Ready?" Chad looked to the back, smiled, then gave Gramps a thumbs-up.

The boat sliced through the waves with ease. Willa and Sue clutched their hats, finally giving up and removing them when the wind proved too strong.

What a glorious feeling, flying over the waves. Finally, they slowed as they entered the Mackinac Island harbor. This time, Willa had shivers as she imagined her father crashing his identical boat right here all those years ago.

Soon Gramps secured the boat at the yacht cove, and they all got out.

Mr. and Mrs. Moore weren't there. Willa looked around, expecting to see them waiting on a bench somewhere.

Chad pulled out his phone and made a call. He turned away from them.

"That was a blast, Mr. Christy." Sue gave Gramps a quick hug.

"Brought back a lot of memories." His hard gaze at Willa made her stiffen.

Gramps ran his hand quickly over his face, briefly covering his eyes. When he looked at her again, she saw only sadness. "I miss Angie so much. Every day."

She stepped into his arms. "Oh, Gramps, I'm so sorry."

Gramps pulled her tight and kissed her forehead then released her. "I'm so glad we have you, though, Willa. I'm grateful of that."

"And I'm so glad I have you." She patted Gramps's cheek.

Colton jogged up toward them. "Was it stellar riding in a vintage speedboat?"

"Incredible!" Sue launched herself into Colton's arms.

The big guy lifted her up off the ground then set her back down. "Time for lunch at the Chuckwagon."

"We'll see you. Thanks, again!" Sue waved, and she and Colton headed off hand in hand.

Chad ended his phone conversation. "My parents will be here soon."

Gramps glanced between Chad and Willa and pointed toward Marquette Park in a gesture that suggested they should go. "I'll meet you over there when we're done."

Chad inclined his head toward Willa. "We'll be there."

Mr. and Mrs. Moore, attired in matching chinos and crisp white shirts, headed up the walkway.

Willa and Chad walked down the narrow dock in the opposite direction of his parents. They crossed the street and soon found an empty bench beneath some trees.

Chad waited for Willa to sit then eased down beside her. "I need to talk with you."

His serious tone made Willa hope that she was finally going to hear more about her birth father. "Great. I'd love to hear what happened that summer."

He quirked an eyebrow. "I loved my brother, and he really did care about your mom. But he was only a kid. We all were."

She exhaled long and low. "I figure that Thad and my mother had a thing, didn't they?"

"Yes." Chad stared up at the sky, now dotted with cumulus clouds. "A teenage infatuation, you could say."

Willa mulled this over. That made sense. Sometimes "good girls" like her mom were attracted to the "bad boys" like Thad.

"Angela. . .your mom was a small-town girl and Thad. . ." He turned to face her. "As much as I loved my wild and crazy brother, I felt he was bad news for Angie."

Nearby, a couple of college-aged guys tossed a Frisbee back and forth. *So young. Like my parents were.*

"But she loved him, didn't she?" She must have.

"Yes." He ran his hand over his cheek. "He was a reckless kind of guy."

"I kinda figured that, from what I've heard."

He stared at her. "I was the quiet one. The conscientious son."

"Gramps said my mom was too." Tim had said the same about Chad.

He averted his gaze. "We had many things in common."

"Like your love of Thad?"

He pressed his eyes closed. "I wish I had known about you."

Willa exhaled a long breath. "Because Thad had died, I guess my mom didn't want to reach out to your family. There'd have been no point trying to make him shoulder his duties as father since he was gone already."

Chad shook his head slowly. "It's not quite like that."

Her heartbeat stuttered at the emotion in his voice. "Then how was it?"

He ran his hand over his face. "I begged Angie to stay in Hessel and not go with my brother that night. The night he died, he'd planned to take her to a beer party on the island. I convinced her that it wasn't a good plan."

"Thank God you did that, or I wouldn't be here."

Sweat shone on his forehead. "You're right, we both loved Thad. Angie and I got word that night about the crash..." He lowered his head.

"You were together?" A prickling of understanding, cold and spreading, coursed through her.

"We'd been at a picnic for the church, when your grandfather came to tell us."

Her mouth went dry. "I thought my grandfather had gone straight to the island to be with your family."

He inhaled and straightened. "But I stayed with Angie."

"Grieving together?"

He looked away. "You know, Angela had a serious boyfriend but had broken up with him. I really liked Angie. She was so smart, so funny, so beautiful. Thad and Angela hung out all that summer."

Did she hear a little jealousy?

He gave a curt laugh. "My wife reminded me a little of Angie."

Where was this going?

His Adam's apple bobbed as he swallowed hard. "I'm almost fifty, and my ex-wife and I had no children."

She blinked at him, unsure of how this mattered. "I'm sorry."

Chad gave a curt laugh. "Turns out she planned it that way, whereas I hadn't."

"Wow. You mean she didn't want children?"

He raised his eyebrows. "Maybe because then she wouldn't have been center stage. She's an attorney. Left me for the most senior member of her firm."

"Sorry."

"When I saw you." He exhaled a whoosh of breath. "I knew right away who you were."

"Thad's daughter?" She looked down, afraid of what his next words might be.

He stood. "No." He turned a slow circle.

When she looked up, his lips were pressed together hard, and a tear trickled down his cheek.

Chills shot through her. "You?"

He dipped his chin. "Angie and I, we were so upset about Thad. We went off to a quiet place. And I guess you could say we comforted one another."

*More than comforted one another.*

"I'm not proud of what we did." Chad shook his head. "We were inexperienced kids who got carried away in an attempt to quell our grief."

"And I'm the result of that?"

"Look into my eyes and tell me you don't see it. Those tricolor Moore eyes that we both have, that Thad had. They skipped a generation with my dad."

"I can't believe after all these years I'm finally learning the truth." She felt a little sick. If she weren't already sitting, Willa would have done so. The answer to what she'd come north to seek out was standing right in front of her. She drew in a steadying breath. "What would you have done if you'd known?"

"Conscientious brother, remember? What do you think I'd have done?"

But then her mother would have had a reminder for the rest of her life of the Moore son whom she'd really loved. Willa lowered her head and closed her eyes. Her mom had been protecting herself, her own heart. But she had been so very young.

"I'm so proud to be your father, Willa. I want to shout it from every corner of this island." He stepped up onto the concrete bench. "Willa Christy is my baby girl!"

She blinked back tears as she looked up at him. "I'm afraid that at thirty-one I no longer qualify as a baby girl." Wait till her family heard about this. Mom would play the suffering martyr, Dad would be stoic, and Clare would want to know everything about Chad.

Chad jumped down. "I talked with your grandfather Christy on the way over."

"Did he know?"

"I think for the first time, today, he saw me without my sunglasses on. I did that deliberately. Looked him square in the eye when I shook his hand."

"What did Gramps say?"

"He started by asking which brother had fathered you." Chad gave a deep belly laugh. "When I said it was me, he pretty much started with one profanity and ended with a few others."

"Sounds like Gramps when he's super riled."

"He calmed down. Eventually."

"Did he think it was Thad?"

"Yeah, he suspected, but he said that your mom was so adamant about leaving things alone. . ."

"And with Thad dead, there was no use pushing the issue?"

"Yeah. But I wish Angie had reached out to me. We both felt guilty about what happened—like we'd betrayed my brother's memory."

"Do you regret it?"

"How could I when I look at you. My own flesh and blood. I just wish. . ."

"We can't change that. But now we both know."

"I'm so grateful to learn about you." He sat down again. "My parents have noticed how cheerful I've been since we met you. I feel like I have hope again."

"I'm glad." She really was.

"And what a cool thing to have our reunion be in that contentious cottage. My father has always considered it a shackle."

"Why?"

"I guess some young woman was murdered on our property. A long, long time ago—"

"Like in 1895?"

Chad's eyebrows drew together. "How did you know?"

"Let me tell you about this journal I found. It was behind a wall in a room we've been remodeling at the Grand."

# CHAPTER TWENTY-THREE

*1895, The next morning*

"Alice is dead?" Lily gasped as she stared at the policeman who'd just knocked on her door and shared the tragic news.

"Yes, miss. Your maid was killed last night."

Lily gaped at the man. "How is that possible?"

"That's what we want to know." The man's tone was harsh. He was about her age, with a thick reddish handlebar moustache and a stocky frame. "You'll need to come with me."

He led her downstairs. As she walked with the man through the lobby, guests eyed her suspiciously. Outside the hotel, a police wagon waited.

Heat seared Lily's cheeks. Was she under arrest? He hadn't said so. But he assisted her into the conveyance.

"We have witnesses who heard you on more than one occasion arguing with your maid."

Too shocked to reply, Lily sat gripping the edge of her seat.

How was she supposed to trust in God when He was allowing all these terrible things to happen? She'd been brought up in a small Kentucky church where members had always encouraged her to rely on the Lord and not on man. She'd always thought they'd really meant that she shouldn't rely on Ma, who was "off" as they all knew. Although she'd heard many great preachers speak in all her travels with Clem, she'd still relied on her weapons to keep her safe.

She bowed her head and prayed. *Lord, give me strength.*

Before long, Lily found herself at Mackinac Island jail.

The sheriff scowled at her. "This is what comes of making a spectacle of yourself in front of all those fancy people at the Grand every night."

"I've done nothing wrong." Lily clutched at the cameo at her throat, a gift from her mother. Mama too had done nothing wrong. Still her name was associated with a tragedy, and she was condemned as guilty by the Kentucky press.

How had things come to this? How had a young maid who'd worked for the Moores ended up so far from Chicago and now dead? Lily clamped her mouth shut. She had no answers.

"All righty then, Miss Lily, we'll get you set up in your new accommodations."

When they locked the door, something broke inside of her. What if Mama had survived, been charged, and forced into prison? Her poor mother with her fragile emotions would have gone utterly mad. Perhaps it had been a mercy that she'd perished quickly in the fire. And to think that Stephen's father had likely caused the tragedy.

After an hour, the policeman returned to her cell and offered her a tin cup of water.

"Thank you."

He leaned in and held up a note. "Did you and Mr. Moore set this up? To kill that maid?"

"What?" She sipped her water, thirsty.

"We know you got this note from Thaddeus Moore asking you to come up to his family's cottage last night."

She shook her head. "I was at my uncle's home, Captain Robert Swaine's, and I'd like for you to send for him. He'll help sort out this whole mess. If you can't reach him, then have Dr. DuBlanc come fetch me from this place."

He growled his assent.

Lily tried to think hard about what she knew about Alice. She wasn't Irish, as she'd claimed to be. She was only fifteen and had worked as a maid for the Moores, but something had caused her to be thrown out. Obviously, some strange thing existed between her and Thaddeus. But what was that relationship? The note from Thaddeus clearly had Lily's name on it, not Alice's. Had her maid seen it? And who was Alice's smoking partner?

Another slow hour passed before the burly policeman returned and opened her door.

She exhaled in relief.

"Follow me."

She followed him to where another policeman set all of her self-protection weapons on the precinct's counter. "Evidence."

A slow grin spread across the officer's face. "Now what would a lady such as yourself be needing with all those weapons?"

The burly policeman scratched his chin. "Oh. Joe, I forgot to tell you that this gal says she has witnesses." He didn't sound repentant in the least.

Lily gaped at him. "So you never sent for Captain Swaine—"

He raised a hand to silence her. "We're busy around here."

There'd been no one brought back while she was there, and the other cells were empty.

An officer strode through the front door, scowling.

The corporal stopped when he reached her and wagged his finger at Lily. "I don't know what you've been up to, but the state police have ordered us to release you and send you back to the Grand. And my chief agreed."

"I won't be held here?"

He grunted his assent.

Lily exhaled in relief. Before long, she'd been checked out of the jail. When they offered her a ride in the police coach, she refused. She'd rather walk and collect her thoughts than be seen in that conveyance again.

She headed up the street. *Poor Alice. Dead.*

"Lily!" Stephen rode toward her on a tandem bicycle. "I just heard. I'm so sorry." He pulled up alongside her on the street.

Tears trickled down her face. "I've never been so humiliated in all my life." Not even when she'd been concerned about others finding out about her mother. Now, with Stephen having confessed his suspicions about his father, she still found herself in a situation could irrevocably harm her reputation.

"Come on and hop on the back, and we'll ride back up to the hotel. Sorry I couldn't get a taxi, and I didn't want to wait any longer. Grabbed this from the rack and came as fast as I could."

She wasn't alone. God was with her. He'd put this man in her life—the last person on earth she ever would have imagined being her special love. His presence right now brought a comfort that defied words. Was this what it was like when you're meant to be the other half of the two who become one in God's sight? The strain of the day began to lift.

"Just don't expect me to launch into a rendition of 'Daisy Bell,' Stephen. I'm really not up to singing today."

To her surprise, he began to sing his own version, substituting her name, as they rode through town and toward the hotel.

They were met at the hotel by Mr. Williford, who escorted them upstairs. "The state police will ask you about Alice." He led Lily and Stephen to a private meeting room on the second floor.

Mr. Williford, a sheen of perspiration on his dark forehead, opened the door. A state policeman attired in full uniform sat inside along with Mrs. Stillman. Mr. Williford closed the door behind them.

The policeman pointed to two empty chairs across from him. "I'm Officer Byrnes. I understand that the deceased, Alice Smith, was your maid?"

"Yes." Lily's mouth went dry.

Stephen pulled her chair out and, when she was seated, took his place beside her.

The policeman's cold gray eyes met hers. "And you weren't too happy with her, were you?"

Lily stiffened.

"Don't answer that, Lily." Stephen leaned in. "What are you getting at, Officer Byrnes?"

The policeman jerked a thumb over his shoulder. "Mrs. Stillman informed me that Miss Lily has complained to her supervisor frequently about Alice, who was in her charge."

*In her charge?* The woman barely acknowledged Alice. "I went to Mrs. Fox twice about Alice's smoking, which was a safety concern."

"Oh. . ." Byrnes's droll tone held doubt. With a mocking laugh, he turned his attention to Stephen. "Did you know your sweetheart went down to meet Thaddeus Moore at his parents' cottage last night?"

"She most certainly did not." Stephen frowned. "What are you playing at?"

Byrnes leaned in. "Mr. Moore sent you a note that said, 'I'll be there to pick you up at ten.'"

Stillman pointed at Lily. "I saw you get in his carriage."

"That would be impossible since I was at the Swaines' home."

Stephen dipped his chin. "I was there."

When the policeman looked doubtful, Lily said, "You can call in my uncle Robert Swaine to confirm that."

"She was on the porch near ten," Stillman sputtered.

"We departed at nine." Stephen stared coldly at Stillman. "Which Robert can confirm."

"We'll speak with Captain Swaine." The policeman shifted in his seat. "What time did you return to the hotel, Miss Swaine?"

"About midnight."

Byrnes cleared his throat. "You were with the Swaines all that time?"

"Yes."

Stillman fidgeted with her cuffs.

Stephen cocked his head. "The hotel manager told me that Alice had fallen off the cliffside and died. Obviously, you think there was more to it."

"We have to rule out foul play, Dr. DuBlanc."

"People said she was found on the cliffside by the Moores' cottage." Lily spoke up. "What in the world would she have been doing over there?"

"That's what we want to know."

"As for the note from Thaddeus Moore, I never saw it. Where did you find it?"

"Mrs. Stillman discovered it on your desk." Byrnes cast a quick glance at the grim-faced woman.

Lily turned to Stillman. "You say you saw me get in the Moores' carriage. What was I supposedly wearing?"

"An ivory lace gown with a matching shawl," Stillman supplied. "And a cream-colored bonnet to match."

Stephen scooted his chair closer. "That's not her attire from last night."

"What about the shoes?" Lily's gut quivered.

Stillman frowned. "Ivory with a buckle, I think."

Lily met Officer Byrne's gaze. "That's what she was wearing, wasn't it? My outfit but with those kidskin pumps? I gave those to her because they were too small for me."

Byrnes dipped his chin. "Mrs. Stillman, you may leave."

Stillman's eyes widened. "Don't you see that she had something to do with this?"

Byrnes raised his eyebrows at the woman. "Being upset with a servant and wanting them dead are two different things, ma'am. You're dismissed."

The horrid woman departed in a huff.

Byrnes tapped the tabletop hard. "I'm going to send for Robert Swaine."

"Seems like Alice may have been intending to meet someone. But who?" Stephen shook his head. "Would she have gone out to see this Thaddeus Moore? Did you know that she had been a servant in their household, Officer Byrnes?"

"We've heard." The policeman leaned back. "Did you ever see Alice with any men?"

"No, but she frequently went out back where people smoked." Lily chewed her lip.

"I heard yesterday that Alice had a male friend, maybe a protector, here." Stephen rubbed his forehead. "Someone possibly in his early thirties."

Mr. Williford stepped forward. "That would be Mr. Diener."

Where had Williford come from? Had he been listening the entire time?

"Diener means 'butler' in German, did you know that?" Mr. Williford cocked his head at her.

"I wonder if there's a connection with the Butlers from Chicago?" Stephen asked.

Byrnes pushed his seat back and stood. "I think that's for the Pinkertons to find out." He left the room without a good-bye.

Mr. Williford took a seat across from Lily. "Never would I have imagined that my restful summer assigned to this region would become so full of mysteries."

"Restful summer?" Lily didn't understand the man. "Working here during high season?"

Stephen crossed his arms and leaned back in his chair. "You're our Pinkerton then, aren't you?"

"Yes, I am. And you're going to help me solve one of the biggest cases

I've had in my career and prove that we Pinkertons don't just break up strikes."

Lily awoke to the sound of birdsong outside her new room in the Canary. She'd not been able to sleep in her suite at the hotel. Nor could she perform for the past few nights. Clem remained and watched over things for her, but he planned to depart soon with Marie.

Light filtered through the eyelet curtains, illuminating a small girl clutching a stuffed rabbit to her chest.

"Oh good, you're awake!" Opal jumped on the bed beside her and shoved her toy bunny in Lily's face. "He wants a morning kiss."

"A kiss?"

"Yes."

Lily obliged.

"Mama always kissed me each morning."

Lily crooked her finger at the little girl, and Opal moved closer, eyes wide. Then Lily lifted her head and kissed the child's petal soft cheek. Opal covered the spot with her hand.

"We've got a surprise for you today, Miss Lily."

She did not need any more surprises. "Oh?"

"Fambly meeting."

"Family?"

"That's what I said." Opal clapped her hands. "Once Sadie marries Robert, then we'll be 'fish-elly in the fambly too."

Lily stifled the urge to laugh at Opal's mangling of *officially*. "Who's going to be there?"

Opal threw her arms wide and flopped back on the bed. "Everybody. Lots and lots of people."

Later Maude came to see her. "I heard about Mr. Costello saying the gowns belonged to the hotel. So I've sent over a trunk with some things to hold you until Uncle Robert sets up your accounts in town."

Lily hugged her cousin tightly. "Thank you. You didn't have to do that." Clem had brought her limited wardrobe over from the hotel. But he still hadn't found her journal.

"Sadie and I can help with your hair, if you want."

"I could use help with the pins in my chignon."

After she'd dressed and Maude and Sadie had secured her tresses, the three of them went to the window and looked out.

"Opal spoke the truth."

"What about?" Sadie cast her a quizzical look.

"About all the people coming."

Downstairs, people streamed into the home.

Maude pointed to the street. "I see carriages parked all the way around the curb."

"Many guests will arrive on foot, though." Sadie sat on the window seat.

"Here comes our cousin, Dr. Cadotte. And Cousin Stan, he left the livery behind today."

"Yes, I've seen him before. Driving." Lily smiled, warmed by the feeling of connectedness.

Jack charged into the room. "Hey you two! Sis and Sadie, get down there and greet people. Miss Ada and Ben are here now." He huffed like a little general.

Maude saluted him while Sadie scowled as they departed.

Jack, attired in a blue suit, extended his thin arm. "Lily, come with me."

"Yes, sir."

"There's a few dozen or so cousins downstairs, all Cadotte relations."

These people were all kin to her. "Why the family meeting, Jack?"

He made a sour face. "I think they all like to gab together but mostly they came 'cuz Aunt Virgie said so."

"Aunt Virgie?"

"My great-aunt Virgie is here, and Uncle Robert wants you to meet with her first—before the others. She was my grandma's sister. But Virgie ain't a sourpuss like she was."

From downstairs, peals of laughter sounded.

"Come on, I gotta take you down the back stairs to Uncle Robert's office. Aunt Virgie and him are waiting there."

"All right." They both left the room.

"Oh, and she's real old." He grinned up at her. "But her house in the middle of the island is even older."

"I see."

"She's Grandma Swaine's sis." He scratched his nose as he tramped down the stairs, leaving Lily far behind him.

When he reached the bottom of the stairs, he popped out from behind the wall. "Boo!"

Lily took a step back.

"Come on." Jack turned and headed down a short hallway then rapped on a paneled door.

"Enter at your own peril," Robert Swaine answered.

Jack opened the door. "I would never lead a lady into peril." The boy affected a playful British accent but failed miserably.

Lily stepped in behind her cousin. A tiny woman attired in a style from decades earlier, her white hair secured in a fluffy chignon, stood at the window, her back to them.

When she swiveled to face them, the elderly woman's eyes widened then filled with tears. She covered her mouth with both hands then lowered them, crossed against her shoulders. "Jacqueline," she whispered.

"No, she ain't, she's Lily." Jack frowned.

Robert pulled a linen handkerchief and handed it to his aunt, Lily's great-aunt.

To Lily's surprise, the older woman scowled at Jack. "I know, you scamp, but she looks so much like my sister did. Like your grandma Jacqueline. Except for her hair."

"Go on, Jack." Robert shooed Jack from the room.

"I'm Virgie." The elderly woman dipped her head almost solemnly.

"She's the matriarch of the Cadotte family." The way Robert said this, so heavy with respect, moved Lily.

"You have ancient roots connecting you to this island, Lily, to this entire area. And we're so very glad you've found your way back home." Virgie opened her arms to Lily.

When she embraced the elderly woman, it did indeed feel like she had found where she belonged. She fought her tears, not wanting to appear at the meeting with a red-streaked face.

Virgie finally released her and squeezed Lily's arms. "You're about to meet the rest of the family. One thing you need to know is..." She looked to Robert.

"We take care of our own," he finished for her.

Lily's weapons had failed her, had even resulted in her being accused and jailed. For the first time since Alice had died, a weight seemed to be lifting from her heart.

Virgie released Lily. "You're about to meet about fifty kinfolk who are going to decide how they can best help you."

"And put this ordeal behind you. All the accusations." Robert drew in a deep breath.

"Do they know about my ma?" Would they be so welcoming if they'd heard about the fire?

Virgie and Robert exchanged a long glance.

Robert rubbed his eyes and then dropped his hands. "Dr. DuBlanc explained about his father, about what he believes are false claims against your mother."

"My dear great-niece, we don't believe in repeating falsehoods in our family. So nothing shall ever be said unless it is from you." Virgie hooked her arm through Lily's. "Now come on. I feel like I am showing off a new baby to our family. Terrance's baby girl has finally joined us."

With those words, something shifted in her consciousness. There was no stopping those tears now. Lily was accepted for herself. Satan's lies, which had followed her for years, would not prevail. And through the gifts from her father and the Father in heaven's direction, she'd found her way home. With God's help, she could overcome the past and start anew.

"Thank you for helping us." Stephen sat across from Ben in Robert Swaine's office at the Canary.

So much had happened in the past week since Alice's death. Since Lily had connected with her extended family, she appeared much lighter in spirit.

But he wanted to clear Lily's name fully. He also wanted to help Mr. Williford, which meant that he had to rely on others. Ben Steffan, as a seasoned reporter, was just the man.

Ben opened his satchel and pulled out several folders. "I've got information that might help us figure out what happened, but according to the *polizei*, they're considering Alice's death accidental."

"Accidental? Weren't bullets found at the scene?"

"*Ja.* And she had faded bruising around her neck, suggesting she'd been grabbed hard a few days earlier." Ben used his hands to show a strangling motion.

"Who'd have done that?"

"My money's on Stillman. A guest saw her roughly pull Alice into her quarters about a week ago."

Stephen tapped his toes against the floor. "But she's not charged with anything."

"I don't know." Ben arranged his papers in three piles.

"And none of the bullets found had hit Alice?"

"No, but there were slugs in the trees near where she fell. It was a *konstruktion* site there for the Moores' new stairway to the water."

"And I heard that her wrist was broken. Is that so?"

"*Ja.* It had been twisted hard." Ben thrummed his fingers on the desktop.

"But no one has come forward?"

"*Nein.* Several people missing, though."

"What? Didn't the police require everyone to stay?"

Ben raised his hands then lowered them, wearing an expression of frustration. "They believe it was an accident, so nein. Mrs. Stillman has vacated her quarters and Mr. Christy *informiert* that Mr. Diener is gone too."

Stillman and Diener? "What possible connection could those two have?"

"It gets more suspicious. Butler is gone as well as his sidekick, Parker. A reporter *freund* from Chicago told me that Hans Butler has been charged with kidnapping underage girls—usually maids in wealthy households—and bringing them up to northern Michigan to brothels. He says there's evidence that will make the charges stick."

"Truly?"

"Ja. And I spoke with Mr. Thaddeus Moore this morning, who informed me that he never sent any message. Furthermore, unbeknownst to his interfering *mutter*, he is engaged. He and his fiancée were taking a moonlight carriage ride when Alice died."

"What's Williford saying?"

"He says nothing but gladly accepts my information. He's promised me that if I don't blow his cover, he'll give me an exclusive once the crime is solved."

"That's if you don't figure it all out first and get your own scoop." One that would clear Lily's name fully.

"Ja." Ben rubbed his chin. "I have a question for you."

"What's that?"

"Have you told Lily that you are in love with her, Dr. DuBlanc?"

# CHAPTER TWENTY-FOUR

*Mackinac Island, 2020*

*W*hen Michael had dropped off Lily's journal the previous night at Kareen's office, she'd agreed to help tie up loose ends. Now, however, Kareen pointed to a seat across from her, her face grim.

She held Lily's journal aloft. "How much do you want for this?"

"What do you mean?" Michael sat stiffly on the edge of the antique Windsor chair.

She stood and crossed her arms over her chest. "Michael. . ." She drew out his name. "Do you think I'm a fool?"

He blinked. "No. Why?"

Kareen took several mincing steps around her desk and stood over him. "Do you want the company back? Do you want money to leave the island? What is it?"

Michael raised his hands in mock surrender. "No, nothing like that."

"I doubt it." A muscle jumped in her cheek. "I'm pretty sure you want to ruin my husband's family name."

"This Parker mentioned is one of Hampy's relatives, then?"

She dropped her arms and returned to her desk. "Yes. My husband's grandfather. Who did time for his crime, by the way. He was only in his early twenties then."

Michael scooted back from the edge of his chair. He'd never heard about the Parkers' pasts nor where they got their money.

"Hampy's grandfather, Gus Parker, turned his life around. He became ultraconservative after he served his time. Gus married a wealthy woman, and they set up Hampy's dad with this hotel. I remember Hampy saying his grandfather didn't trust anyone, though."

"That journal made it sound like he was a scary dude."

"Humph! And you want to rub my nose in my grandmother's past."

"What do you mean about your grandmother?"

She grabbed the journal and lifted it. "Alice, of course. My beloved grandmother whom you have exposed as a former prostitute. She was so young."

Gaping, Michael couldn't manage to speak.

"And don't sit there looking all innocent. I've heard you had Colton bring in a mystery crew. You dig up dirt and you throw it all over my family!"

"Wait a minute. First of all, that isn't my intention, and secondly, Alice died."

Kareen huffed out a breath. "Of course, she did—at eighty in Oshkosh."

"No. This Alice Smith, the maid, died here. On the island. At the Moores' home in 1895."

A furrow formed between Kareen's brows. "No."

"Didn't you read the whole journal?"

"Didn't have time. I scanned to the middle."

Michael stood and extended his hand for the journal. She passed it to him. He opened it to where the entries had ended. "Read this." He handed it back to his boss.

She put her reading glasses on, a pair of bright red cat-eye frames. "This isn't right. It can't be." She shifted back in her seat and removed her glasses, her expression perplexed.

"A different Alice, then?"

"My grandmother Alice was born in 1880, which would be when this fifteen-year-old maid was born. Grandma lived on a farm in Wisconsin and went to the city, where she worked as a servant. Then she came to Michigan. And my grandpa Carl, who was a good bit older than her, brought her to the Grand and they worked together. They met again later and married."

"Sure sounds like it could've been her."

"Carl Diener was my grandfather. His stepbrother, who anglicized his name to Butler, was my horrid great-uncle, who died in prison." Kareen swiveled away, her back to him. "From what we'd heard, Hans Butler did some really bad things."

What did Butler get convicted of? Was he found to be a trafficker? "You said your grandfather Carl met up with your grandmother Alice later. Where?"

She laughed. "Would you believe at a cemetery in St. Ignace?"

"A cemetery?" *Weird.* "Why were they there?"

"She said they were both sent a letter requesting that they meet there to remember a friend who had died. A maid they knew from the Grand."

"And that's how they got together?"

"Yes. Grandpa Carl was astonished to find her there." Kareen rubbed her lower lip with her thumb. "Oh my. I think one story she'd shared was that he'd thought she was dead. That might fit with this journal's story."

What was it that Willa had said the other night? Something about a large dog's skeleton being found in a grave, in a coffin accidentally dug up in St. Ignace. Dad had mentioned it too. *Bizarre.* "I think I might know what could have happened. Maybe not all of it but part."

"You're really not here to blackmail me?"

"I can't believe you'd think that of me."

"If you'd grown up with all these skeletons in your closet, you'd understand. My grandma Alice was positively paranoid and a recluse. Now I can see why."

"I'm glad I didn't know about my ancestors' secrets." Michael shrugged. "Lily and Stephen had to do the heavy lifting themselves."

"Did they marry?"

"Yup. And I'm sure you'll keep the DuBlancs' secret under your hat too."

"I didn't get that far. I was more interested in what she wrote about Grandma Alice and Grandpa Carl."

"Would you be willing to tell Willa what you know?"

"Is that all you want?"

"Yes." He raised his hands and lowered them. "I want Willa to get some closure with this." Especially now that she knew who her biological father was.

Kareen went to the far wall and stood in front of a painting of a woman in a lacy dress. "Believe it or not, that's me on my wedding day in 1960. I'm wearing Grandma Alice's gown."

"Nice portrait." In it a very young Kareen beamed with happiness.

"My father paid a bundle for that painting. Hampy loves it." She tilted the frame from the wall and opened the safe behind it. "Grandma wouldn't attend my wedding. But she insisted I wear the gown. And she gave me her little journal that she told me I could read when she was long dead."

"And did you?"

Kareen closed the wall safe and pulled the hinged portrait back over it. When she turned, tears glistened in her eyes. "No. Grandma died the day after Hampy and I were wed. Heart failure."

"I'm sorry."

"I know she wasn't happy with the wedding. But I thought she must have approved since she gave me her dress to wear."

She handed him the book.

"Do you mind if I open Alice's diary?"

When she nodded, he flipped the diary pages to the middle. "It's the same handwriting. I'm pretty sure."

"As what?" Kareen wiped at her eyes.

"As what's written in the back of Lily's journal."

Kareen flipped the leather journal over and looked at the back pages. "That's Grandma's handwriting."

"Wait till Willa hears this."

"And we read that." Kareen pointed to the diary. "I've always been afraid to do so."

"I can see why, now that I've heard about Lily and Stephen's parents. Maybe it's better not to know."

"Maybe so."

"But it might help us better understand what happened."

"How about we all get together tomorrow?"

"Is your private patio available after dinner?"

"Yes. Bring Willa here, and I'll have Hampy with me. Let's put Grandma Alice's memory to rest, and maybe her diary will have something about your ancestors..."

"Lily and Stephen," he supplied.

"Yes, maybe there'll be something about them in my grandmother's diary."

"Is it okay to show this to Willa first?"

"Maybe you two should look through it first in case there's anything too shocking."

"I've got strawberry mocktails all around." Kareen offered a frozen strawberry drink to Willa, Michael, and her husband.

"Thanks." Willa took a sip and set her delicious drink on the glass patio tabletop.

"I think I could have used something stronger for this recitation." Hampy Parker faked a moan.

Kareen shushed him. "Go ahead, Willa, and start reading."

"First of all, I want to tell you about two pages that were stuck together in Lily's journal, but I opened them last night." She looked expectantly at Mrs. Parker. "Alice wrote them."

"Let's hear it."

"She wrote this as an entry days before she supposedly died."

*When I told Stillman that I'd never forgive her for what happened to me in Traverse City, I thought she would choke me to death. If Carl hadn't knocked on her door to work on her room, I wonder if she would have. My neck still hurts.*

*I know you read what I write, Lily. I'm sorry to have used your journal. Do not trust Mrs. Stillman. She was the madam at the brothel that Carl Diener rescued me from and brought me here. I've forgiven him for bringing me to work for his half-brother, Mr. Butler. He says he didn't know what was happening. When he learned Parker had taken me to Traverse City, he followed me there, but it was too late.*

*When I arrived at the Grand Hotel and found Stillman here, I almost left. But I told her straightaway that if she said nothing about me, then I'd say nothing about her. I've since learned that she had the same arrangement with some influential men who have visited the hotel and recognized her. Lily, she's the one who tried to burn down the mercantile in town this summer—she thought Sadie had overheard her talking with one of the brothel's influential patrons. She threatened to blackmail him. The sad thing is that I don't think Sadie heard anything at all, and she could have been killed trying to get into that burning building.*

"And today in the St. Ignace newspaper, look what I found in the history column." Willa grabbed her iPad and read: " 'The young woman found dead this past week has been identified as one of the Grand Hotel's maids, Alice Smith. Miss Smith's tragic death was ruled a terrible accident. Mr. Williford, of the hotel, accompanied Miss Smith's remains, in a casket constructed by islander Garrett Christy, to St. Ignace for a pauper's burial as no family could be located.' "

Kareen gasped. "I'm certain that no one ever contacted my great-grandparents! Especially since she wasn't dead!"

"No Williford on the Grand Hotel's employee rolls." Michael wrapped his knuckles on the tabletop. "Yet here he's reported as such."

"We'll have to tell David Williford, because I'm pretty sure his ancestor was the Pinkerton involved." Willa glanced at Kareen Parker, who wouldn't be there if her ancestor hadn't received so much help and divine intervention.

Hampy frowned. "Probably that doctor and that first Garrett Christy were in on it too."

Willa raised her hand. "Wait a minute. You'll love this next bit. From the history column again from 1895: 'Islander's favorite pet dog Izzy, Dr. Cadotte's beloved Labrador retriever, known and loved by all, died of old age. We will all miss Izzy's wagging tail and hearty greeting. Let's all lift a bowl of water to his memory.' "

Michael laughed. "Skeleton of a large dog found in that coffin?"

They all nodded.

"Oh my goodness." Kareen clapped her hands over her mouth. "I wonder if Grandma was like in..."

"Witness protection sort of?" Hampy asked.

Willa's hands shook as she opened the first page of Alice's diary. "Regardless, I'm so relieved she wasn't killed."

"Although not for a want of trying by some people." Michael made a shocked face. "We found an article written by Ben Steffan for the *Mackinaw City Courier*. In it, he wrote that the slugs at the scene were from two different guns and came from two different directions on the grounds. He hypothesized that one person fired at another, who fired back. Also, Hans Butler had been seen leaving the property that night near the time of the supposed death, as had another man."

"Only fifteen years old, and people wanted her dead." Kareen clutched her husband's hand.

"Mr. Parker, are you ready for this?"

Hampy lifted his cocktail glass. "Anyone got a shot of vodka to spice this up?"

"No," Kareen hissed.

Mr. Parker waved his hand. "Go ahead. I grew up having it drilled into me that I had to be a stand-up guy since my grandfather was a con."

"And my grandmother was a recluse who kept her family close." Kareen sipped her drink.

Willa displayed the diary and the journal. "First of all, I learned that Alice was not illiterate. She also wasn't Irish. As you'd said, Mrs. Parker, she'd grown up on a farm in Wisconsin and she'd attended school. So Alice wrote in the back of Lily's journal because she needed an outlet, and she didn't have her own diary. Carl Diener, who became her husband, gave her the diary when they married. Here's an entry from it:

> *Dear Diary,*
>
> *I thank God for all He has done for me to take me out of the pit I was in. Four years ago, I left home for work in Chicago, against my mother's wishes. She was right. But I went anyway. I wasn't good at maid work. When young Thaddeus Moore complained because he thought I needed more training, his mother got rid of me. I met Carl then. He owned a business in Chicago that provided servants to the rich people. But if we didn't work out, he moved us to Mr.*

*Butler's clubs. I cried most of the time at the club, because the*
*men who frequented the place were always asking favors*
*and nasty things. Carl says he didn't know anything about*
*what his half-brother was doing, but when I couldn't do*
*my work, I was taken away. I was transported by boat by a*
*cocaine addict named Gus Parker—*

"Cocaine addict?" Kareen exchanged a shocked look with her husband.

"That's what it says." Willa shrugged apologetically.

Michael set his drink down. "Could be how Butler got him to do his dirty work."

They all fell silent for a moment.

"He was probably only in his midtwenties then." Hampy raked his hand over his face.

Willa nodded. "Okay, so Gus Parker was Mr. Butler's bodyguard." She looked down to continue reading:

*Gus transported me with some other girls to a brothel outside*
*of Traverse City, Michigan. I do not wish to recall anything*
*there except this—when I'd been there, in hell, for over two*
*weeks, Carl Diener himself came and found me.*

Kareen pumped her fist in the air. "Go, Grandpa Carl!"

They all raised their glasses. "To Grandpa Carl," Hampy said.

After the toast, Willa flipped the diary toward the end. "Alice actually kept this diary off and on for most of her life." She displayed the last entry from 1960. "It's kind of sad but kind of good."

"That's right before our wedding." Kareen took the diary and looked at it.

Alice had written that she'd been beside herself to learn that her grand-daughter was marrying the grandson of the man who'd tried to kill her.

Kareen began to cry and handed the book back to Willa. "Read it."

*I wasn't sure if I'd ever get the stains out of that dress. I was*
*such a foolish girl. I wore Lily's lace gown to meet Thaddeus*
*Moore. I'd planned to tell him the whole awful thing he'd*
*caused by complaining about me to his mother. But it was*

*Mr. Butler who sent me that note. Then Parker called out to me and raised his gun. I started running when I heard another shot. I was sure I was about to die, but I turned and saw Mr. Williford shooting at Parker. I ran to where some stairs would allow me to escape, but they weren't completed. When I slipped, I thought I'd fall. I saw Parker run off, and I thought I saw Mr. Butler too. Mr. Williford grabbed me and pulled me back up onto the stairs.*

*Everything after that was chaotic. I don't like to think about what all those men had to do to get me to the mainland safely, as if I were dead.*

*As I was washing the gown, appalled at the idea of my granddaughter wearing that in her abomination of a marriage to a Parker, I was sure the old stains would never come out. I thought—I wish Gus Parker could be there to see that dress. I wish he'd croak right there when he remembers what he did. But Gus is gone. He's been dead for years, Kareen told me. And as I washed that dress, God spoke to my heart. "I washed you clean, that dress clean, years ago when you gave your life to Me." When I lifted Lily's gown, it was spotless. Spotless. I sat and cried a long time. I'm ready for heaven now. And I trust that God will bless what I thought was an unholy union.*

When Willa looked up, moisture was glinting in the men's eyes, and Kareen was reaching for a tissue. Were they as convicted as she felt? God could set aside the past and heal their hurts. And there were new beginnings.

Time to let go of her anger toward John. Time to start a new chapter in her life.

# CHAPTER TWENTY-FIVE

## *1895*

*L*ily clutched Stephen's arm as he led her down the hall to her old suite at the Grand Hotel. Guests and employees had greeted her so warmly that she felt a little guilty about cancelling her contract. But she'd heard that Ben was doing a wonderful job playing piano for the audience.

Stephen stopped by the doorway. "I'm sorry, Lily, about your journal still being missing. Maybe you can think of someplace it could be where we haven't looked."

She pulled her key from her reticule, unlocked the door, and they entered. The storage area access had been walled over. "They were supposed to have left a small door to access the storage area."

"Maybe with Mr. Diener leaving and Alice's death, the crew rushed it through. Or because the hotel intends to close the suite off, it no longer matters."

"I can't believe they're planning to seal this place up."

"Superstitious I guess." Stephen rubbed his chin. "Miss Smith's life was cut too short."

"Poor Alice never got to use that costume jewelry that Miss Ivy Sterling left behind. I'd told her to keep it as I had my own things, and I didn't wear a lot on stage."

"No doubt Mr. Costello grabbed that like he did all of Ivy's clothing."

Lily opened the wardrobe. Empty. She went to the desk.

"I'll look in here for your journal, although I don't know why she'd have it since she was illiterate." Stephen went to Alice's door.

She pressed her eyes shut, her heart beating rapidly. She needed to get out of here.

They spent what seemed like ages looking—to no avail.

"Come on, my love, let's go." Stephen closed Alice's door.

Her face warmed. "Am I your love, then?"

"If you're to become my wife, then I imagine so."

Lily shook her head as she left the room. For someone used to dealing with emotional issues, he was remarkably slow to communicate feelings with her. Stephen followed her. As she turned the lock, she heard him say something.

She turned to face him. "What was that?"

"I love you, Lily, and I want you to marry me. Even if your mother may have used my father's pipe to start the fire to kill them in a pyromaniac frenzy."

She quirked an eyebrow at him. "I love you too, Stephen, and I'll marry you. Even if your father did leave his pipe behind and his act of forgetfulness caused that inferno."

He dropped down on one knee right there in the hall, his face flushed. "I have this all backwards and created the worst proposal in history."

He was right, but Lily offered him a hand up. "What matters now is the rest of our lives."

He pulled her into his arms and kissed her. The warmth of his body pressed to hers, his lips so firm and wonderful as he kissed her over and over again, Lily was sure she'd melt. When he released her, she looked into his passion-glazed dark eyes. Could this really finally be happening?

"Would next week be too soon?"

When he kissed her again and his arms felt like home, she knew her answer.

Applause broke out from somewhere along the hallway. Lily swiveled around.

The actress, Miss Laura Williams, although rumored to have been Uncle Robert's sweetheart, was actually married. "Bravo," the beautiful woman called out. She stood next to her husband, wounded war veteran Thomas Kinney, in his wheelchair, both clapping.

Was Lily's father even now applauding them in heaven? Free from his wheelchair, free from pain. Tears sprang to her eyes. Maybe that little treasure chest of Papa's had held the clues to bring her home to where she belonged, right here in this place with this man.

She looked up into Stephen's dark eyes. "Next week would be perfect."

# CHAPTER TWENTY-SIX

*2020*

*W*illa mounted the brilliant blue carpeted steps, punctuated by yellow starburst patterns, on her way with Michael to the cupola in the Grand Hotel.

"I've really enjoyed our time together, Willa."

She didn't want it to end. "So have I."

He pointed to the dark blue wallpaper with multisized cumulus clouds covering it. "What did Aimee say about your suggestion to replace it with something simple?"

She grinned, glad he couldn't see her face. A check from Aimee and a brief contract would keep her on the island a while longer. "Oh, you know Aimee."

The faux antique light fixture overhead was a goner too in her redesign. And the metal grate overhead would be painted to minimize its visual interference.

"Aimee and David sure were excited to hear about how his ancestor worked here as a Pinkerton."

"I think David felt vindicated."

Michael laughed. "No plaque, though."

"But David put a ring on it at their dinner last night."

"A fast mover."

"He's over thirty, like us, so he probably knows his own mind."

"Like you know how you feel about that turquoise-and-white-striped-canopy in the cupola?"

"All right, just because I've complained about it—"

"Since the first time you and I met up here after work for business." Michael arched an eyebrow.

"It bugs me."

"You're not supposed to be looking at it. You should be looking at the view."

As they entered the bar at the top level of the hotel, she knew she could look at this man every day for the rest of her life. Since their evening with the Parkers and after a lot of prayer, Willa was feeling that nudging in her heart that told her Michael could be part of her future even if her birth father, Chad, was right and the Grand's redesign projects would be going to Vern Yip.

Michael led Willa to a seat by the windows that extended all the way around the room, stopping at the bar. They placed their orders. He had to know where he stood with her. Willa's contract was coming to an end. He had it on good authority that Vern Yip would be the new designer going forward. But he'd not spoil this time with Willa.

He reached across the small table and took her hand in his. Willa's hand was so warm, so soft, so right. "I didn't bring you up here to talk about work. I want to talk about you."

Her eyebrows shot up. "Personal then?"

"Definitely." He ran his thumb over the top of her hand. "I understand how adoption and your mom's death could have impacted you. I mean, that's major."

"It is, it was. But I think coming up here this summer and meeting my father and grandparents has helped with healing. God put me in the right place at the right time."

"Yes, He did." Michael thanked God every day for her being in his life.

"And I'm glad we got to meet." She squeezed his hand.

The waitress set napkins and their Cokes down, but they didn't release hands.

When the server left, he leaned in. "Willa, you know some about my love life. Heck, Bianca made sure our so-called relationship was blasted all over social media. But what about you? Why aren't you married? You're beautiful. You're so smart and talented." *And I love you.*

"Thank you." She released his hand and took a sip of her pop.

"There's nothing on social media ever linking you to anyone." He splayed his hands.

"Have you been cyberstalking me?"

"No." The muscles in his neck tightened.

"Well. . .maybe." She laughed, and he relaxed.

"I'm sorry, Willa. I'm asking too much." But he wished that he could understand and break through whatever was holding her back.

"No, I think it's a good question. Especially if. . ." She gave him a long soulful glance with her beautiful eyes.

"If we're going to take our friendship to the next level?" Could she tell how broad his smile was behind his mask?

"Yes. I want that."

"I do too." *More than anything.* "But when are you leaving?"

"Aimee gave me a reprieve." She made a swirling motion around the room. "A short contract to come up with a redesign for the cupola."

Joy surged through him. "No kidding?"

"Nope. But she had the nerve to offer me a wedding discount if I needed it later. I don't think I'd ever take her up on that."

That was a short-lived joy spurt. What was she implying? "Why not?"

She sighed. "When I graduated from the Savannah School of Design, I was having my dream come true. And my mother was investigating wedding venues for me—including here at the Grand Hotel."

"Really?"

"Yes. But my BFF from school, John, my soulmate who understood me so completely. . .He apparently believed that my designs were actually his."

"Huh?"

"We'd started dating our freshman year, just casually at first. But by our junior year, we were inseparable. He was happy-go-lucky, so charming, smart, and everybody loved him. He was born an extrovert, was warm and witty, whereas I had to learn at school how to reinvent my introverted self. I had to develop a persona for the business aspect of selling my designs.

But John was way ahead of me on that—he passed some of my designs off as his own."

"He stole your stuff?" *What a scumbag.*

"He wormed his way into my heart, motivated partly—I learned later—because he thought I was the best design student. And he was lazy."

"Seriously?"

"The betrayal was crazy bad—to know I was used like that."

"I know the feeling." *Bianca had perfected it.* "Didn't the faculty back you up?"

"They did. They were so supportive, but at that point the deed was already done."

"What happened?" He frowned. He hated that someone had misused this wonderful woman.

"A firm with far deeper pockets than the one John pitched my designs to picked me up to do an overhaul of all their European resorts. So I left."

"Sounds like God brought you through it."

"Yes. He put people around me who believed in me and my work. And of course now I'm grateful we never married."

"I saw my pastor yesterday while I was on the mainland. He thinks the same thing about me and Bianca. Or as he put it, 'Ya dodged a bullet, Mike, eh?' "

"Like Alice Smith did all those years ago."

He tapped his hand to his chest. "I really got convicted by her testimony. She literally dodged a bullet. But she eventually forgave the man who'd ruined her life."

"I was touched too. And I've finally forgiven John."

"Good." He took her hand in his again. "My pastor said, 'Time to move on from what happened.' And I think he's right."

Willa seemed to look into his very soul. "Time for both of us to knock down those walls around our hearts."

# AUTHOR'S NOTES

*T*he Grand Hotel really was sold in September 2019 after being in the Musser family for generations. Considered the gem of the Great Lakes, this stately hotel transitioned from local ownership to an international investment group, KSL. Pivot Hotels & Resorts, the lifestyle and luxury operating division of Davidson Hotels & Resorts, now manages the property for KSL. In the changeover, legal challenges ensued. World-famous designer Carlton Varney filed suit against the hotel, saying that many items there had been on loan to the Grand Hotel but were his property. He had been associated with the Grand for decades. He also alleged age discrimination against the new owners, who no longer requested his services. So that was the kernel for my story, with a fictional resort designer who comes in to pitch her services once the renowned decorator, Varney, was gone.

As mentioned in the story, there really were extensive, luxurious changes to the Esther Williams swimming pool. The famous HGTV designer Vern Yip was actually hired by the Grand Hotel for pool and other redesign work. Also in 2020, COVID did result in reduced occupancy not only at the Grand Hotel but also at other hotels on Mackinac Island.

There is a lovely marina in Hessel, Michigan, by Les Cheneaux Islands and an annual vintage wooden boats festival. Les Cheneaux Islands Antique Wooden Boat Show is a big draw to the Eastern Upper Peninsula in the summer. None of that is associated with fictional character Garrett Christy III, though.

To get to and from Mackinac Island, you must in general use water transportation, usually ferries (although there is also an airport on the island). Sadly, part of the inspiration for my fictional character dying in a boat crash was a real-life crash, with a teenaged driver in the Mackinac Island harbor in 2020 while I was there. In the story, the crash took place three decades earlier, however.

This dual-timeline novel includes the third section of what was originally planned as the 1895 story with Lily as heroine in the Brides of Mackinac series. *My Heart Belongs on Mackinac Island: Maude's Mooring* from Barbour was a Maggie Awards winner and a *Romantic Times* Top Pick. Character Sadie Duvall's 1895 story was published as the novella "His Anchor" in the *First Love Forever* collection from Barbour. "Love's Beacon," appearing in the *Great Lakes Lighthouse* collection, has some characters from this story. And the independently published *Butterfly Cottage* contains many of the characters from the 2020 part of this novel. Garrett Christy is a recurring character in my books and in particular one of the main characters in the Christy Lumber Camp series. And I have other Christys at the Straits of Mackinac during Pontiac's Rebellion in *Mercy in a Red Cloak*.

I "borrowed" many names for this story. Thank you to the many friends who allowed me to do so. Real-life Sue Pentland is a social worker. My son-in-law, Colton Byrnes, asked to be put in a story and here he is! Michael David Williford is a DJ at the Straits and is married to the former Aimee Laferier. Michael and Aimee were my hosts in St. Ignace while I was researching for this story, and both have work histories in the hospitality industry on the island.

Dr. David Buck is an excellent optometrist—but his practice is in Virginia not Michigan. By the way, lupus can indeed attack the eyes, as well as cause mood issues when someone is in a lupus flare. The idea for Willa's (and the twins') unusual tricolor-ringed eyes was inspired by a server at a local restaurant. I'd never seen anything like them. They were beautiful—so I appropriated them for this novel!

There is a real-life Jack Barnwell, who is known as the premier landscaper on Mackinac Island. His gorgeous book, *The Gardens of Mackinac Island*, was very helpful to me, and I highly recommend it.

I was a psychologist, both a licensed and certified school psychologist and a licensed clinical psychologist, for over twenty-five years. I hope that my insights as a former psychologist, used in writing about my characters' emotional difficulties, will help readers understand how failure to deal with past trauma can cause all manner of difficulties. My previous business associate, the wonderful clinical psychologist Dr. Mary Svendsen, continues to practice in Charleston, South Carolina. It was fun having her be the one to have helped fictional Willa in this novel.

# ACKNOWLEDGMENTS

I always thank God, without whom I wouldn't be able to write, and my family—especially my son Clark J. Pagels, often my brain-storming partner. Kathleen L. Maher, my critique partner, always has my literary back.

Thank you to my agent Joyce Hart and acquisition editor, Becky Germany, for believing in my story. Thank you to Becky Durost Fish, my editor, for working with me to make this manuscript shine! Much appreciation, also, to all the staff at Barbour who work to make life easier for us authors: Laura Young, Shalyn Sattler, Abbey Bible, Ellie Zumbach, David O'Brien, and more!

I'd like to thank my early beta reader Sherry Moe, and beta readers Tina St. Clair Rice and Anne Rightler for galley help, as well as the Behind Love's Wall Promo Group members, and my Pagels Pals reader group members. The #1K1HR Facebook group members, especially Ruth Logan Herne and Deb Hackett, have been great virtual accountability partners.

Blessings to Dr. David Buck and crew, especially Michael Bunting, Audri Stang, and Judy Orellana for keeping me in glasses. (Four pairs and counting in the past ten months!) Much appreciation to Dr. Daniel Carlson, my chiropractor, and rheumatology nurse practitioner Misty White for keeping me moving after long days at the computer.

The Addicted to Mackinac Island Facebook group, particularly leader Linda Borton Sorensen, a talented photographer, have been great encouragers. Also the Island Bookstore, owner Mary Jane Barnwell, manager Tamara Tomac, and saleswoman Jill Sawatzki are so supportive of my Mackinac Island books and a blessing.

CARRIE FANCETT PAGELS, PHD, is the award-winning author of over twenty Christian fiction books, including ECPA and Amazon bestsellers. Twenty-five years as a psychologist didn't cure her overactive imagination! A self-professed history geek, she resides with her family in the Historic Triangle of Virginia but grew up as a "Yooper." She returns in the summer to the Straits of Mackinac—her favorite place on earth! You can connect with her at www.CarrieFancettPagels.com, where you can sign up for her newsletter via the Contact page. Carrie regularly features giveaways—including some bonus material related to this book.